Ruffled

FLOURISHES

FLOURISHES

a serio-comic novel of washington, d.c.

PETER ROUSSEL

bright sky press

HOUSTON, TEXAS

bright sky press

2365 Rice Blvd., Suite 202 Houston, Texas 77005

10 9 8 7 6 5 4 3 2 1

Library of Congress Cataloging-in-Publication Data

·Roussel, Peter, 1941-
Ruffled flourishes : a novel / by Peter Roussel.
p. cm.
ISBN 978-1-933979-42-7 (pbk. : alk. paper)
1. White House (Washington, D.C.)--Fiction. 2. Press secretaries--Fiction. 3. Presidents--Fiction.
4. Washington (D.C.)--Fiction. 5. Political fiction. I. Title.

PS3618.O87R84 2009
813'.6--dc22
                                                              2009003329

Book and cover design by Cregan Design
Edited by Al and Nora Shire

Printed in the China by Asia Pacific Offset

To the memory of my father, mother and brother
and
for my sister
and
To all those dedicated individuals who have served
through the years in the
Office of the Press Secretary, The White House

Ruffles and Flourishes: The musical fanfare that, along with *Hail to the Chief*, signals the entrance of the president of the United States at official ceremonies.

Author's Note: This is a work of fiction, all of its characters and events being imaginary creations of the author. Any similarity to persons living or dead is unintentional and purely coincidental. However, having served in the White House under two presidents, the author did observe numerous verbal exchanges between members of the press and others. These, along with other sources, served to provide inspiration for this book.

CHAPTER ONE

REPORTER: Is there anything a guest at tonight's state dinner
              should avoid?

SPOKESMAN: **Gas.**

Sox St. Louis, deputy press secretary to the president, sat watching what
was happening outside the White House, particularly on that stretch of
Pennsylvania Avenue where every day there flows past a human phantas-
magoria. He relished the moments when he could look out at life unfolding
on the other side of the fence that separates America from its leader.

It was during these brief reveries that he had discovered a commonal-
ity: life on both sides of that fence is a theatre of continuous performance,
comedic and dramatic.

Today, like always, he could look out on the White House grounds
and watch as visitors departed the West Wing, heading toward the outside
world of the street and potential encounters with camera-laden tourists
gawking and arching their necks for a better peek at the sights. Once outside, those same visitors might also find themselves tripping over rowdy
schoolkids underfoot on the obligatory field tour, America's youth
unleashed at 1600 Pennsylvania Avenue, their parents grateful to have
them ravaging someone else's house for a change.

If taxes, death and stale beer at domed stadiums are the constants of
life, then add one more thing to that list—the parade of people that daily
drifts along the two blocks in front of the White House, many of them
with amazingly blank expressions on their faces, seemingly nonplussed by

their surroundings.

A pomp-free passing in review, it includes the famous, the unruly and unwashed, various age groups, nationalities, races and colors, mixed in with a polyglot of sometimes chanting demonstrators, beady-eyed vagrants and hapless street people aimlessly roaming up and down that history-rich slab. On some days the scene can be mindful of the grimy sort of meandering that one associates with a crowded carnival midway.

Here, people shuffle past menacing iron fences, their spires spiking the sky as silent sentries framed against the precisely manicured grounds of the North Lawn, separating Joe Six-Pack citizen from the sometimes slightly mildewed house on the other side. The same iron bars against which thousands of tourists' noses have pressed for a better view, a less-obstructed snapshot, a glimpse of the mighty, a sighting of something grand and noble, a wisp of anything so that they may tell others they have joined the club reserved for those who have known a moment of rapture at the country's most prominent address. Its zip code, 20500, they have probably found less inspiring.

Every day Sox watched as members of the White House press corps visited that zip code as participants in a form of journalistic hysteria-on-the-hoof, spinning in and out of the northwest gate, their faces hellishly lit, rushing to sniff out a fresh news break or to feed at the bountiful trough of rumors inside. Strangely, he had sometimes felt sympathy toward them as captives hopelessly caught in a hammerlock of fear at being beat on a story. Yet, he had seen enough to know they were not members of a fraternity but competitors in a human destruction derby. Nearing the end of each working day there arose a sound from their ranks he had come to dread, a ghoulish drone of desperation, an unnerving buzz of helplessness hanging over their work area behind the briefing room, drifting up from the crowded carrels where they labored and sweated. It would come late in the afternoon around four o'clock, deadline time. It was a dirge for the defeated who were about to come up empty—no story for that day.

That's why he always preferred watching the people casually ambling along on the avenue outside. Nobody out there ever seemed to get nervous around four o'clock. None of them seemed worried about being on deadline. For the most part, they remained merrily oblivious to the kilotons of angst being generated by reporters inside as they relentlessly pursued new news.

But if today the place was a home for mega-stress, he wasn't showing it. He appeared to be on cruise control. The rigid strain of task and duty that so often muscled his face, was missing. At least for the moment. Tilting back in his chair and deftly angling it so as to better expand the view through the floor-to-ceiling window in his tiny West Wing cubicle, he laced his hands behind his head and drank deep of the elixir of quiet, an infrequent visitor to his office. Gazing out on the avenue, he was envious of its inhabitants. There they were, pursuing a lifestyle of seeming calm compared to that behind White House walls where outbreaks of news leaks were a staple on the daily menu. Those along with microwaved Mexican food as the Thursday blue plate lunch special in the White House Mess. All of it added up to screwy things sometimes happening there.

The president had once reminded Sox that working in the White House was "like a giddy romp through one of life's imperfect minefields." Perhaps. But too often he had seen the detonators on those mines explode. Too often he had observed bruising battles of one-upmanship and grabs for power that placed one in the line of fire merely by showing up for work. It was a world where decision-making could be a treacherous, body contact sport. A high-stakes arena where dialing 911 to combat the daily outbreak of stress was of no help. Life's exit ramp for the meek was the door of the West Wing lobby.

Even as an in-house refuge, his pint-sized office, with its strategic view of the driveway and North Lawn, could be a source of hazard and embarrassment. Like when the president of Egypt had last come to visit. His motorcade had pulled up under the West Wing portico, where such state visitors disembarked only a few feet from Sox's window—a window on the world. A window where sometimes the world watched the watcher. Sox had been engrossed in a phone call when the Middle East leader arrived. To gain a closer, if more unsteady, look, he had tilted his chair

13

back to better eyeball the distinguished visitor *mano a mano*.

Emerging from his limousine with a grand flourish, the Egyptian had instantly found his welcome beclouded by disruption from a bizarre spectacle in the nearby window. It had become a tableau of pure slapstick where Sox, with both feet teetering perilously close to the edge of the desk, had turned, lost his balance and flipped over headfirst, his body going haywire, face, arms and legs splattering wildly against the divided panes of glass. He finally came to rest in a spastic, ungainly pile, spread-eagled in oafish splendor, a grotesque human still life. Managing to keep his diplomatic composure intact, the Egyptian leader watched with a puzzlement that was more sorrowful than amused. It was not a pretty sight.

Crudely impaled against the window, Sox's shame abruptly turned to horror as the visitor's security guards, reacting to the thud of a body hurled against wood and glass, snapped to battle-ready positions, their steely gazes riveted on the window, hands darting inside suit coats, fingers curling nervously around triggers. It took only a second for them to see the watery, mangled lump sprawled against the glass was not a threat to their boss' security or the peace process. What was in danger, as a result of this incident, and was dutifully noted by the press, was the reputation of a president of the United States who would tolerate such bozo-at-the-circus antics on the premises. Sox had seen the world through that window. And the world had occasionally seen him. Bottoms up.

But today, and now securely upright in the same chair, he wistfully turned his gaze and thoughts back to the great avenue beyond, this despite the chatter from nervous reporters gathering outside his door and rendering him hostage in his own cubicle.

Seldom was there ever escape from the wave after wave of reporters drawn to his office, hovering there and using his tiny corner of White House turf as a campsite where they could nose around for information. The "rumor lounge," some called it, but always they were there, escaping the tiny crawl spaces to which even the mighty networks were assigned in the back of the briefing room, scrounging, grubbing, prying for crumbs of news that a press spokesman might drip-drip to a favored few, leaving the majority to come away empty-handed but grateful just for the temporary change of venue. It was all part of the verbal small arms fire, the testy game of words that played out almost daily in this strategic corner of the West Wing, the combat zone into which the White House press corps and presidential spokesmen waded each day.

He felt secure in his office, and a part of history. After all, the West Wing had been around since 1902, a pretty durable place considering it had originally been erected as a temporary office structure.

From his window he watched as technicians from the networks came shuffling up the walk. Soon they would begin their daily ritual of preparing lights and cameras in the various North Lawn "stand-up" areas assigned to each news organization and where their correspondents reported nightly to the nation. None of them seemed in much of a hurry.

"Dammit, Sox, what the hell is going down?" cried a voice outside his door, its tone shrill and angry.

"We hear the Russian ambassador is on his way over here," another voice challenged. "Why isn't he on the president's public schedule for today?"

They were in heated overdrive—limber lungs and short tempers. Business as usual. His closed door was of little help in buffeting the onslaught. But he was used to it. Such froth had become an essential part of the daily upper press office scene. Those who toiled in this part of the White House had long ago become accustomed to these outbursts, a hen scrabble that had become sort of a Muzak for the West Wing.

Despite the ranting, he continued to stare out toward the street people, wanderers oblivious to this outbreak of media frenzy.

"Get your ass out here, Sox!" another voice screeched.

"Yeah, we want a readout on this meeting with the Rooskie!"

"What in hell's fire is going on here?"

Rat-a-tat-tat. Rapid-fire salvos from the press to a press spokesman who today had no answers. An empty quiver.

Of the three spaces in the upper press office, Sox's was the runt of the litter, a tiny hole at the room's far end, a crumb of a space but a jewel of a location. Its view of the real world—life outside those gates—far surpassed that of the Oval Office. That was a problem for all administrations, Sox contended, the president's office being so totally detached from just plain folks. But from Sox's office, he could see everybody. With the mere turn of his head, he could watch the comings and goings of heads of state. And in the case of the president of Egypt, he could also use that site to humiliate himself in front of world leaders. But most important for one holding his position, he could use that spot to monitor press activity on the lawn and driveway. The trouble was, they could monitor him, too. If one looked closely during many of the network newscasts, one could clearly see his office window in the background, and sometimes the occupant of the room. It was a nationwide visibility that served as a reminder to always keep his fly zipped.

While staking out his office each day, reporters also disdained it: "So small you have to enter it sideways." Another wag hung a sign on the door: *Retirement Room for Reporters. Nice view. Nice chair. No leaks. No information. No stories.* But as far as Sox was concerned, no matter. It had that glorious window looking out on the driveway and North Lawn. As far as he was concerned, it was the best nook in the building for watching history happen, the press be damned.

His assignment to that office had been considered a badge of achievement for dutiful, if not notable, staff work in the less visible though equally competitive trenches of the White House bureaucracy. A perk. And why not? He had paid his dues and earned his spurs.

It had not, however, been a course traveled minus setbacks. One of these occurred during his stint as editor of the first document delivered to the president each morning, a ten to twelve-page review of the overnight and early morning news reports. It was to this news digest that he assigned the lofty title: *Compilation of Reports About the President.* Regretfully, it was the president who had pointed out the unfortunate acronym he had chosen: *CRAP.*

Earlier in the administration, he had served as deputy to the deputy for political affairs. Had there been a deputy to the deputy to the deputy, that would have knocked him down yet another peg and made it an utter impossibility to cram such a wordy title onto the single line of a business card. Fortunately, no other such deputy was ever appointed.

But now he was a bona fide presidential spokesman with his own office in the West Wing. And not just anywhere in the West Wing. He was deep in the gut of the West Wing, his own office in the administration of President Carl Crayon.

"Rumors, Sox, rumors!" screamed a reporter, the lathered chant outside his door intensifying.

"Russian rumors, Sox!"

"Your silence stinks!"

"Yeah, stop the stonewalling, cut us some slack and pop with some fresh copy!"

"Fresh copy—that means answers!"

It was a full-court press by the press. The more he gazed out the window, futilely trying to tune out the grumpy babble pouring in over the office transom, the more the painful reality crept over him that he was once again mired in spokesman's hell, the press-versus-spokesman combat zone where no cease-fire in place had ever been known to exist.

He was naked in the thick of the fray—no facts, no ammo.

If one had real clout in this White House, one was "in the loop," part of the "need to know" informational circle. He was so far out of that loop, and he knew he was, that it was sometimes difficult for him to confirm rumors about rumors. Often, he just didn't know. Now here he was, blindly plodding along and trying his best to function as a credible presidential spokesman. Something was going down. But what? Once again, one of the president's spokesmen, one of his links to the outer world, one of Old Glory's voices, would be the last to know.

"You're suckin' eggs, Sox!" cried one of the voices on the other side of the door. "The Russian embassy says there is a meeting today. What's the White House say?"

At last, a query he could handle.

He pressed his hands together in an upside down "V" and shouted: "The White House is an inanimate object, a wooden frame structure. Therefore, it is incapable of thought, speech or reaction to reporters' questions. If a piece of the wood ever does learn to speak, I'll see that you get the story first."

"Smart-ass," the voice muttered.

A spokesman was only as good as the information he possessed. In this case, he had zero. But no need to let the press know. They'd figure it out soon enough. For now, serve up lots of noncommittal drivel and try to make them think he knew something about the ambassador's reason for being there.

Neither was there reason to let them know he had not even spoken to the president in two weeks, save for a brief, ill-begotten exchange prior to their watching a movie last weekend in the White House theatre. While settling in to view a goodies-versus-baddies western entitled *Chase, Catch, Condemn*, he had attempted to jolly the president and first lady via the shameless sort of groveling that always dented his pride a bit, but never so much so that it stopped his being an occasional kiss-ass when there was a moment to be seized. Referring to the film's title, he had airily noted: "Gee, a movie about running, snagging, and a prophylactic." His venture into big-time brown-nosing proved a bust. No one had laughed. Or weakly smiled. Or spoken to him the rest of the night.

"Sox St. Louis, get your butt into ramming speed and give us a fill on this Russian-U.S. hen party!" a fresh voice challenged. Its nerve-rattling nasal twang was painfully familiar.

Sparta St. James, though still in her thirties, with sunny, deceptively soft facial features that suggested a benign spirit within, was hardly that. A whip-hard network TV correspondent, her face, unlike those of many of her colleagues, was not painted, tinted or heavily caked with cosmetics to hide the pressure-induced stress of her job. Neither was her hair overly sprayed to assure plastered-down presentability. She didn't need it. Her eyes were weapons enough. Two electric ovals, news-seeking killer-bee beacons that flashed defiantly in unison and could force withering submission from those foolish enough to impede her path to a story. Breaking news was a competitive elixir from which she drank deeply, a feisty hard-charger who was the journalistic embodiment of a one-person wrecking crew.

In recent years her name and reputation for roughhouse in the White House had been the butt of snide pressroom cracks, mostly by competitors who had eaten her dust.

"When that saint goes marching in, it'll be to the briefing room—not some heavenly perch."

"Sparta St. James is at home in the company of saints—the New Orleans Saints."

"Sox and Sparta may be named Saint—but saints they ain't."

None of it ever drew a blink from her.

He hunkered down further in his chair, annoyed yet determined to tune out Sparta's tinny, unsettling voice.

Once during a similar stakeout, and well aware of the press' fondness for free food and drink, he had created a diversion by unexpectedly throwing open his door and yelling: "Food bag! Food bag! It's on the house!" What followed was a Daytona stock car race within White House corridors, the hurtling bodies pounding those in their way en route to the gratis goodies. Momentarily forgotten was that he had succeeded in diverting their attention away from a breaking and potentially negative story. But there had also been a dark side to the turn of events. An overzealous radio reporter, while chomping down on one of the freebie nougat-laden caramel bars offered, had bit fiercely into the tip of his tongue. The resulting scream was of spine-curdling anguish, the poor fellow lending further texture to the moment with a string of profanities, many of which referenced the mother-son relationship and were so voluble in their fury as to have interrupted a reception for religious leaders that the president was hosting in the nearby Roosevelt Room. Sox never used that tactic again.

"Hey, Sox, S-O-S! Get out here ass-fast and give us some guidance," growled Sparta, her raspy impatience mindful of a wildly screeching buzz bomb in search of a target.

"Facts, fella, facts!" another voice echoed. The second voice was unrecognizable to Sox and was quickly swallowed up in the snarling ferment his closed door continued to hold back.

Today's press office chaos, like many days, was a source of ongoing bemusement for Sox. Such a tiny quadrant of White House space. And yet it was here that each day there occurred a monumental taffy pull for information—the government versus the press.

In geographic terms, the arena for this tussle extended from his office down the nearby narrow hall to the three steps that led to the lower press office and the little theatre that served as the briefing room. Its original title was the West Terrace Press Center, but as a room with a small stage where heavy doses of drama and ad hoc humor occurred, Sox could think of it only as a theatre. Sometimes of the absurd. Underneath its floor lay the indoor swimming pool, drained and no longer in use. The growth of the press corps, particularly with increased members of the electronic media, required evicting reporters in 1969 from the stately coziness of the West Wing lobby where they had been permitted to freely loll about while monitoring the comings and goings of Oval Office visitors. The space shortage was solved by covering over the pool and converting it into a briefing room.

On days when the room was full to overflow with reporters, lights, cameras and questions, one could feel the floor sink and sway a bit, reminding all present that even covered over, an empty swimming pool still lay beneath. Some reporters sat over the deep end. On days like this, Sox could only hope that the floor might collapse.

"Sox! Sox! Sox!" A tongue-lapping chant rose from the mob outside, an outcry that boomed across the intimacy of the upper press office and spilled out into the corridor between it and the Oval Office.

It was in that hallway early in the Crayon administration that a diminutive, owlish-eyed member of the president's economic advisory team, an infrequent visitor to the West Wing, had been buffeted by the sheer force of such chanting while en route to the nearby men's room. That he should have been panic-seized was understandable. Such outbursts were unfathomable in his monastic-like offices in the nearby Executive Office Building. Fearing demonic forces had penetrated the security of the building's inner sanctum, the little guy fled in horror and remained so shaken as to avoid any further use of that particular lavatory.

Frustrated, Sox bit into his lower lip, stifling the urge to respond. The trouble was, with what? Verbal blanks such as "No comment" would only serve to inflame the lather. "No comment"—utterly useless pap. Sox's life knew two kinds of hell: a press corps denied and women scorned. Well, maybe three: Sparta St. James scorned *and* denied. "No comment" was of no help in any of these cases. The press rampage continued unabated.

Kicking back in his swivel chair, he propped both feet up on the window ledge. It was not easy to tell the press something when you didn't know anything. And yet, the press always seemed to think that a spokesman for the president was an insider privy to most everything. Even a deputy press secretary. For an instant he considered checking with senior staff in the president's inner circle, but just as quickly dismissed the idea as an exercise in futility, reminding himself of the empty bag he had sometimes been handed in the past. First, it would be: "Don't tell the press anything." Not tell them anything? Easy. He didn't know anything. Then, when pressed, they might suggest he try: "When we have something to say, we'll say it." Brilliant. Yeah, try getting an enraged press corps to chow down on that slice of bone. Then, as a last resort, they might daringly recommend he pull out that stop-the-presses chestnut: "I have nothing for you on this."

The first time he had ever filled in for his boss, J.Y. Katy, the press secretary, and conducted the daily press briefing, Sparta had cut him off at the knees for doling out such slobber from the podium. "Those are the most meaningless statements I have ever heard!" she scolded. She was right.

The cries by the wolf pack still outside the door interrupted his thoughts.

"Get the hell out here with some answers!" an angry voice insisted.

"Sox, cut us some slack. J.Y.'s not around, and I'm coming up on the big D—deadline. How about filling in the blanks for us!"

"You've got a Russian coming to the house—why?" someone else shouted.

"Come out, come out and give us some star-spangled spin!"

He continued to ignore their pleadings. There was no choice. Instead, he turned his attention back out toward the passersby on Pennsylvania Avenue while thinking how he wished some of those senior aides, so ready to lob him those non-responses, could hear this press rancor and have to deal with it. But no, he was alone right now on the front line of the West Wing press bedlam. A western front that never seemed to be quiet. He was the only leper left in the colony. Even J.Y. had disappeared, leaving him alone to be whipsawed by the press gang currently hanging around.

And where was J.Y.? And how was it that he was always addressed only as J.Y.? Shouldn't every press secretary be addressed by a name, not just initials? But since in this case those initials stood for Jaxson Yesterday, it was readily understandable that it would always just be J.Y. "I didn't want to go through life being called Jax and people trying to figure out why my first name was the plural of Jack. Or that I was a game played with a small rubber ball."

The restlessness of the reporters outside Sox's door was becoming a growth industry, a case of media jitters on steroids. And they had settled in for the long haul. Okay, screw it, he told himself. If the senior staff wasn't going to take him into their confidence, then why should he be left alone to do this heavy lifting? It was white-flag time. A bailout deserved a bailout. It was not his turn to give blood. He was out of there.

Impulsively, he bolted upright, springing to the door and throwing it open. He was ready to slog for every inch of territory, to peel through the human glut that had turned the upper press office into a media campsite, a tangle of bodies invading desktops, chairs, cabinets and any other space capable of accommodating anyone interested in lounging, perching or just hanging out. Today was not an exception. On just about any day, much of the press corps roosted here. Here they could not only stake out the press spokesmen, but could also keep tabs on their media competitors, just to make sure no one got a leg up. It was one big happy family, with daggers always poised.

As Sox emerged, a nattering shell-burst erupted across the room.

"…cut the…"

"…games…"

"…this crap about a meeting?"

"…the American people have a right to know."

"What is happening?"

"…can't leave us hanging…"

"…damn producer ragging my ass to nail this…"

"Where's J.Y.?"

"…two-step with the Russians?"

"…some reaction now…"

Nothing like fresh meat in the arena to send the press into a volcanic froth, he thought.

Determined to penetrate through the mob, he extended and locked his elbows at a battle-ready angle, a technique he had learned in blocking drills during his undistinguished high school football career. Bracing himself, he plunged headlong into the forest of faces, their taunting accompanied by hands randomly grabbing at him, the perpetrators partially obscured among the welter of bodies, a room choked in human gridlock. Steadily pummeling his way forward, he retaliated with wild swings of his elbows, causing some to step back, but this overt physical act did nothing to diminish the unrelenting hail of questions dogging each step.

Enduring a self-imposed silence and holding his tongue, he grittily tunneled ahead until coming within arm's length of the door at the opposite side of the room. It led into the West Wing hallway and would be his exit to freedom, a point beyond which, according to an unwritten code, no reporter would venture, unless escorted by a White House staff member.

At the center of the jostling was a bouncing pepper pot in the person of a radio reporter whose in-your-face intensity burdened his every step. Vocal mortar fire at point-blank range from a little guy brandishing a big, menacing microphone. His jumping-jack effort to stay close had brought him to the brink of sartorial meltdown, his ill-fitting shirt crawling up the back of his rooster-thin neck so that it seemed he might ooze down inside the collar and disappear.

While wishing that might occur, Sox launched a counterstrike with a path-clearing body block—a wind-sucker which helped free his line of sight to the door. By penetrating through a few more bodies, he would no longer be a press office P.O.W. History would record it as an escape achieved without the use of tactical weapons of mass destruction, save for a few slightly off-center elbows jabbed into the southern extremities of certain male reporters.

But his freedom march was not quite finished. A glance over his shoulder confirmed that Sparta was closing fast, bobbing towards him in hot pursuit. Reaching the door, he turned and braced himself. Fortunately, her progress had been slowed by the necessity of engaging in hand-to-hand combat herself with other bodies crammed into the small space. Frustrated, she abandoned the land route and went airborne, climbing atop a desk and frantically waving in his direction, establishing eye contact and forming an overstated question mark with the circular sweep of her hand. He looked past her, a non-response which served to incite her going ballistic and unleashing a Richter-scale scream with gale force.

"What's the old man up to?"

Surely that was loud enough to be heard in the Oval Office, he thought. Numbly, he stared at her and all the other inquiring faces edging close. Before him was a human freeze-frame of anticipation, an amassed White House press corps primed for response.

He had nothing to offer. He knew nothing, thereby could say nothing. Of course, if he did know something, that was a problem, too. That meant getting clearance to say something. He'd just have to tap-dance. Pretty much the norm. That was the vexing part of being out of the main informational loop. He was left to wade into all this and play the interim holding act, his role being to let them beat up on him whenever J.Y. was absent. It was a case of the hopeful pursuing the helpless, a charade played out on a nearly daily basis. And based on the theory that once in a while he might slip up and actually impart some useful tidbit of news, however thin it might be.

He had now succeeded in pushing forward far enough to grab the door's handle. It had required a mighty effort to secure that turf, and turning to face his pursuers, he kept the handle firmly clutched in one hand. He had no idea what he was about to say, but having said it, he could now be sure that his exit would be immediate and with no further hindrances.

"Listen, everybody…uh…" he stammered, his voice barely rising above the noise level which instantly dropped at his utterance. "I'd really like to help everyone here…so…uh, let me just say…"

As he fumbled for words, the room pulsated with the urgency of pens and pencils scratching across notepads. Then, as if on cue, they paused, an expectant hush settling over the room, like everyone had come to the end of a sentence on exactly the same beat. He cleared his throat and continued.

"I really am trying…I'm trying to…"

He hesitated again, watching as they wrote down each of his words. It was incredulous because his words were…nothing. Blather. Gibberish. Substantively zero. Yet they were willing to meticulously transcribe the stuff as if he were reciting the Ten Commandments. It then occurred to him that maybe this was the time to pull out that venerable chestnut of spokesman stalls—answer a question with a question.

"You asked about the old man?"

"Damn right!" Sparta snarled.

"Well…uh, that is, which old man? We've got a bunch of them working here."

As the words left his mouth, he turned and flung the door open, escaping into the muted stillness of the hallway.

Moving toward the lobby but still not out of shouting range, he could hear their derisive yelps rising and hanging over the area like a drone emanating from lathered locusts. Drawing further away, he welcomed the small comfort of hearing their anger quickly dissipate into isolated bursts and sputterings, like erratic sparks from a high-voltage line broken loose from its mooring. Finally there was the soft thud of the thick press office door closing shut, sealing him off and enshrouding the hallway with an austere calm, like there had been a lightning strike, but just as suddenly it had died. He sighed uneasily. He had done his job. He hadn't lied. Yet he felt unfulfilled, as did the reporters, partners as they were in incomplete lovemaking. Media interruptus.

He passed on through the West Wing lobby, since 1934 a waiting room for world leaders, captains of industry, noteworthy citizens and streams of lesser visitors. The West Wing lobby—that small but elegant arena just a few paces from the Oval Office. The room in which fleeting bits of casual conversation sometimes find their way into the pages of daily newspapers. Or end up as bits of historical trivia in doorstop-thick books that record the passing scene of the presidency. The gathering place that on a daily basis shares scraps of time with the movers and shakers of the world. The lobby which, in itself, is a theatrical event.

He continued past couches and chairs, perches often occupied by the powerful and famous, including at the moment the secretary of state and a delegation of Chamber of Commerce executives. Today's scene was also inhabited by those occupying less lofty echelons in the nation's labor pool, most notably a pizza deliveryman who had arrived simultaneously with a troop of Boy Scouts and lustily announced at the reception desk that he was anxious to unload the specific item that had been ordered, "a large with anchovies," and be on his way.

While the flustered receptionist was busy phoning around the complex to locate the pizza's recipient, the deliveryman sought to engage the secretary of state.

"Hey-a, Mr. Sec, whasa hoppinin?"

His grunted greeting netted a curt nod from the worldly secretary, the latter's reserve seeming to discourage any suggestion that the requested food item whose pungent aroma now amply filled the lobby might be his. To be sure, it was a pretty wayward mix of folk who had gathered there today, with most of them cautiously eyeing each other. But that was pretty much the activity of choice in this room, there being no stacks of dog-eared magazines with which visitors could occupy themselves. Nobody worked crossword puzzles while waiting here. It was strictly a paradise for people-watching.

Dodging through the Boy Scouts, Sox smiled at their jittery excitement, a notable contrast to the sham nonchalance of the executives. Who were they kidding? Behind those smug exteriors they were just as eaten up with the fidgets right now as the Boy Scouts. Probably more so. Sox chortled to himself as he recalled what a frequent high-ranking visitor had once observed: "No matter how many times one warms the pines in that lobby, one never fails to experience a parched dryness in the throat and an active case of the flip-flops in the gut."

Out on the driveway the afternoon's radiance was settling over the grounds, the sun-shower penetrating the latticed greenery and raining glisten on the white facades. The lawn was busy with gardeners and handymen darting in and out of shrub-shrouded nooks, and beyond was a parade of pedestrians, the haze reducing them to blurry silhouettes as they traveled the sidewalk, some filling its expanse in columns of three and four abreast.

As he shuffled toward them, Sox's feet skidded on the carpet of soggily matted leaves left spread across the driveway from the earlier morning dew. With the sun knifing through massive spreads of clouds, he gathered himself and looked directly upwards, at first shading his eyes, then letting the rays hit him direct. It felt good to stand out there, even if only for a moment to be away from the myriad pressures churning inside those walls. He could be a non-spokesman for just a few minutes, albeit frustrated and unfulfilled, his latest efforts having been void of any hint of accomplishment.

He kept walking toward the street, pausing to greet some of the network television crew members who had drifted outside to bathe themselves in the afternoon's warmth. There on the North Lawn's emerald expanse, they puttered at non-essential tasks, including stretching their legs in the sun. As they crept about, they seemed to be in slow motion, laboriously uncoiling large spools of cable or leisurely tinkering with their camera equipment. The evening's newscasts were still hours ahead, but these technicians seemed needful of being occupied, even if only with minor tasks. All this lethargic activity was confirmation of a reality about life on the White House beat that was seldom perceived by the public. The work here, like on any job, could be a bore.

He slowed as he passed by a slightly overweight television correspondent taping a report, probably a syndication piece. The reporter was nattily attired from the waist up in a blue blazer, red pinstriped shirt and crew tie. Below his waist, out of camera sight, he wore only a pair of tight-fitting, paint-smeared cutoff jeans and mud-encrusted sneakers. He continued to flub the opening as the camera rolled, cursing with frustration each time he stopped. He was already on "take four."

At last Sox reached the northwest gate security post. The guards, most of whom usually recognized him, were his friends, except for one who always requested to see his pass. "You have a nondescript face—I can never remember you." The last time this occurred, Sox quickly produced the pass, brandishing it with a scowl and savoring a small victory as the chastened guard sheepishly grinned at having again initiated this nettlesome act of repetition, sort of like a dutiful beggar. Now as he walked past, Sox checked but didn't spot him. Instead, the guards on duty nodded politely, one of them smiling and saying "Hello" with his lips, a pantomime since all sound was blocked by the imposing sheet of protective glass that encased the post.

Finally, he was out on the street, stepping from behind the fence onto the great avenue, an excursion into reality and life's scruffier side which now swept him along, rubbing elbow to elbow with an unshaven, wooly vagrant, a down-at-the-heels regular around there. As a tenant of its nearby alleyways, he was well-known to the White House guards who often spotted him bedding down on the Ellipse or in Lafayette Park. According to reliable sources, it was also a sure bet that he never strayed too far from the liquor store that was within walking distance.

Everywhere were people—grabbing, pushing, soliciting, posing, preaching, one even pissing, and no one giving a damn about Sox, who he was or where he worked. Breaking free from the weaving scrabble of bodies, he moved toward an elderly man in the distance, a drifter creeping along, slumping with visible agony as he took each step. His shoulders were slack under the crush of an unwieldy cardboard sign, but he still plodded onward, much like Christ on his way to Calvary. Coming closer, Sox could see he was holding a battered harmonica in his free hand and pressing it weakly to his swollen lips, attempting to play a low, mournful tune. He was protesting something, as have so many in front of those gates, and Sox waited until he could clearly read the old-timer's sign. Its ragged letters were a mixture of red and black scrawl.

INSURANCE RATES COULD BE LOWERED
IF PEOPLE WOULD QUIT HAVING WRECKS.

Sox looked into the sadness of his beady eyes, swollen and nearly shut, a man bent but not defeated. His face was powder-pale. The old fellow cocked his head to better study the presidential spokesman, his eyes slowly blinking open and shut, flints of an undimmed spirit. Then, without further pause, he took up his tune and began walking again, a lone vagabond gradually engulfed by the mass of humanity roaming the avenue.

Sitting on a nearby curb were other recruits to the ranks of the down-trodden. One of its more shabbily garbed members wore dark glasses, crudely taped together with Scotch tape. He sat against a lamppost, a tin cup at his feet. A small, handmade sign sat to one side, its message proclaiming: *Blind Since Birth. Donations Welcomed.* It was an intriguing declaration, given that its intended beneficiary was partially hidden behind the sports pages of a newspaper, absorbed in the results from an area racetrack.

A nearby companion, unwashed and unlaundered, had opted for the candid approach. Across his lap he clutched a piece of cardboard, soiled and weather-warped, its penciled message offering a refreshingly frank plea: *Why Lie? I Need A Drink.*

Sox jogged across the street, surveying the littered terrain of Lafayette Park, a landscape pocked with makeshift signs and billboards of various sizes, colors and purposes, some bearing faint kinship to the garishly painted advertising seen on outfield fences in some minor league baseball parks. As a showcase for one's artistic wares, and even the crudest art forms, it served as a makeshift national museum for graffiti.

The subject matter for today's displays included the obligatory roll call of causes: *abortion (pro and con); taxes (let's nuke 'em!);* and *acid rain (Mr. President, acid rain is not a rock group!)*

Most of the messages, however, were more of a muddle.

BRING BACK RUTHERFORD B. HAYES!

I GOT JESUS. I WANT JUSTICE!

YOU JERK (AND YOU KNOW WHO YOU ARE!)

IS ANYBODY HOMELESS IN HEAVEN?

MY CHILD IS NOT NOW, NEVER HAS BEEN, AND NEVER WILL BE AN HONOR STUDENT AT ANY SCHOOL, ANYWHERE!

HAVE A NICE DAY OR A NUCLEAR WAR. THEY BOTH SUCK!

LISTEN TO THE DEAF. THE DEAF HAVE A VOICE, TOO!

THE PEOPLE KNOW A TURKEY WHEN THEY SEE ONE!

HELL IS NOT THE ONLY OPTION—SEEK OUT THE LORD!

MR. PRESIDENT, CONGRATULATIONS—YOU'RE STUMBLING TO GLORY!

LET'S UN-DO HISTORY!

PEACE IS KINDA NICE!

THIS CITY IS A CIRCLE JERK!

THIS CITY IS A GOAT GRUNT!

SPIN PATROL—DEFENDERS OF AMERICA!

He stood mesmerized while reading some of the less-intelligible offerings, attempting to decipher their content made fuzzy by tortured usage of the English language. It was a short-lived reverie.

Suddenly a long, black limousine, which he instantly recognized as Russian-made, negotiated an abrupt turn and wheeled into the North Lawn driveway. Pausing as a member of the uniformed division of the Secret Service poked his head in the window on the driver's side, the car idled long enough to belch several puffs of gray smoke from its exhaust; then, as the gates swung open, it began slowly snaking its way through the grounds in the direction of the West Wing entrance.

Nervously, Sox launched into an all-out sprint for home. Having drifted through the park past H Street, he now darted back across it, zigzagging between two look-alike sedans, the type that are a Washington contradiction—bland, but eye-catching.

He was racing now, weaving around pockets of people scattered about the park. The afternoon was heavy with humidity, so much so that as he ran he felt droplets of sweat oozing down his forehead, the excess moisture dribbling into his eyes and blurring his vision. His face glistened brightly, but his thoughts remained clear. And inwardly he was raging. Dammit, he thought, the Russian ambassador cruising right up the front driveway in full view of the press corps. Subtle. About as subtle as a strip show on the South Lawn in the midst of an arrival ceremony for the pope. Might as well drop a dry fly on a lake of starving piranhas. Once again, he was out of the information loop. Once again, as a supposed insider, he was an outsider, no better informed on White House business than the protestors in the park. What the hell was going on? Why was the Russian ambassador here?

Out on the lawn, network television crews and correspondents scurried to catch up and track the Russian's arrival, jostling for position, some boldly jogging along in tandem with the car, jabbing microphones at its rolled-up window, vainly trying to peer inside and glean some offhand comment as to the purpose of the visit.

Sox slowed down long enough to flash his pass at the guardhouse, jogging in place, then breaking into a sprint again before catching up with the others. Once there, he found himself an observer immersed in the journalistic froth surrounding the vehicle as it slowly, unevenly lurched along, making for a jerky progress that served to discourage those reporters running alongside from getting too close. Finally it reached the West Wing portico and slowed to a stop.

Still wheezing and panting from his impromptu romp home, Sox gulped down air, his body slumping, his legs a rubbery wobble, hands grasping at his knees for support. Hunched over, he watched as the flag-laden superfortress disgorged its passenger, a craggy-faced eminence of diplomatic bearing who indeed was the Russian ambassador.

Instantly the air was flooded with a sheet rain of questions hurled his way, most of which blended together in a garbled hum, a few bits rising from the clamor.

"Mr. Ambassador…purpose…this meeting?"

"Mr. Ambassador…this unusual?"

"…rumors…the president…trip…"

"…and why aren't you on the president's public schedule for today?"

Suddenly a voice boomed out louder than all the rest—so powerful, so dominant, so assertive that it seemed to demand a response.

"Hey, Mac! You got a score on the Dodgers game?"

The ambassador hesitated, the surprise in his face riveted on the reporter who had shouted the question. A collective groan rose from the mob, an emotion that burdened them only for seconds before the yelling resumed. The ambassador ultimately had no results to offer on the Dodgers game, pausing on the portico's steps to noncommittally shrug, then ducking inside to escape the circus his arrival had jump-started.

Everyone began breaking away, rushing back toward the press room and their tiny work cubicles at its rear. From there, pursuit of the story would now shift to the telephone and the badgering of well-cultivated sources sprinkled throughout the tiers of influence in Washington's foreign policy spectrum. Sources? A Washington buzzword for leakers.

The uproar quickly subsided. For the network camera crews left behind, it was back to business as usual. And that business was pretty much just hanging around. For large chunks of each day they had no other option than to sit out on the lawn and wait for something to happen. The axiom of the White House beat was: "Ten hours down. Two minutes on." There were great chunks of idle time for them—between briefings, between visitors, between events and the occasional spurt of news. But the rules of the game were such that no one could afford to stray too far for fear of missing something unexpected. A happenstance. A quick blip. Like today.

Once the doors closed behind the ambassador, most of the members of those crews drifted back to the lawn and their stand-up areas, discharging videotape cassettes from cameras, fussing with lenses and other busywork. Still others resumed prone positions of leisure on the North Lawn grass. Amidst labyrinths of coiled cables they created makeshift perches from which to absorb the sun's tanning rays and combat the tedium by devouring dog-eared paperback novels. The Russian's arrival was but a momentary diversion from such literary pursuits which they now took up again in their crudely arranged nests.

One of their members who had missed the arrival ambled over to join his colleagues.

"Hey, who was the dude in the striped pants who just came in?" he asked, directing his query at no one in particular.

No one looked up. One of the technicians, unshaven, a ham-fisted wide load of a man, was sitting with his feet casually propped on an equipment box, his back strategically angled against a camera stand. In two stubby fingers of one hand he deftly cradled a tattered paperback, its precise angle of elevation requiring minimal hand-to-eye coordination. His eyes fluttered listlessly as he read, the corners of his mouth beginning to sag with the onslaught of a yawn. After a moment he shifted his position slightly, all the while his eyes never departing from the literary epic in which he was absorbed. Finally, with a vacant detachment, he looked up, his eyes sleepily settling on his inquisitor.

"Dunno, just got here myself," he said wearily. Then he paused, took a deep breath and belched coarsely.

"Probably a UPS delivery."

CHAPTER TWO

REPORTER: Is the President fat?

SPOKESMAN: I don't know. We haven't weighed him lately.

Sox slammed his office door shut. Frustrated, he swatted at the imposing stack of pink phone message slips stacked on a corner of his desk, sending them airborne and randomly fluttering down throughout the room, adding another layer of silt to the family of debris that had been gathering without interruption in the tiny office. While aspiring to the goal of an orderly work environment, he had fallen lax in his housekeeping with the result that sloth had gone on a rampage.

The disarray had become a glutted mess that spilled across the room. It included days-old newspapers, spools of unraveled wire service copy running off in all directions, file folders, briefing books, baseball cards, press releases, photographs, T-shirts, a bowling ball, cassette tapes, an athletic bag crammed to overflow with tennis racquets, athletic shorts that by their odor confirmed their absence from any recent visit to a laundry, books, magazines, books piled upon magazines piled upon books, campaign buttons, bumper stickers, a clarinet, a manual typewriter, mounted above which was a sign stating, *Endangered Species*, various White House perks, cufflinks, tie clasps and a Lucite frame containing a small piece of cork with the following inscription underneath:

This fragment of cork was part of the floor installed in the White House Oval Office in 1934. The floor supported six Presidents of the United States before it was removed in 1969.

He slapped aimlessly at one of the pink slips as it floated downward, missing and grabbing only air. Slumping in his chair, he stared vacantly out at the street. He was not a happy camper. Nor was he in a receptive mood to reengage the press fury erupting outside his door. But the intrusive reality was that it wasn't going away. And for good reason. Today's story had new legs.

"Sox, how about it!" a voice cried out, enraged and brimming with urgency.

It was immediately followed by others, bombs away.

"This guy's in the Oval Office right now!"

"Why no photo op?"

"…no pre-brief…"

"…nothing on the schedule…"

"…zip…"

"What's Larry Lunchbox in middle America supposed to think—that they're in there trading Tupperware tips?"

"…raises lots of questions…lots of questions…"

Sure it does, Sox fumed. The same questions he'd like to ask a few people himself. Like the president. Like J.Y. It was days like this that made him envy the network crews and their downtime out on the lawn. Unlike them, however, he didn't have a cheesy paperback to help make the time pass. He looked wistfully at the rubble around him. There was nothing risqué in that mess—no escapism.

The facts he knew as of this moment were these: a) the Russian ambassador was in the Oval Office holding a previously unannounced meeting with the president; b) the press was going berserk waiting for answers; c) he had no clue as to what was happening; and d) Sparta had rejoined the ranks of those bellowing outside his door.

"Crayon's plate is slopping over with problems!" she shouted. "The Russians are playing games! The Congress is gridlocked! He's got a $400 billion deficit, and there's not one damn taxpayer-paid spokesman who can give us a fill on what's going down right now!"

She was right. But he could only remain mute while drawing brief solace from another voice that chimed in: "Life ain't fair, Soxy—what the hell!"

Where was J.Y.? He tried buzzing him on the phone intercom. No answer. Probably over sniffing around the Oval Office. Nothing to do now but gut it out and wait until somebody was willing to bring him up to speed.

Up to speed. Up to speed. Up to speed. Up to what speed? He chuckled to himself thinking about that phrase, one heard tossed around the West Wing to such an extreme that a vomiting spasm would be welcome if it meant relief from hearing that jargon. Verbal flapdoodle. A language of a world within a world.

He hadn't been on the job long when, after several weeks of bouncing between meetings, some of which seemed interminable, he discovered some of his colleagues were disciples of this highly specialized lingo. The White House, it seemed, was the site of the Olympic Games for cliches.

He could only feel sympathy for those future historians of good patience who in recording the sequence of great events during this period would be left with a grab bag of catchy phrases to puzzle over, unravel, decipher, translate and in general try to figure out what the hell they all meant.

For Sox, this roll call of phrases included some repeated every day to the point of nausea:

"What are the downside risks on this?" (He always wondered: Why is no one ever concerned about the upside risks?)

"Does it look presidential?" (Asked with regard to the planning of just about every event, trip, ceremony or movement, mercifully with the exception of those movements relating to the president's bowels.)

"Let's go the full nine yards on this." (He always wanted to meet the guy who deemed why it should be nine. Why nine? Why? Why not thirteen? Or twenty-eight? How about six? Was this a constitutionally mandated number? Why nine?)

"Let's 86 (scrub) that." (Once he had tried to inject a patriotic flare into an otherwise gray meeting when, at the appropriate pause, he said: "Let's 76 that." No one laughed.)

Such phrases had become so embedded in his consciousness that days passed by when many of his conversations consisted of little more than chain links of this bilge loosely strung together. "Up to speed…let's 86 that…the full nine yards…downside risks…," etc., etc., etc.

Many of these lines were saved for the endless stream of staff meetings. Hard as he tried, he could never "get a handle" (another one of those phrases) on why so many meetings were necessary. They popped up everywhere—mushrooms in an overcrowded field.

The slightest pause in the decision-making process would activate these gatherings, the cry going up: "Staff meeting! Staff meeting!" From all directions eager bodies would dutifully appear to fill the furniture, like central casting had instantly answered a request to provide a room brimming with shiny faces full of resolve. Such meetings would include senior staff meetings, congressional relations staff meetings, press office staff meetings, domestic policy staff meetings, scheduling meetings, advance office meetings, pre-advance scheduling meetings and a bevy of other meetings to find out what went on in other meetings. It was a paradise for those inspired by the tedium of going to meetings.

A typical day would have Sox jockeying in and out of a half-dozen such sessions. They were epidemic in their extreme. Many were held in the Roosevelt Room, across the hall from the Oval Office, where it was convenient for the president to make an impromptu drop-by. Or so it seemed. The key always was that it appear like an ad-lib gesture on his part: "…heard the brainstorming going on in here…just wanted to drop in for a second to say hello and…" Sometimes it might be a legitimate whim, but otherwise it was carefully planned in advance to make sure such a quick hit had a spur-of-the-moment look to it. Spontaneity was a coin of the realm in this White House—as long as it was well-planned. As one of the scheduling office staffers confessed: "The hardest part with him doing all these unscheduled appearances is finding time in advance to schedule them."

The end result of all this was that a lot of decisions were left hanging in these meetings. But those who demanded them and those who went along for the ego surge of being in on the action seldom seemed to mind, even though the problem at hand often remained. They knew what everyone knew: later on, the president, in consultation with individual advisors, would make the "final decision calls" himself.

Still, the meetings kept everyone busy, if not productive. If they accomplished little, they did serve to fill cavities of time for lesser aides and hangers-on who knew that should a decision actually be made at their lower level, the president or some other senior official could unravel it later if necessary.

Another favorite meeting format was the corridor conference, a group of three or four on foot, in motion, on the run. A senior official had once confided to Sox his enthusiasm for such hallway confabs, endorsing the technique thusly: "I like to do things on the fly, make decisions then. It's hard to say no to a moving target."

He was pondering that wisp of erudition when the clang of the phone snapped him back to immediacy.

"Hi, Sox, it's Flaxen Day…uh, remember you met me on a flight about six months ago…"

Flight? Flight? Flight? What the hell flight? If it wasn't Air Force One or the White House-chartered press plane, he hadn't been on any other flights recently. At least not any commercial flights. Still, the silky purr in the voice at the other end seemed to suggest possibilities beyond sylph-like innocence. That was pure speculation on his part, to be sure, but even if not, its alluring tone was a diversion far more palatable than the journey through spokesman's hell in which he was currently mired.

"Give me that again," he stammered, the focus of his attention shifting from the continuing taunts and gibes by reporters waiting outside, a world of torment and panic just a few feet away, to the breezy eagerness in her voice, a far more enticing alternative.

"You had been to Texas for the weekend," she said softly. "It was on the flight back…I was one of the flight attendants…I noticed the White House tag on your briefcase…you gave me an autographed photo of the president and suggested that you would personally show me the White House…that I could take a tour sometime…you…do…remember…don't you?"

Contact. Flashback complete. The trip had been a weekend when he rushed home for twenty-four hours. No politics. No government business. It had been for a cameo appearance at a college reunion, where in the midst of some whiskey-inspired ego-flexing, he brazenly launched an attempted conquest of one of the class' yearbook beauties. Given his high-flying position at the hub of worldly decisions, he figured bedazzling her would be a cinch. He figured wrong. All he notched was a big suck of wind and maybe a record-setting mark for the meltdown of hopes while attempting such a score. For all his inside-the-Washington-beltway bravado, her interest extended little beyond polite indifference, a ho-hum tolerance for his prattling on about being "in the decision-making loop" at the White House. She soon set her sails for brawnier game, the balding offerings of a pudgy mastodon from the ranks of their bygone football team, leaving Sox to spend the rest of the evening nursing his punctured ego, sulking around the room and looking as if his rear end was on his shoulder. To his consternation, two things continued to plunge throughout the night: his spirits and her neckline.

But the occasion was not a complete washout. By virtue of his single status, he managed to choke down his rejection long enough to gamely accept the ever so slightly coveted class award as the *Best Aging Bachelor.*

But Flaxen Day…Flaxen Day…oh, yeah, it had been on the flight back when he was upgraded to first class. Pretty spectacular, she was, a Texas Venus with a tantalizing hint of spicy perfume that teased the air as she moved up and down the aisle. How he had ached for the chance to more fully inhale that aroma. For the chance to stroke the tiny wisps of dark curls so delicately entwined at the back of the neck, then gathered enticingly in the upward sweep of a bun. He imagined how exciting those curls might be if left untangled and allowed to spill freely across the soft shoulders and down toward the alluring hint of curves. Then to succumb to the mysteries behind the smoky, emerald eyes, dancing sparklers so casual and demure one moment, then animated and childlike, snapping wide in awe as he regaled her with slightly more than embellished tales of his life in the shadow of the Oval Office. Just thinking about her made him feel better about the world, even if no one would tell him what was unfolding between the president and the Russians.

Then he remembered how his seat companion, a piano salesman and self-proclaimed arbiter of good taste, had dispelled any notion of being a bore when, after several drinks, his eyes became riveted on Flaxen's shimmering assets, prompting him to lean over and lustily whisper: "There goes a star-spangled piece…of America." His observation confirmed Sox's belief that even those of the blue-blooded world of highbrow culture were helpless to resist the allure of a well-turned ankle.

"Remember, Sox, you said if I was ever in Washington and had some time, that I should definitely call you…that you could invite anyone over to the White House to visit anytime…well, I'm laying over at Dulles," she said, again interrupting his thoughts, her earlier upbeat tone giving way to a harder, not-to-be-denied edge.

He laughed nervously. "Laying over" he repeated silently to himself. He liked that choice of words. A thought to savor, in the case of Flaxen Day. He wished there was a hold button for expectations, given that he was currently entrapped by the press, not to mention the press of work. What was he to do? At the same time, he found himself extremely reluctant to leave unfulfilled the hopes and dreams of such a deserving goddess of flight.

"Look," he said, coming alive and shifting into a business-like tone, "it's sort of a tough day we're having here. I mean, we're talking some possible heavy lifting with the Russians. The full nine yards (that dreaded phrase again, but he was desperate!). Sure, I could do what I said…have you come over here, but…it…uh…that…is…this isn't probably a good time to be conducting guided tours of the West Wing…maybe sometime later?"

"I can be there in thirty minutes," she gently insisted.

Before he could respond, the door flew open. It was Buddy Uncertain, a member of the presidential Secret Service detail.

Leather-tough, with a shirt-shredding torso that defined raw muscularity, he was an imposing mural of tanned fitness and coordination. Slamming the door harshly, he left in his wake frantic pleadings from the glut of reporters massed outside, ranting for a break on news from the Oval Office meeting. Sox wondered, what next? Now here was Uncertain kerplunk in the middle of this, someone whose presence would raise new suspicions and further feed the press frenzy. Might as well have Julius Caesar come strolling in, too. Or Julius Erving. Dr. J. That would be okay. At least they could shoot some hoops outside on the South Lawn driveway. Much better than having to dance through press hoops inside.

Uncertain slowly removed his dark glasses, then easing into a chair, he pulled close and leaned forcefully across the desk, his eyes drilling Sox with laser-beam intensity.

"We gotta talk," he said forcefully.

Despite that command, Sox was determined to finish with Flaxen.

"Okay," he muttered into the receiver, "how about in an hour?" As he spoke, he pointed a finger at the receiver and formed the words "personal call" with his lips to convey his annoyance with the intrusion, leaving Uncertain frowning with impatience.

"Great. I'll see you then," Flaxen said, clicking off.

He dropped the instrument into its cradle and turned his attention to his visitor. He had hated to cut her off so sharply, but an agent like Uncertain seldom came to visit, much less burst in like this. Such an unexpected drop-by was definitely a cause for concern. Also, it was not wise for a press spokesman to cold-shoulder an agent. Their respective work in behalf of the president was a daily commingling, and deals on media coverage situations were an accepted way of life. The press office depended on the cooperation of the agents. On the other hand, that could be a one-way street. The agents depended largely on each other.

Many of the agents were Sox's friends—and he was theirs. Uncertain, however, was an agent to whom he'd never felt especially close.

"We've got a problem in the East Wing," Uncertain said tightly.

"Really…?" Sox replied cautiously, relieved that the problem wasn't related to the meeting currently under way in the Oval Office.

"We've got demonstrators in the public tour line. They've tied themselves to the guardrail with their belts and are demanding to remain there until they've been granted a meeting with the president. We'll handle it, but we were wondering what you plan to tell the press about this."

Another wave of relief surged over Sox, and he pushed back from the desk, casually planting his shoes one atop the other, a reaction that clearly annoyed Uncertain, his jaw tightening.

"Why…we'll do nothing."

Uncertain stared at him with a fixed puzzlement.

"Nothing?" he exclaimed.

"Yeah, nothing. You won't have to do anything either. Relax, it'll all be over soon."

Uncertain leaned in closer, his eyes narrowing with skepticism.

"Oh, yeah? How come?"

"Key-rist, man, it's simple."

"It is?"

"Sure."

"How so?"

Sox leaned across the desk, his head swiveling left and right as if to assure that what he was about to whisper was intimately confidential.

"Trust me, Buddy."

Uncertain looked at him apprehensively, then inched closer so that Sox's lips were nearly embracing his.

"You know why they'll leave on their own?" Sox whispered.

Uncertain nodded uncertainly.

"Biological factors."

CHAPTER THREE

REPORTER: You said my story based on your briefing yesterday was overwritten. Why?

SPOKESMAN: Because I was undertalking.

"Your guest is here. Shall we clear her?" the guard at the northwest gate asked, the chesty brittleness in his phone voice exuding all the warmth of a Washington cold snap.

Oops. In the crush of dealing with the press on the Russian situation and Uncertain's pesky concern over tour-line antics, Flaxen Day had completely dropped off the radar screen of Sox's priorities. The only trouble was, she hadn't forgotten.

"Yeah…sure…why not," he mumbled wearily into the receiver. "Go ahead and clear her in."

Why not compound the day's problems big-time? A day that had quickly become a broken string of pearls scattering wildly in all directions. Oh, well, what's one more body crammed into the press office? But what a body. He'd momentarily salve his frustrations with a survey of her shapely frame, then he'd resolve the matter by asking one of the guards in the uniformed division of the Secret Service to take over and provide her a brief tour of the Red, Blue and Green ceremonial rooms.

Normally a looker like Flaxen might warrant the personalized Sox St. Louis tour, but with the Russian matter dominating today's agenda, he reluctantly concluded he'd have to rain-check that experience for now, bite the bullet and choke back any hormone-incited impulses, thus keeping her impressive proportions in proper proportion.

But wait—what was the commotion outside? From his window it looked like another firestorm erupting—bodies hurtling, cameras being knocked about, tripods wobbling and the tranquility of the grounds shattered by another press melee of some sort. But what? All the foot traffic was chewing up chunks of White House lawn, baseball-sized divots being gouged in the grass, leaving it dimpled like a large green domino. Sparta had long ago relieved him of any notion of reverence she might have for that acreage: "Some people think of this as hallowed ground. Hell, it's just another yard with crabgrass."

He stood up on the window ledge to try and better see what the fuss was all about. At the same time he could use the vantage point to check out Flaxen as she made her way up the driveway from the guardhouse. But unfolding before him was mild rampage—arms pumping, yanking, shoving, a row of overturned folding chairs, all of it unleashed by garrulous network technicians who were abandoning their camera positions in the stand-up areas and romping up the driveway, the centerpiece of their attention still indiscernible but apparently newsworthy. One of the network correspondents had also joined the chase, and unknowingly was creating his own minispectacle. It was the reporter Sox had seen earlier looking very proper for camera shots strictly from the waist up. Below the waist, another story was now sadly unfolding. Due to some shredding of his cutoffs in the posterior area, he was providing those into serious butt-watching a sight that was expansive, insightful and, for him, unfortunate.

For an instant Sox thought there might have been a security penetration and that guards had pursued and seized the occasional gatecrasher or some other unwarranted intruder. But then an even more unsettling thought occurred. Could it be? Yet one more surprise today about which he was uninformed? Something—or someone—had definitely triggered new press interest, at least among the network camera crews. As the bodies began to disperse and his view of the hubbub became less obstructed, he was even more perplexed. There was no limousine. No phalanx of security guards. No trappings associated with royalty or other notable visitors. As the lapdog giddiness began to ebb, parting and giving way to the furor's epicenter, he could at last see what had brought a world-class workforce of America's premier news organizations to heel.

It was Flaxen. Project pulchritude. She was even more dazzling than he remembered—a silky blaze. Despite being surrounded by a crush of bodies, she seemed unperturbed by it all, looking fresh and eager, with an easy, laughing smile which illuminated her face, her head tossing play-fully from side to side. As she came nearer to the building, he could see her eyes anxiously flashing from point to point, glistening in the late afternoon sun with emerald purity.

With arrival at the West Wing entrance, the human convoy which had somewhat enfeebled her progress began to fall back, like playful young colts in a field who had scrambled to chase a rainbow, only to find it disappear just as quickly. Their thinning ranks did not diminish their continuing to stare as she passed under the portico and approached the same door by which the Russian ambassador had only shortly before preceded her. There she gave a tentative smile and said "hello" to the stiffly braced young Marine in charge of door duty. Amazingly, rather than looking at her, his eyes remained riveted on a point in his straight-ahead line of sight, without the slightest peek in her direction. It was an extraordinary feat in military self-discipline, one duly noted by the media onlookers who agreed that, by virtue of this occurrence, one of two ensuing actions should promptly occur. Either the soldier should be accorded a ribbon-bestowing ceremony befitting one who has earned a significant promotion in rank, or else he should be given a medical discharge from the armed forces of the United States due to an unfortu-nate and catastrophic loss of eyesight.

But the same media kibitzers felt reassured by his presence there, knowing that it signaled the president was still in the Oval Office. Anytime the president departed, even if remaining within the grounds, so would disappear the military presence from guard duty at the West Wing entrance door. It was one of the media's ways of keeping tabs on the president's whereabouts, or at least his presence in, or absence from, the Oval Office.

Sox continued to watch as the pack, like stragglers from an army in retreat, disgruntedly returned to their outposts on the lawn. There they would once again take up the business of idleness under grand conditions, fidgeting with their cables and cameras, lounging and wandering, and waiting for something else to happen.

One of their members who had lingered behind to savor the visual feast until the last possible moment saw Sox staring out his window and yelled at him: "Hey, Sox, ho-hum, one of your budget advisors is here."

Others paused in their journey back to the lawn to toss out their own verbal footnotes.

"The economy stinks, but those are the best statistics the White House will see this year!"

"All of you are wrong. That's the new ambassador to paradise."

One of the technicians came rushing back down the driveway, his raspy voice modulating in an urgent tone simulating a network newscaster delivering a fast-breaking story. Mockingly, he directed his bulletin at Sox, to the point of acting out the scene as if he were on the air and reading from wire copy.

"This just in. Near-riot rocks White House. Identity of mystery guest still undetermined. President officially designates North Lawn as a disaster area. Declares a state of emergency for all eligible males in White House press corps. Details at five."

Sitting in the West Wing lobby, Flaxen took a deep breath and tried not to appear awestruck as various persons of note passed by. She quickly discovered that this was a place where people-watching could be an indoor sport without pause. Here was the secretary of state whizzing by en route to the Oval Office. Here was the director of the National Security Council whizzing by en route to the Oval Office. Here were members of the U.S. Olympic team being escorted to a Rose Garden ceremony. Here was a plumber being escorted to a West Wing toilet in need of repair.

The receptionist, a pleasant-looking woman in her early thirties, nodded briskly to each passerby as they traveled past her desk. Attractive in an overly scented and swept-combed way, she seemed to Flaxen a beacon of character and efficiency, carrying out her duties with a no-nonsense gusto that suggested someone smitten with the elixir drawn from the occasional gusts of power dispensed from her perch. She was a greeter, a handshaker of the famous and mighty. But far more important in the continual in-house White House grope for power, this woman was a purveyor of presidential perks. She, too, had her power base. During the lulls, she remained earnestly engaged with telephone busywork, most of it, Flaxen noted, consisting of the doling out of tickets for coveted seats available in the presidential box for forthcoming attractions at the Kennedy Center.

Occasionally she paused in the midst of her telephoning to glance over at Flaxen who she sensed was a bit overwhelmed by the surround-ings, much in the way a child becomes wide-eyed upon entering a circus tent for the first time. Though impressed by the aura of history-in-the-making which hung heavily over the lobby, Flaxen still could not help thinking of the similarity to her own work—they were both servants to the public in a rarefied atmosphere. She doubted, however, if the receptionist was interested in a job swap. No one here was being asked to raise their tray table or bring their seat to a full, upright position. But what about Air Force One? Didn't the same rules apply there? She made a mental note to ask Sox about that. Speaking of the press aide, where was he? She had been waiting for almost fifteen minutes, and even though it was like being backstage on a world stage, with a who's who on parade, she was eager for new thrills. She was ready for her tour.

In the meantime, might as well try to fill in some blanks about the place. "Is the press office in this area?" she asked hesitantly of the recep-tionist, an uneasy stab at small talk.

The receptionist looked up abruptly, eyeing her cautiously.

"Yes," she answered crisply, then nodding, "just on the other side of that door."

Flaxen stared thoughtfully at the door, an imposing barrier, ominously thick and darkly polished.

"What else is on the other side of it?" she asked, her eyes growing wider.

"A lot of history," the receptionist answered dryly.

Flaxen felt momentarily annoyed. Surely that was a recycled answer, probably served up with slight variations to other visitors who had preceded her through these portals. Since there still was no sign of Sox, she decided to press on with the inquisition, the receptionist's abruptness be damned.

"This is such high-level work you do. I guess you've seen many famous people pass through here."

"Yes, including celebrities who aren't even famous," the receptionist sniffed. "Actually, we've had—"

Before she could finish, the plumber burst through the door and into their midst, hitching up his faltering, tool-laden work pants. His rubbery face expanded as he offered a gap-toothed grin at the receptionist, then at Flaxen. "I'm lookin' for a wench who's seen my wrench," he growled lustily, wiping away beads of sweat streaking across his grimy face.

The receptionist greeted him with icy silence, her eyes flaring with scorn, two defiant heat-seeking missiles.

The plumber decided not to tarry. Sheepishly, he bowed his head and slipped silently back through the door, avoiding any further eye contact except with the floor beneath his shoes.

"Your question was about…?" the receptionist asked, stiffly regaining her composure.

"Famous people…celebrities…world leaders. You must see them all the time."

"Yes…yes, certainly," the receptionist repeated. "As a matter of fact, just last week this lobby was graced with some of the greatest artists."

Flaxen's mind raced. Greatest artists? Living artists? Paintings on loan? Was there an exhibition in town?

"From what period?" she asked hesitantly.

The receptionist shook her head, her face shrouded in the sort of pity reserved for class dunces.

"No, no, you don't understand," she responded. "We had them alive and in the flesh, all over this lobby. Surely you must have read about their visit here."

"Well, I'm relieved to know none of the French impressionists were able to rise from the grave, even to visit the president."

The receptionist shook her head again.

"No, dear, I'm talking about the Golden Gloves boxing team. Now *there* are artists who really know how to put someone down on canvas."

"Oh," Flaxen sighed. "Of course."

CHAPTER FOUR

REPORTER: What can you tell us about the new Chairman of the Federal Reserve Board?

SPOKESMAN: He's a short man with high interest rates.

"Welcome to pandemonium on Pennsylvania Avenue," Sox said.

Flaxen peered up at him, her face aglow with anticipation. He knew in that instant that affairs of state between Russia and the United States had for him just ceased to be a priority. At least for the next thirty minutes. Before him was an eye-filling vision, so fetching and flawless in its purity that not even the pedestrian blandness of an airline uniform could subdue it.

He stood there entranced by the softly curved features of her face, the high cheekbones, the merry bounce in the dimples, the elfin-smooth skin. As she unwound effortlessly from the chair to greet him, he made a visual tour of her figure, a survey whose results were undeniable: she was a pluperfect beauty with a pluperfect body.

"Hi," she said warmly, moving close and grasping his hand with an intimacy that accelerated the flutter in his pulse. "It really looks busy here. Am I a bad girl for dropping in now?"

Bad girl? He should be so lucky. The softness of her lithe fingers as they cozily interlaced with his made him quickly forget his press problems. All the day's earlier frustrations now seemed distant, the stuff of science fiction. The Russians were on hold. The press was on hold. His hormones were not on hold. Never mind that a recent memorandum had been circulated informing the staff that no tours were to be conducted in the West Wing until the president had left the Oval Office for the day.

Before he could slip his other hand around her sleekly inviting waistline and steer her toward the waiting sights, they were interrupted by a sudden burst of bodies thundering through the lobby. At the center of the hubbub was the secretary of state pouring out a stream of nonstop commands to a gaggle of runty aides scrambling along in his wake, each frantic to stay closest to their boss' side but each inevitably falling back, like pint-size pinballs caroming off an electronic game's bumper.

"Forgot a briefing paper," the secretary said, casting a frown in Sox's direction, his ruddy face creased with layers of tiny furrows, his eyes rolling to the skies with frustration. Despite his overt display of impatience, Sox noted that the president's chief foreign policy advisor was still not so utterly preoccupied with the great global issues and their impact on mankind that he couldn't resist stealing an admiring glance at Flaxen, visually sizing her up, then continuing on through the lobby, his aides still scurrying to keep pace.

Briefing paper? Sox wondered if in the true spirit of White House gamesmanship he wasn't angling for an excuse to keep the president waiting for a few extra minutes, just to give credence to the line that had been floated around town that when the president says, "Jump!" the secretary of state is one member of the Cabinet who doesn't wilt and say, "How high?" Ah, the good old secretary of state, on the run, consumed with high-stakes U.S.-Russian games of some sort, late in reporting to the "old man," but still willing to forsake diplomacy for a brief moment to assess the contours of a comely White House visitor.

"That's a grabber," Flaxen exclaimed, "rubbing elbows with the secretary of state! Does this happen a lot?"

"Sure," Sox exaggerated, "pretty much standard fare. Just another day in the main loop."

He knew what he had just said was a charade, false bravado, but necessary for reassuring her perception of him as a personage of note in these quarters and "really thick with the key senior staff." He would need all the cannon fodder he could possibly apply to this project. Debbie Dim Bulb she was not. Already she had handled herself remarkably well, her poise and reserve amidst the boys-will-be-boys press rowdyism that welcomed her to the grounds serving as indicators of a cool, sophisticated mark. But first rattle out of the box she had already been given the Fourth of July, the secretary of state making tracks to the Oval Office—stellar theatre starring a powerful Potomac player. Heady stuff, he reasoned, even for a worldly flight attendant who had lapped the earth.

Thus far today his efforts as a press spokesman had been one big washout. No information received. None dispersed. But with a whiff of her intoxicating perfume teasing the air, an aroma that had even his hangnails itchy with interest, he was convinced the day was salvageable, with fulfillment now coming via the role of tour guide rather than by his trying to penetrate the Ziploc informational seal surrounding the Oval Office meeting. It was a matter of priorities, and his had undergone a drastic change in the last thirty seconds.

"Are you absolutely certain you aren't too busy to show me around?" she purred.

"No problem," he boasted. "A day at the beach."

It took only a few steps down the hallway for the vocal spasms of the news-hungry reporters sandwiched into the upper press office to reach them.

"There's a media army encamped in there that we'll definitely want to avoid," he said.

But it was too late. The squirmy overflow had bunched so tightly against the office's door that it heaved open, bodies staggering out into their path. Nodding guiltily but lingering to take note of the company Sox was keeping, they gathered themselves and waded back into the overpopulated office. Sox knew that room had no tour sights to offer. The Roosevelt Room, to the right, offered no promise either. Milling about in it were various State Department and National Security Council aides as well as Russian embassy officials. Straight ahead was the Cabinet Room. It was his first tour stop of choice. But no need to tell her that yet.

They moved past one other room with access to the hallway—the bathroom. A plunger and other rudimentary tools had been left strewn outside in an untidy pile. From inside they could hear anguished gasps by the plumber seized in efforts to dislodge the source of the unit's blockage.

"What's that all about?" Flaxen asked.

"That's a secure room," Sox said, unsmiling and trying to brush the question off while hurrying past.

"Right," she murmured, taking note of the tools. "The indoor plumbing."

Her discovery served to remind him that it was the same bathroom where he had once kept a major television network correspondent waiting outside. "Hell, if I'd known it was just you in there, I wouldn't have bothered to knock," the correspondent had laughed. Sox felt grateful to have preceded him that day, for while occupied therein his eyes had roamed to the wall and made an incredulous discovery of graffiti scrawled on a White House wall: *George Washington sat here.* He had been tempted to add a postscript: *So did his deputy press secretary.* Thinking better of it, he erased it all, figuring the world of bathroom wall culture could endure without such additions to its literature. In retrospect, he was also relieved that the American public would be spared such gems of prose via one of its television networks. After all, this was the White House, not an outhouse.

They reached the Cabinet Room, and she leaned inside. There were fourteen chairs surrounding the long oval table evenly on all sides. Shadows from the late afternoon sun danced gracefully across the rigid tops of the chairs and down the length of the table. The room looked more tranquil than Sox had ever seen it. He pointed out the president's chair, which was slightly taller than the rest. It sat squarely mid-distant from each end of the table facing in their direction. Several of the chairs had small metal plates attached to their backs, indicators of service in other Cabinet positions in this or prior administrations. One of the chairs had four such tiny plaques on its back, lined up vertically, a governmental badge of accomplishment, mindful of a military medal with additional insignia of commendation hanging from it.

"Sox, do you ever see the president?" she asked, her gaze riveted on the chief executive's chair.

"Absolutely…uh, sure…of course…hey, I'm a player around here."

"But does he know your name? Who you are?"

"Certainly…he knows my name…everything about me. I'm in and out of the Oval Office all the time…you know, photo ops…I see him plenty…the secretary of state…lots of heavy lifting with the heavy hitters…"

Her attention slowly moved away from the room to the nearby closed door of the Oval Office. He sensed in her an enlarged thirst for a thrill surpassing that of viewing an empty Cabinet Room, a thrill he was most definitely incapable of providing. In self-defense he planted himself between her and the door, outside of which several jut-jawed Secret Service agents were appraising them with steely-eyed intensity. The greater part of that intensity of inspection, he noted, was directed at Flaxen, her ankles to her eyebrows, rather than to himself. She seemed to him anything but a national security threat.

"I'd show you the Oval Office, but unfortunately some folks are in there right now," he said matter-of-factly, a gentle pop to her bubble of hope. "That's why you see the Secret Service agents stationed in this hallway."

Nearby was a marble bust of Abraham Lincoln. She paused to admire it, her eyes mistily filling with awe. The moment of reverence proved brief, a spell broken by her making the appalling discovery that someone had wadded up a chewing gum wrapper and stuffed it in the ear of the sixteenth president of the United States. Crass disrespect for the Great Emancipator. Poor fellow. Sox made sure the intensity of his revulsion for the deed equaled Flaxen's. That accomplished, he decided to forego mentioning that it was also the same statue that some members of the senior staff patted each morning for "good luck" as they passed by, a symbolic gesture akin to athletic teams which perform a similar ritual with old championship game trophies as they depart a locker room onto a field of battle.

With options fast evaporating, he decided to keep moving. Just past the Oval Office the hallway curved slightly back toward the Roosevelt Room on the right and, to the left, a series of senior staff offices. At the far end was the office of the chief of staff, Quad Sands. Some called it "the sandbox," but a lower-level aide once summoned to its historic confines for a reprimand had gone further and acidly dubbed it "the quicksand box." As time passed and others were summoned for the same purpose, the name stuck.

Sox's modified game plan now called for a cursory pass by there, then back to the lobby where he could dump her off and bank the points he had scored today for use on a future and more intimate occasion.

Adjacent to the quicksand box was an outer office where two primly mannered secretaries were menacingly perched, their eyebrows arched with suspicion.

"The gatekeepers," he whispered, returning their vigilant glares with an uneasy smile.

Knowing that they diligently watched over their boss' turf with a huntsman's scent for the kill, he dared not approach even to suggest Flaxen be accorded a brief glimpse into the inner sanctum. Just to be in its proximity was to bask near the trough of power. He had at least given her that whiff.

"All roads may lead to the Oval Office, but they usually make a pit stop here," he said, his tone implying a firsthand intimacy with the area.

"Are you in and out of this office a lot, too?"

He nodded affirmatively.

Before she could react, they were distracted by stirring among the agents back at the opposite end of the hallway, muffled voices, and then a rush of activity as the Oval Office door swung open, the corridor filling with bodies in a closed-ranks formation. At its center a voice was engaged in high-spirited banter and moving in their direction. As the phalanx of brick-shouldered agents grew closer, the voice's owner and other members of the group came into view.

"It's…it's…it's the president!" Flaxen gushed excitedly.

The press spokesman gods had not been kind to Sox earlier in the day. Now it seemed he was being dealt a fresh hand. He was about to be in position to serve up the Number One attraction in the house. Everything was about to be so right. And yet, everything was about to be so wrong.

Quad would want to know what in the hell he was doing conducting a tour of the West Wing while the president was engaged in Oval Office talks with the Russians? He'd also want to know why this fluff in the airline uniform was worthy of such glorified treatment? And why Sox wasn't in the press office helping hold the press at bay? And what, if any, were his prospects for employment elsewhere?

With the presidential entourage steaming their way, he had less than ten seconds to mull his fate, perhaps the final thoughts of his career within those corridors. The options were basic: cut bait, haul ass and immediately hustle her out of there; or, bet the ranch that Flaxen and her traffic-stopping assets could carry the day. He shrugged, bit down on his tongue and made his choice.

"No sweat," he said, forcing a weak smile. "I'll introduce you."

Their horizon was now dominated by the approaching human juggernaut of the president, a protective convoy of Secret Service agents, Quad Sands, the secretary of state and other tailgating aides of lesser rank. Sox grabbed Flaxen and hurriedly pre-positioned her for maximum exposure, his strategy vested in the belief that even with the conservative constraints of her flight attendant's uniform, she still might be capable of bringing a brief hiatus to the affairs of state. The fact that several sets of high-level eyes already appeared to be wandering her way, seemed an encouraging sign. Still, he was consumed by grinding jitters, like a jackhammer had been plugged into his innards. And why not? His White House career was clinging to the shirtwaist and skirt of an airline flight attendant.

"Mr. President, excuse me," he said, veering into the chief executive's path, "but there's someone here who would very much like to meet you."

The president broke stride and paused, his face tightening with impatience over the delay. He leaned through the forest of bodies surrounding him and appraised Sox, then settling on Flaxen. She returned his examination with an eager smile, her face flushing slightly, a blush of crimson suffusing the glow in her cheeks, her eyes growing watery with glee. Softly, her glistening lips parted and whispered, "Hello." The president glanced at Sox again, then smiled warmly at her.

"Are you sure it isn't the other way around?" he asked, shifting toward her with a casualness that suggested any prior hint of annoyance was now null and void.

Through clenched teeth Sox gasped for intakes of White House air. The scowl on Quad's face was a bullet he'd have to dodge later, but it was the immediate moment that now harbored his every concern—ensuring the president's approval and Flaxen's exultation, his tickets to a potentially safe and pleasurable future.

"Mr. President, this is Flaxen Day."

"Well, yes, how are you?"

"Very well, sir, thank you."

Her hand, trembling, went limp in his and remained enclasped there as he studied her. Sox stepped back, leaving them to share center stage.

"The uniform—you fly, of course. Well, just consider being here like working the cabin in first class."

She laughed politely, but remained silent.

"Have you ever toured the White House? Ever seen the Oval Office? Go on down and take a look," the president said, tossing his head toward the latter. "I think I put my tray table up and placed all carry-on items in the overhead compartment."

She laughed again at this wafer-thin stab at humor, this time feeling emboldened enough to lightly place her hand on his shoulder as if needing to brace herself in the wake of this mirthful onslaught. Nice touch, Sox thought.

"We could use her on Air Force One, eh, fellas?" he goaded, never looking back at his cadre of aides, all of whom nodded affirmatively. "Well, I'm late for a meeting in the Situation Room."

Slowly he let loose of her hand and started to walk away. Turning and looking back over his shoulder, he noticed Sox, to whom he had not spoken or acknowledged. Sensing the gravity of the situation in the press spokesman's terms, and clearly wanting to rectify the omission, he strode back toward them, pointedly stopping directly in front of Sox.

"Oh, and how are you today, Bill?" the president asked grandly.

The words boomed out loudly down the quiet hallway.

Flaxen's jaw dropped, the wrench of surprise in her face pronouncing

Sox guilty.

All he could do was watch helplessly as the president walked away, then tried to face Flaxen but instead dropped his head with a measured slowness, like the final-act curtain in a theatre, so low until it rested against his chest.

Flaxen stared at him with eyes flashing angrily.

"Bill!"

He groped for an explanation, but it was useless.

"In and out of the Oval Office all the time?" she mocked. "Knows exactly who you are? Bill?"

Outside, the sun was setting over the majestic grounds. Inside, Sox wondered if he would ever see her again. He didn't look up. He couldn't. He could only hang his head in defeat. There was nothing else to say.

CHAPTER FIVE

REPORTER: Is the president going to stand for reelection?

SPOKESMAN: Well, he's certainly not going to sit for it.

Sox staggered into the darkened stairwell of his apartment, a basement efficiency in Georgetown. Many were the nights he would arrive home similarly late, but often with spirits racing and energized by events of historic scope that had passed before his eyes during the day. This was not one of those nights.

Dejected, deflated, rejected—the day's events had left him with a holocaust of the spirit, a mopey listlessness that even made freeing a tacky advertising flyer from his front door a challenge. He peeled away the solicitation from where it had been wedged in the door's screen. It was on pink paper and beseeched him to sign up for half-priced ballroom dancing lessons. *Have fun, meet new friends, impress your partner*, it implored. Launching it into wadded flight, he reasoned he must be on every sucker list known to mankind—direct mail, phone, computer—his life was plagued by such crap. Now dancing lessons. On pink paper. In his door. A perfect ending to a self-inflicted mess of a day.

Entering the apartment, he was greeted by the nerve-jabbing ring of the phone, an interruption that would undoubtedly repeat throughout the night and all the nights the rest of the week, since he was saddled with phone duty. It was an assignment that rotated among members of his office, being available after office hours to take press calls. This week he had drawn the short straw. Wading through a celebration of litter that ran freely to all corners of the room, he struggled to liberate the phone from a pile of formidable muck under which it was fighting to be heard.

"Yeah—what?" he barked, still wrestling to untangle the receiver from debris.

"Hello, Bill…I mean, Sox."

Instantly he recognized the president's voice and gulped deeply.

"Uh, yes…hello, sir."

"I understand from some reliable sources that I may have caused you a little problem with your lady friend today. I'm sorry, it was a momentary name lapse on my part."

"No problem, Mr. President," he insisted. "You've got a lot of big-ticket items teed up right now, much more important than what happened today. Actually, I got just what I deserved. If you see someone walking around the West Wing tomorrow with a charley horse between their ears, I'm your guy."

"Well, I appreciate your understanding. I can assure you it was unintentional. I guess I was somewhat distracted—"

"Hey, Mr. President, who wouldn't have been? We're talking some great gams there, great stats."

There was an uneasy silence before the president responded, his voice suddenly growing firmer.

"*She* isn't the distraction I was talking about. There are some other things going down right now, some delicate talks with the Russians. I just can't add any more."

"I understand, sir."

"I hope you do because what we don't need are any press leaks. This place has more holes in it than a saltshaker. We don't need that right now. Maybe one of these days I'll get to announce a secret before it appears in the morning papers."

Sox thought it was amusing the president should be worried that his deputy press secretary might be doing some leaking on this Russian thing, especially since this particular spokesman's knowledge base on the matter was zero.

"Yes, sir."

"Well, button it down. Oh, and how about that lady—good gams, good stats?"

"I think she's history, sir."

"So am I. Good night."

"Yes, sir. Good night."

Hanging up, his spirits were in a free fall toward deep funk. The president's call had left worrisome loose ends jangling in his mind. Notably absent from the conversation had been any hint of specifics about the Russians, none of the gritty little fill-in-the-blank details so essential to the aid and comfort of a presidential spokesman, the fodder necessary for keeping credibility intact while providing safe passage through press room minefields ladened with prickly "I gotcha" questions.

He had come up empty again. It was one thing to chase a skirt and strike out. No sweat. He'd have other innings. But here was the boss on the line, hammering away about leaks, like he was confiding with some Oval Office insider privy to hush-hush diplomatic traffic, when in fact he was just talking to Sox St. Louis, your basic White House minnow. And yet the leader of the Free World had found it necessary to bluntly remind him about this. Hah! Not to worry, Mr. President. Impossible. No loose lips here to sink any ships. This mouth is closed until further notice, due to the lack of information. Leaking? Yeah, but only in the john tonight after sucking down a few beers.

Besides the humiliating day at the office, Sox was also confronted by another heavy burden: the residue of neglect represented by his apartment's considerable untidiness. Wearily, he surveyed the scene.

Everywhere clothes were scattered like confetti—shirts, socks, suspenders, athletic supporters—much of it dangling from makeshift perches. Adding aromatic texture was a hodgepodge of half-empty food cans, their pungency indicating sardines as the favored meal. Into the scant free areas of floor space were crammed books, the stacks towering unevenly upward, several of the piles teetering and swaying to the wind-rattling rhythms of automobile traffic bouncing along outside. Further busying the landscape were badges of past political campaigns—bumper stickers, buttons, yard signs, ribbons and pennants—strewn haphazardly on shelves, adorning them in meandering, aimless patterns of display.

The centerpiece of this cataclysmic mess was the fireplace, itself not in use, or capable thereof, due to a congestive overflow of refuse spilling from its innards. Above it a red, white and blue placard was on display, neat and orderly in a simple gold frame, the care and precision of its workmanship offering a singular spot of distinction amid the squalor. It read: *William Shakespeare had a lousy press agent.*

Leading away from this carnage was a narrow hallway which fed into a thin strip of space that served as a kitchen. He wandered back there, pulled a TV dinner from the cramped confines of the refrigerator and dumped it into the stove, his thoughts remaining elsewhere. Sometime later—he wasn't exactly sure of the hour, having nodded off—he awoke to the acrid smell of smoke invading the apartment. Racing back to the kitchen, he pulled out the charred dinner's remains, tossing the gooey fragments into the sink. It was then that a vexing question arose in his mind: Was he supposed to have cooked it at 220 degrees for 40 minutes? Or at 440 degrees for 20 minutes? Whichever, it was a disaster. He had obviously made the incorrect choice by at least several hours.

"Soup's on," he mumbled resignedly, tossing the baked aluminum aside.

Soon thereafter he readily succumbed to drowsiness. It met little resistance, enfolding him as he read a book that had caught his eye, one which he had purchased at a used bookstore several months back, keeping it hidden away in a safe cache for deployment on such a dreary occasion. It seemed a most appropriate literary choice for the evening: *The History of Mud.*

At 3 a.m. the phone's unnerving ring jarred him back to reality. He was tempted to ignore it, but even in a groggy haze remembered his obligation—phone duty. Before he could answer, the immediate challenge was to find the phone and free it from entanglement in the vast waste area under his bed. Once, during an overnight visit, a female guest had peeked into that awesome pit and, taking note of the clutter, had dubbed it "the landfill of the forgotten."

It was rumored that buried in it were the highly sought 1952 Topps Mickey Mantle rookie baseball card and an autographed photo of Steve

McQueen. So far, no one had summoned the courage to mount an exploratory thrust into the area. Thus, the rumor remained unconfirmed.

He continued groping for the phone, at last managing to brace the receiver under his chin, sans hands.

"Hi-ho, Sox, it's Sparta."

"Why am I not surprised?" he whispered, his voice still choked with sleep.

"We just got a rocket from our Russian bureau that Radio Moscow is playing Rachmaninoff's *Prelude in C Sharp Minor*. You know what that means?"

"That the music video can't be far behind?"

"No," she bristled. "But it might mean that Navikoff has died. Been lots of rumors about this guy's health."

"Navikoff?"

"Yeah, Navikoff."

"Navikoff?"

"Yeah, smart-ass, Sergei Navikoff, the president of Russia."

"Okay, so what?" he said, extending the stall and struggling over whether to come fully awake or cut her off and crawl back under the covers. "Russian presidents have died before, and the rumor game about this guy has been going on for weeks. Maybe they just needed to play some slow-dance tunes for a change."

"Look, just check it out, will you? Is that why the Russian ambassador was over today? Maybe he knew something. Maybe the latest papa bear has bellied up. Confirm it for me one way or another and give me the U.S. reaction—fast."

"Confirm what?" he protested. "With all the rumors and speculation, we've already buried this guy about five times. I'll let you know if I get anything."

He slammed the phone down, an impulse telling him he should immediately call the Situation Room. On the other hand, no other reporter had called—none of the wire services, no panic, no tumult from any other press citadels—which suggested Sparta was probably flying solo, a fishing expedition. And the people in her Russian bureau had probably gotten Rachmaninoff confused with somebody else's tunes. Once again, the rumor game. Now at 3:30 a.m. he was in no mood to play. Just to be safe, he'd lie there and rest his eyes for a few minutes, then make a call. He pulled the downy comforter up over his head and closed his eyes, never anticipating success for the urge to which he now surrendered, the still veil of slumber.

CHAPTER SIX

REPORTER: Has the president selected a date yet for the next summit meeting?

SPOKESMAN: Of course not, he's a married man.

There are four doors by which to enter the Oval Office. Some might be willing to die just for the chance to walk through one of them. That was the fate for which Sox now braced—death in the Oval Office. Slam-dunked by the president of the United States. His career as a presidential spokesman—over. It was one thing to walk into that room and bask in its historical aura. It was another to be called on its carpet.

He was about to know that experience, having been summoned to wait in the tiny reception area that separates the Oval Office from the Cabinet Room. His early-morning presence had been requested there by the commander-in-chief. The purpose had been described thusly by Quad: "The president has expressed a desire to drop-kick your rear end through the West Wing and across the North Lawn with such velocity that you clear the pointy spires of the protective fence—maybe."

As he waited, Sox mulled his twofold choices. He could leave, find the nearest airplane propeller coming his way and walk headlong into it. Or he could wait.

What had brought him here to face such punishment was Sparta's call last night. That damn call. Navikoff hadn't died yet, much less five times. Sparta had quoted Sox's answer on-camera in a stand-up piece for her network's morning show. To make matters worse, the wire services had picked it up: "When asked to comment on rumors concerning Navikoff's death, White House spokesman Sox St. Louis said, 'We've already buried this guy about five times.'"

Even though he had since gotten the wires to pull the quote, it was too late: it had already made its way across the Atlantic. Moscow had not been amused. Nor had President Crayon.

All he could do now was wish. He wished it were yesterday. He wished he could be getting puke-drunk and inhaling the politically power-inspiring mists of a Georgetown pub. He wished he could get so drunk, hungover and cotton-mouthed dry that he'd wake up feeling like a rugby team had left its used socks in his mouth. He wished he were dangling from charred roots at the edge of hell. Anywhere. Anything. Just not the Oval Office.

His career was about to end, and what did he have to show for it? Some memories. Some yellowed newspaper clippings. And—how could he forget?—a collector's item, a roll of plaid toilet paper from Crayon's last campaign.

Quad and J.Y. arrived and flanked him on each side, like guardians of a prisoner in custody. The three of them stood in a semicircle around the desk of the president's secretary, their heads cast down in a prayerful bent like repentant schoolboys, waiting while the secretary typed, tended to paperwork and generally ignored their presence. In between erratic staccato-bursts on her computer, the quarters were muted with an imposing early-morning silence. Except for themselves and two Secret Service agents in the hallway, they were alone.

Cocking his head toward the glass doors that opened to the colonnade, Sox could see the images of workers out in the Rose Garden busily unfolding chairs, obviously readying the area for a ceremony. His mind raced over the president's schedule for the day but recalled nothing that would warrant such activity. He remembered that the president was due to sign a proclamation declaring this Zoo and Aquarium Month. But a Rose Garden ceremony? Surely not.

He leaned over to J.Y. "Did I miss something? Has a bill-signing ceremony been added to today's schedule?"

"No," J.Y. whispered. "What they're preparing for out there is the ceremony where the president will sign the document commuting your death sentence."

Quad and J.Y. chuckled lightly but drew indifference from Sox who remained intrigued by the scene outside as additional workers drifted into that arbor of splendid isolation, methodically unfolding more chairs and aligning them in precisely symmetrical rows. It was a dazzling display of geometry-on-the-hoof as practiced by crack members of a finely tuned and chair-tested government labor force.

One of the phone lines on the secretary's desk buzzed. She snapped it up, listened for a moment, then brusquely disappeared behind the large wooden door leading into the Oval Office. It was that entrance that Sox whimsically referred to as "Door number two," the one which required the greatest number of steps to reach the president's desk, about twenty paces. He only wished it was twenty miles. Too late, as the secretary returned and directed them into the stately inner sanctum.

A quick appraisal of the room indicated nothing much had changed since he was last there two weeks ago. That occasion had been for a brief photo opportunity to welcome the newly appointed ambassador to the United States from Upper Volta.

"How come there's no Lower Volta?" Sox had chuckled. No one, especially the president and the ambassador, had cracked a smile.

As his eyes traveled around the room, he noted two minor differences that had occurred since his last visit. The desk was a bit messier, with several cigarettes loosely scattered amongst the formidable tide of memoranda arrayed in slightly uneven rows, a pungent bite of stale tobacco choking the air. Better it should be called the Odor Office, he thought.

Secondly, at the epicenter of the desk's clutter was a small wooden plaque. It read: *Disregard This Plaque.*

With Quad and J.Y. lingering behind, Sox felt trapped, a deer in the headlights. The only sound in the room, other than fragments of a phone conversation in which the president was engaged, came from the nearby grandfather clock. Its pounding sway was ominous and heavy, a grim metronome to accompany the tempo of his carefully measured steps, each softly planted and muted by the furry thickness of the deep carpet.

The president sat with his back turned as he finished his call, then abruptly spun around and slammed the phone to the desk, leaving all present to note that ramming-speed was evidently not his forte, the receiver missing contact with its holder, becoming entangled with its cord and settling at the desk's edge in a gnarly pile.

The president eased from his chair, eyes glaring, a missile gathering roar for a launch. Fitfully, he wadded up a piece of wire service copy and hurled it at Sox.

"Here it is!" he raged, his face turning brightly crimson. "Jesus H. Palomino! This…this…this no-brainer deluxe! A flesh wound opened up by your stupidity…in the name of Uncle Sam's jockstrap, what are you going to do about it?"

Sox stared helplessly at the crumpled paper as it settled onto the carpet. He wanted to explain, but explain what? He had screwed up. He could say he had only been kidding. That Sparta was a friend he thought he could trust. That he had no idea she would actually quote him or that the wires would pick it up. Weak. Lame. He knew such an argument would have about as much impact as a goldfish's hiccup. He was as defenseless as a goalie for a dart team.

His tongue was now twisted so deeply into the side of his cheek that any words of explanation were out of the question. His thought processes were still intact, however, and telling him that he'd had a hell of a good ride in this job, but that the time had come when his privates had finally gotten caught in the blade sharpener. Time to bend over and kiss the goodies farewell.

In this moment the president was as red-assed as Sox had ever witnessed. Steamed. Hacked. Twisted off but good. But despite his fury, Sox also saw a man who was tired. The eyes, reddened by anger, were lid-heavy, and the puffiness in the cheeks was dry and colorless.

"This could only have been the work of a world-class yo-yo," the president said sharply. "Do I have a world-class yo-yo as one of my spokespersons?"

Sox looked up. "I…uh…that is…Mr. President…"

"Couldn't keep your powder dry, huh?"

"Mr. President…"

"Here we are on the verge of signing on with the Russians for a summit on terrorism, working closely with Navikoff, trying to delicately smother the big bear with love, and you take a swan dive off the three-meter board reserved for the brain-dead."

"Mr. President…"

"No, that's all right, your president will clean up the manure pile you've dumped. I've already started. I've called the ambassador to explain it was just a sleepy press spokesman having a mental meltdown."

"Mr. President…"

"No, I'll make the explanations. I'll do the calling. The backing and filling. The heavy lifting. The damage control." He paused, sucking in air to gather momentum for a new rip. "You…you're on the respirator. Your future under this roof is kite-string thin. One more screwup like this and your next government assignment will be in the deepest bowels of this red, white and blue bureaucracy."

Sox sensed Quad and J.Y. shuffling in place from somewhere to his rear, but no one stepped forward nor spoke. It was clear that he was without defenders in the room, and rightfully so. It would be a solo crucifixion, so he might as well go down swinging.

"Sir, it was after three in the morning when I got the call…I was…groggy," he said, wincing as he bit his lip.

"Three a.m.? Why weren't you making hey-hey with that airline babe you were parading around here? She fills out a skirt pretty damn well. Hell, at least that would have kept you busy so you wouldn't have had time to open mouth and insert foot."

"Sir, I was the press phone duty officer for the night. Sparta would have called about that story regardless of whom, I mean, what I might have been doing."

The president hesitated, seemingly intrigued by the suggestion that Sox might not have been alone when he took the call. It was a short-lived lull.

"This has really hurt us," he said, snapping back. "Trust me when

I tell you that the ambassador's had his verbal shredder plugged in this morning—carving a revised rear end for yours truly. And let me assure you that the message he had for me was not anything resembling 'Merry Christmas.'"

Sox lowered his head, hoping the presidential ranting was about to run its course. Instead, the president looked past him toward the rear of the room.

"Hey, fellas, what should I do—glue his gonads to a salad fork and serve him a la carte at the next state dinner?"

"I think we've got an even better punishment in mind, Mr. President," Quad called back, a secretive smile forming at the edges of his mouth.

The president nodded, then clenched his teeth, fiercely punching at the air in front of Sox with a jabbing finger, an act that made his fury all the more imposing.

"Okay, let's hope you've learned—no more 3 a.m. smart-assing with the press. Next time, be alert, be serious and not waxing wise with Sparta or any other damn newsies."

"Yes, sir," Sox whispered weakly.

Without hesitation, he turned and headed for the doorway where J.Y. and Quad were waiting with grim faces, but the darting glances between them suggested that it might only be mock solemnity. As he beat it out the door, Sox decided that only four things could possibly be moving faster in Washington at that moment: light, sound, free advice and bad advice.

"Well, you're still standing," Quad chuckled.

"Yeah, barely," Sox muttered. "Somehow I have the feeling that I won't be getting the employee-of-the-month award."

"Ah, yes, but since we now have a truce between you and the president, that only leaves the terms of punishment to be determined," J.Y. reminded.

Sox looked at him warily.

Punishment? What punishment? He waited for an explanation, but Quad and J.Y. only smiled benignly as he continued to squirm. Then it dawned on him—oh, no—the daily press briefing—a bungee jump into hell. As much as he hated the briefing, he also knew in a perverse way that one day as a citizen on the outside, he'd miss it. Its action. Its intensity. Its high. Still, for him to conduct it was a torture. Mega agony. The daily briefing—"the best free show in town"—a daily joust where no mercy was shown in going for the jugular and reporters were always eager for a whiff of fresh meat.

In the briefing room was a small stage and podium, a monument to disaster for those who stood behind it and were slow of mind and thick of tongue. Here one could be hung out to dry by a press corps that delighted in watching briefers wilt, an intellectual strip show before a ravenous audience.

Sure, he thrived on byplay with the media, but the briefing was another matter. It was a chance for reporters to vent, to unleash full-bore and sometimes keep the briefer tap-dancing out there for an hour or more. It was a time and place where they had the briefer by the short hairs.

He watched as J.Y.'s eyes began to dance with anticipation for what Sox now knew was inevitable. Sure, the press secretary was happy—why not?—he was getting off the hook today by serving up his deputy as the sacrificial lamb. Damn the briefing—a verbal caesarean section. He was roadkill every time he had to stand up there and perform. They knew that's why he was content with the deputy job and never wanted to be press secretary where one was expected to conduct the briefing at least once a day, if not more, even though occasionally lobbing the duty off to a subordinate.

And as Sox was painfully aware, they remembered how once when conducting the briefing his nervousness had triggered his lower extremities to let go. The pee had penetrated his light tan summer suit with a spongy artistry that made it a news item as far back as the fifth row, thereby bringing a new and entirely unexpected subject matter to the fore.

He hated the briefing. He'd do anything else. Revoke his Mess privileges for a month. Make him scrape the bird dung off the tennis court. Make him make passionate love to Sparta. Anything. Not the briefing. Not today. Hell, not ever.

CHAPTER SEVEN

REPORTER: The president has appointed a blue-ribbon citizen's committee to review equality for women. Are women getting aroused?

SPOKESMAN: I certainly hope so.

"Shall I make the five-minute announcement?"

Sox looked up apprehensively at the young female press office staffer idling in his doorway. Missy Fore was a short-termer, having been on board only two weeks, a find of J.Y.'s. She was a little too bubbly perhaps (a couple of long days in this office would cure that), but pretty in a wholesome way—fresh, eager and attractive. No matter. The briefing was about to begin.

"They said I should ask you if you wanted the announcement made. Do you?" she asked earnestly.

He remained silent, pensively studying her. He figured if she stood there long enough and stared back at him hard enough, she might sense the landfill of dark emotions gathering behind his falsely calm façade—anger, self-pity and sheer terror. She continued to fidget back and forth in the doorway. Understandable. Not only was he nervous, the staff was nervous for him.

"Yeah, go ahead and make the damn announcement," he mumbled, his face so deeply furrowed it looked like he had made a weighty decision akin to pronouncing the last rites. Maybe he had. His.

As she disappeared down the hallway, his attention returned to the Q&A guidance sheets the staff had prepared for him, only to have his concentration broken by a blast from the press room speaker system: "The daily briefing will commence in five minutes." It was Missy's perky voice. "Today's briefer will be Sox St. Louis."

The announcement unleashed a torrent of whoops and cries from the area of the briefing room, a disturbing outburst. They were waiting. The thundering herd. It was a savage arena he was about to enter. Damn, Quad! Damn, J.Y.!

The tumult continued, intimidating chants and other shouts of challenge as he continued to pore over his guidance notebook. At the top of each page was listed a current issue highlighted in capital letters. Beneath these headings were suggested questions and answers relating to that topic.

The further he read, the queasier he got, his gut flip-flopping in a dyspeptic rumble. But there was no use complaining. And to whom would he complain? Many of these non-answers masquerading as answers were by his own hand. He was about to walk out on that podium and get his clock cleaned by the White House press corps.

He turned the pages faster, searching for areas where he could embellish answers and at least fulfill the dictum once offered by a colleague during his days as a lowly congressional aide on Capitol Hill: "Say just enough to make 'em think you've said something profound when, in fact, you've said nothing."

He could only hope the pages he now held in his hands would help him fulfill that mission, but he sincerely doubted it. What he held in his hand was basically a lot of gobbledygook.

DRUGS

Has the president made a decision on key elements of his drug package that will be sent to the Hill?

I anticipate specifics will come as decisions are made based on recommendations forwarded to him by appropriate members of the Cabinet and his domestic policy advisors. He can then consider action on those recommendations.

ECONOMY/SPEECH

Is the president giving consideration to a prime-time speech on the economy?

I have nothing to enlighten you with on that matter.

POSSIBLE FOLLOW-UP

But are you ruling that out?

When we have something to announce, we'll announce it.

FEDERAL RESERVE BOARD

Any reaction to the latest action by the Federal Reserve Board on interest rates?

We make it a policy not to comment on such actions.

HOMELESS AID

Will the Administration endorse the levels of support in the House-passed bill for aid to the homeless?

We'll look at it.

SOCIAL SECURITY

Has the president received the initial report of the bipartisan Social Security Task Force?

Yes.

Does he plan to take action on the recommendations?

He will review their report and certainly consider the views offered with regard to any future recommendations he might make.

WHITE HOUSE STAFF

Can you confirm the stories suggesting major staff changes are soon to occur at the highest levels of the White House?

It serves no useful purpose to comment on such stories.

Page after page it continued, unfettered by any notable substance until finally he reached the end. On the last page an enterprising press office staffer had provided the ultimate bailout guidance. The page was headed:

NO COMMENTS:

I don't want to go beyond that statement.

I wouldn't want to pass judgment on that.

I haven't heard the president express a view on that.

I don't respond to "rule in" or "rule out" questions.

I've taken you as far as I can go on this subject.

I just don't want to get into that.

I'm not prepared to elaborate any further.

I can't steer you one way or the other on this issue.

We're studying all options. No decision has been made.

I've said all I can say on this.

IF ABSOLUTELY NECESSARY:

I prefer not to comment.

It was all a lot of "no comment" goo tied up in fancy ribbons. A few words pretty much saying absolutely zilch. So what was the problem? After all, wasn't that his mission—to go out there and say as little as possible? To keep the administration at arm's length from any minefields? No comment. No controversy. No firestorms. And most importantly, no second-guessing of any of his responses by senior White House staff. Call it the ultimate overkill on playing it safe. Call it survival. Do all that and still figure out how to factor in some advocacy for the administration's positions along the way.

J.Y. ducked his head inside the door. "It's feeding time at the zoo."

Sox frowned at this reminder of last call before the briefing, the loneliest of times for even the slickest of spokespersons, much less the occasional practitioner of the art. He had ventured into this violent pit of press-presidency combat before as the briefer, so shouldn't he be feeling total self-assurance in the discharge of this duty? Fear should be on a holiday for anyone who could handle this, right? Why, then, had there been for the last hour a Jell-O-like quiver working at the base of his spine, an unsettling tingle that was now advancing all over his person? No secret—he was scared—a condition which had created another urgency, one addressed by advice from J.Y.: "Don't take the podium in the briefing room without first taking a piss." Great idea. Anything to delay going into that room.

No question—he felt such wisdom warranted translation into Latin and enshrinement on the briefing room entry door. It was a proven philosophy, visionary thinking he had seen borne out many times during lengthy briefings where distress was not only manifested in the briefer's ability to fend off tough questions, but also to maintain bladder control. He might flub a few answers today, but he would not again pee in his pants. Besides, he was again wearing a lightweight tan suit. Bad choice.

"It's time, fella," J.Y. repeated, waiting patiently at the door.

Sox shrugged halfheartedly, wondering if the sympathetic way J.Y. was looking at him had anything to do with the twitch in his innards now having possibly spread to his face.

"I'll be in my office listening on the speaker and squeezing for you," J.Y. said, clenching his fist in close proximity to his groin area.

"You're absolutely, positively sure you don't want to take the duty today?"

J.Y. rolled his eyes and threw his head back in a feint of mock laughter. "Nice try, but I'll pass. Besides, I have to face that firing squad every day. You—you're due for a time in the tube. And speaking of tubes—here's one for you."

Three staffers from the lower press office emerged from behind him, their arms intertwined to form a patchwork cradle under which a well-battered tuba teetered under their uncertain support. Twisting and turning to angle the massive musical instrument into Sox's office, they eased it down in the only corner of the room not occupied by garage sale bric-a-brac. Given the nature of the room's other varied contents, the presence of a tuba could only pass for mundane.

"A tuba?" Sox blurted.

"Well, to be precise, a sousaphone!" one of the staffers exclaimed.

Then it dawned on him that any delay in facing the briefing, short of nuclear cataclysm, was a moment to be cheered.

"A tuba! A sousaphone! A what-the-hell!" he shouted with unrestrained delight.

"We figured you might want to take a couple of blows on this before going down to the briefing," J.Y. chuckled. "Vent up here—not down there. There's already enough hot air in that room."

Other members of the staff from the lower press office edged into his junk-ladened room, one of them proudly announcing: "It's a bass sousaphone. When you let 'er rip on this one, it should get the attention of just about everyone awake in the Western Hemisphere, as well as ships at sea and orbiting spacecraft."

"Absolutely!" Sox agreed. "Let's give it a go—a heads-up blast at the hellhounds downstairs."

They carefully lifted the instrument over his head, then down and around, the great horn settling over him in a snug fit. Eagerly wetting his lips, he sucked in hard and puffed. Nothing. Not even the slightest froggy belch. Again he puffed mightily into the oval mouthpiece. Nothing. Again. Again. Again. A half-dozen tries later, huffing from the heels, there finally emerged a puny squeak, sour, tinny and off-key.

Defeated for the moment, he smiled and nodded his appreciation to the gathered staff.

"Thanks, everybody, for giving me the chance to be a blowhard who needs to blow harder."

Everyone laughed, then began exiting to make ready for the briefing.

He unraveled from the instrument and laid it on top of the pile of rubble that had been growing in one of the office's corners. Seeking any other diversion to delay that which awaited him, he flipped on the TV to check the noontime headlines. The male and female anchors were delivering the news with tightened jaws and a stilted sense of purpose, each trying their best to lend a "This just in!" urgency to an otherwise ho-hum report on the leading economic indicators. The female was perfectly coifed and clothed, no errant strands of hair or unbuttoned buttons, so flawless that she appeared porcelain—and, from the way she shifted in her chair, ill at ease. Her overly moussed male co-anchor smiled through clenched teeth, his to-and-fro swaying behind the desk a mildly annoying flaw in an otherwise self-assured manner.

Sox could only speculate, but the anxious demeanor of these noon-time news pixies seemed to suggest that perhaps the male had just broken wind and was afraid to show it while the female needed to but was afraid to show it.

Missy's voice again filled the room via the squawk box on his desk. "The daily briefing is about to begin."

This time her tone was so breathlessly intent, he worried that attendance might swell in anticipation of a thunderstroke of major news occurring. If only they knew. Today's briefer was coming to the podium with a barren notebook.

His eyes wandered to the sousaphone. Its husky barrel had slipped and toppled over facedown, settling on the floor in an awkward heap. There would be plenty of time later to unlimber his lungs and coax a thumping note or two from its brassy bowels.

It was time to step into the flying airplane. There could be no more delays. Slowly he began the walk down the short and narrow hallway leading to the lower press office and, adjacent to it, the briefing room. If there was a walk to the gallows, White House-style, it was the walk to the briefing room. Especially if one was the briefer. It was a Pennsylvania Avenue version of the Bataan Death March.

Cradled under an arm was his notebook crammed full of the neatly typed, triple-spaced "no comment" press guidances, those and fifteen other pages of non-answers. All of it would be about as useful as a clothes dryer in a nudist colony. At best, it might initially fool some of the press into thinking that with such a weighty volume of material in hand, he might definitely be there to impart news.

Hearing cheery expressions of "good luck" from J.Y. and others did little to calm the angst that continued to rage in his gut. Good luck on conducting the briefing? Might as well wish him good luck on being in the on-deck circle for the electric chair. He veered left at the end of the hallway and passed the circular guard desk separating the upper and lower press offices. A barrel-chested member of the uniformed division of the Secret Service sat there with arms imposingly crossed, his biceps bulging tautly against the short sleeves of a neatly pressed white shirt, its collar and chest areas showily adorned with gleaming brass insignia.

"Hey, super flak, how many kills and probables gonna happen in that room today?" the guard grunted.

"By them or me?" Sox answered sarcastically.

"Ah…" the guard responded, throwing his hands up in surrender, then making an exaggerated sweeping motion and waving him past as if Sox had needed to stop for clearance at this checkpoint and was now free to proceed. "You know the way, don't you? Be sure and turn left at the bottom of the hill."

It was a downhill trip that didn't take long. There he was confronted by the sliding wooden doors leading into hell's den—the briefing room. He turned and surveyed the lower press office staff, all of whom fixedly stared back, pity welling in some eyes.

At the front desk nearest the doors, Missy was scrambling to keep pace with the nonstop clanging of the blinking phone lines—"Press office, please hold….press office…please hold…please hold…press office…please hold…hello, press office…" It grated on him to hear the phones answered that way. This was, after all, the Office of the Press Secretary, not just any press office.

In the midst of the phone blitz, with receiver lights flashing on hold everywhere, Missy managed to frantically look up, pausing to delicately form the words "good luck" on her lips.

He looked at her impassively. "Maybe this will all calm down once the briefing starts."

"I haven't been here long, but this seems calm compared to some days," she laughed, grabbing another phone.

He took a step back toward the sliding doors.

"You'll do great, I'm sure," she added.

Yeah, sure, he thought, reminding himself that someone had once said there were 10,000 ways to say "no comment." He figured he'd probably use 9,999 of them today.

"Well, we're pretty cramped for space down here, so try not to take too many prisoners," she laughed again, clicking another phone on hold.

That Missy—so unfettered by worry, he thought. He'd love to stay and tarry, but the sliding doors were waiting.

He pressed hard against them, sliding his fingers in between and wedging them apart about an inch. These were the same doors that always seemed so pliable on days when he wasn't the briefer. Today it was like prying apart blocks of cement.

His hesitancy now reinforced in his mind yet another unwritten credo that existed between reporters and White House staff. Once those doors were opened and the briefer entered the room, there was no turning back until the briefing had concluded. The one exception might be the commencement of hostilities for World War III. In the meantime, the standing rule was that the briefer did not leave that podium until the senior wire correspondent in attendance released him or her with "Thank you." There was no greater sin than to do otherwise, something Sox had never seen occur. Today, however, had possibilities.

He started to pull the doors wide, then realized there was one last thing to do. He had almost forgotten about the press secretary's prayer. Might as well give it a go, turn to the heavens and beg The Almighty for help. He leaned back against the doors in a forceful brace, tilting his head down so it settled against his chest, reverential and still. He wrinkled his eyes tightly closed, the wavy flutter of eyelashes dancing lightly across his face. He gulped for calm air and in a low whisper, recited to himself: "Oh, dear Lord, please help me to utter words which are gentle and sweet, words which tomorrow I may have to eat."

Opening his eyes, he watched as Missy remained consumed with juggling phone lines, exhaling in frustration, taking a deep breath and pursing her lips determinedly in anticipation of the next wave.

On the other side of the doors he could hear the taunts and cries of reporters now anxious for his arrival. This was it. There was nothing else to do but go forward and gut it out.

"By the way, Missy," he called out firmly, "when you answer those phones, remember this is the Office of the Press Secretary, not the press office. A press office is where they press pants."

Without looking back, he turned on his heels, threw open the doors and strode resolutely into the briefing room.

CHAPTER EIGHT

REPORTER: Would it be accurate to say that the president is completely surrounded by yes men?

SPOKESMAN: No. Actually, his advisors work in a semicircle.

Entering the briefing room, that lobe of gritty workspace tucked in amidst White House grandeur, Sox was promptly greeted by a barrage of shouted questions, all at boombox level.

"Here he comes—the spin patrol!"

"Kill the briefer!"

"No, maim him!"

"Yeah, let's just nick him."

"…hit him high, hit him low…"

"…torture rack…"

"How about the Germans?"

"How about the Norwegians?"

"How about the Middle East?"

"How about those New York Mets?"

"…budget negotiations…"

"…jobs bill…"

"…confirm…"

"What about…horn…blowing…in your office?"

"Yeah…what about that?"

"…Speaker…leadership meeting…"

"How about a trip schedule?"

"How about a trip!"

"Can you rule out…nomination…this week…"

"…respond to the rumor about Navikoff coming here for a meeting?"

"Yeah, are there any preconditions…"

"Say…what about the Middle East?"

"Get the briefer!"

"No, gut him!"

"Yeah, take no prisoners!"

"No immunity granted!"

"…National League of Cities…?"

"Or, for that matter, the National League?"

"Kick ass…"

"But don't take names."

"Does the president know that…"

"A full house beats a flush?"

"And rock crushes scissors…"

"And paper covers rock…"

"And I'll bet the pickings from this briefing will be slim enough to file on toilet paper."

"Hey, Sox, is this going to be a briefing or a diaper change?"

The verbal grenades, seeking to render their target wobbly, were nonstop.

He had heard such pre-briefing ranting before. It was the press' signature in this, their romper room, these first jabs serving to remind that he was now helplessly stuck in the crosshairs of their sights. Equally troubling was the thought that this was only a sneak preview of what was ahead, a wake-up call for one who had had the temerity to cross this threshold and present himself behind its podium.

At times like these, there seemed a bona fide comparison—press corps and Marine Corps. This room was a media beachhead, the podium the target on which they were locked and loaded with a rolling barrage of questions.

Stepping up onto the blue-carpeted riser, he scanned the faces facing him, the jeers continuing, unabated.

"B team! B team! B team!"

"Z team! Z team! Z team!"
"You owe me a dime, Sox!"
"Here comes one of the spinners."
"Isn't that a vocal group?"
"So much for the lounge act. When's J.Y. coming out?"
"…stop the bleeding…"
"Hey, Sox, do you have any guidance on the president's latest bowling score?"
"Do you have any guidance on anything?"
"Can you confirm the graffiti on the wall in the West Wing bathroom?"
"Can you get us the phone number?"
"Is it an 800 number?"
"We've got a briefer who is…"
"Confused."
"Can you spell Mississippi backwards?"
"What's the capital of El Salvador?"
"What's the capital of South Dakota?"
"Name the presidents of five countries?"
"Name five countries."
"Who was the MVP in the American League in 1956?"
"…not enough chairs in this room…"
"That's why you have knees."
"Hey, Sox, you've got a blonde hair hanging out your fly."
"Maybe he got lucky on the subway this morning."
Sox gazed out numbly at their frenzy, a room gone haywire.
"Hit it, baby!"
"Go!"
"Wait a second!"
"Jesus Christ!"
"Carl Crayon is a monster."
"What about the Russians?"
"Yeah, what's happening? Give!"
"Is the president going to the Super Bowl game in January?"
"Wait a second!"

"…hold your job…"

"Wait a second!"

"Sox needs some prepositions."

"And active verbs."

"Even fragments…"

"But no figments…"

"Is this a joke or serious?"

It was standing-room-only, with reporters mashed against one another, including in the 48 squatty theatre-style seats. In the back, the camera platform swayed rhythmically under the heft of beefy network technicians and other sweat-ladened crew members who were similarly pressed against each other in fleshy gridlock. Arising from this area was a gamey aroma, a salty stench akin to that which inhabits locker rooms where moldy socks have been tossed and left for some time.

The aisles, too, were overflowing with the clutter of still photographers and other latecomers vying for nooks of space. Some of the more inventive stragglers had shunted out space in the windowsills on the north side of the room, coiling themselves into the frameworks.

One of the few in the room who enjoyed the luxury of legroom was the amply proportioned stenographer positioned at the front. She was one of a team who produced the transcripts of each briefing, usually within an hour, which was a boon to reporters up against the time crunch of a tight deadline. She sat idling in front of her machine, seemingly oblivious to the fever blister bursting around her as she dully munched on an apple. Perched off to the left of the podium, she had plenty of space, an inviolate parcel of briefing room real estate reserved for members of the stenographic pool. In the case of today's broad-beamed occupant of that space, such acreage was particularly prized for its functional application.

Settling in behind the podium, Sox surveyed the six front-row seats, each of which was assigned to a representative of a wire service or television network. All the other seats in the room also were assigned, a policy which encouraged bitching by those reporters omitted, but which garnered applause from most of the White House media population. At the very least, it assured the majority of credible Washington news

Flourishes

organizations at least one seat at the briefing. While today's full attendance was an exception, there were many days with no "headline grabber" topics on the front burner when the room more resembled the bleachers at a spring training ballpark—one could easily stretch out and languish in the splendid isolation of empty rows.

Seated next to Sparta was Patrick Y. Just…Y. That single letter was the extent of his last name. It resulted in him constantly being greeted as if he were a question mark—"Patrick, why?" Like all good wire service reporters, he was a bulldog, a hard-charger, tireless and driven: "I'm on deadline!" "I need a reaction right away!" "Is that your quote or the president's?" "The American taxpayers deserve a better answer than that!" "Give me a response, not recycled claptrap!"

He enjoyed rankling J.Y. at the briefings, seizing on his non-responses with a line that had become a Patrick Y trademark and which he uttered with a nauseous, high-pitched twang: "Unacceptable! Ab-so-lute-ly unacceptable!" Sox always enjoyed J.Y.'s curt response: "Accept it, pal." It was one he'd probably be using before the end of today's briefing.

He looked down at Sparta, hoping she might pick up on the message he was trying to silently transmit through beseeching eyes: *I'm your friend. How about we loosen it up a notch and take it easy on the briefer today?*

But she only glared back, her eyes lit with aggression.

"No deals," she snarled, her forefinger spiking the air in his direction. "No deals!" As she repeated it, she half-turned to the crowd behind to make sure everyone in the room heard and understood her admonition.

No deals. Message sent. Message received. He understood. She wasn't about to roll over for anybody. This was the press' workroom, and she was making sure that everyone there—friend or otherwise—was going to view him in that context for as long as he stood behind that podium. No exceptions. There would be no busman's holiday just because a relief pitcher had been trotted out to perform. She was coming after him and signaling everyone else to do the same. The hell of it was that he knew she was right. She was absolutely right. He had just stepped behind the briefing room podium. That podium's edge was where friendships ceased. At least, temporarily.

Opening up his briefing notebook, he purposely kept his hands busy in the hope that no one would notice his mild case of the shakes. He grabbed for errant notes, memoranda and loose scraps of paper, setting them aside and fumbling for pages with the day's announcements—the president's schedule, ambassadorial appointments and other miscellany. All of it was non-news which would only serve to postpone the inevitable—the moment when he would have to cut the fluff and get on with the business of answering questions; when cornbread would have to replace Fig Newtons.

He looked down at the stenographer who had finished her apple and was now impassively chewing gum while fiddling with the headset that plugged her into the podium's microphone system. A glass of water sat on a shelf under the podium. He clutched it, gulping its lukewarm contents like his thirst meter was on empty.

His eyes peered over the podium, seeking the back wall platform with its jumble of cameras, lenses and lights angled at him. Anticipating his first words, red lights under the lenses began to blink on. He shuffled the papers in front of him a final time, bringing the page with the president's schedule to the top of the pile. Sox cleared his throat and his gaze settled on the rear of the room, taking aim at one of the cameras. Then, in a measured, low cadence, he began to speak, his words accompanied by the toneless thud of the stenographer's machine.

THE WHITE HOUSE
Office of the Press Secretary

PRESS BRIEFING
BY SOX ST. LOUIS

The Briefing Room

12:18 P.M. EST

MR. ST. LOUIS: I used to come off the bench in high school basketball, so this role is not—

Q: That's serious stuff.

MR. ST. LOUIS: —totally alien to me. Let me go through the rest of the president's public schedule for today and some announcements.

Q: They really saved the big news for you. (Laughter.)

MR. ST. LOUIS: The president and Mrs. Crayon will return from Camp David on Sunday afternoon, with Marine One due on the South Lawn at 4:30 P.M.

Q: Can you confirm that Crayon and President Navikoff are discussing meeting here soon?

Q: Yeah, and while you're at it, can you confirm that you were taken to the woodshed by the president for prematurely burying Navikoff?

MR. ST. LOUIS: Let me, uh, just say that, uh, as regards the second one, I did do a belly flop into the wading pool of superpower politics.

Q: Sure that wasn't a cesspool?

Q: And what about the rumors?

MR. ST. LOUIS: What rumors?

Q: About a possible meeting between the leaders?

MR. ST. LOUIS: We don't confirm rumors from this podium.

Q: Well, if you won't confirm that, then how about some guidance for our Super Bowl planning in January?

Q: I don't give a damn about the Super Bowl! (Laughter.)

MR. ST. LOUIS: As you stated, that game isn't until January, so it's—

Q: Will he be making the perfunctory presidential phone call to the winning team's locker room?

Q: Yeah, and what's the record for the longest amount of time a president has been kept on hold by a Super Bowl winner?

Q: Yeah, can you find out?

Q: Back to the Crayon-Navikoff rumor.

MR. ST. LOUIS: I told you, we don't confirm—

Q: Why was the Russian ambassador here yesterday?

Q: Yeah, and why wasn't he announced as part of the president's public schedule?

MR. ST. LOUIS: Continuing on with the announcements—

Q: Are they going to meet soon or not? Yes or no?

MR. ST. LOUIS: When we have something to announce, we'll announce it.

Q: —garbage—

Q: —purple prose—

Q: Ab-so-lute-ly unacceptable!

Q: Why don't you at least say they are willing to meet at any time—

Q: —at any place. I mean, there is a common interest in their trying to enhance the economic and security aspects of this world, isn't there?

Q: Neither of them is interested in blowing up the world, are they?

Q: Or bankrupting the world?

Q: What's the president going to be talking about on his trip to Houston next week?

Q: Wait a minute—is there going to be a meeting or not?

Q: And how about the Super Bowl?

MR. ST. LOUIS: No comment.

Q: No comment on the Super Bowl? Incredible!

MR. ST. LOUIS: No, I mean no comment on the meeting.

Q: Is your plan to depart from normal procedure and tell the truth today?

MR. ST. LOUIS: Continuing on with today's announcements, the president will have a meeting today at 3:30 P.M. with Master Paul Painter.

Q: We've been up all night prepping for this one.

Q: Who?

Q: What?

MR. ST. LOUIS: That meeting will be available for writing pool and open photo coverage. Does anyone know who he is?

Q: Yeah, he's a little kid.

MR. ST. LOUIS: At 12 years old, he is president of the national organization, Youth for the New Century. He's their boy of the year. He lists among his heroes: Moses, the pope and Willie Mays.

Q: Like I said, we've been up all night prepping for this one.

Q: Stop the presses!

Q: Who does the kid think should be the next ambassador to Sri Lanka?

Q: Who cares? Could we please get to the news?

MR. ST. LOUIS: —and still continuing with the announcements, the president has authorized the immediate release of an additional 40 million pounds of surplus cheese from the Commodity Credit Corporation's inventory. This is in addition to the previous release made last month.

Q: Whew!

Q: Break out the Air Wick.

Q: Who cut the cheese?

Q: We're whizzing right along here with some major news items.

MR. ST. LOUIS: Oh, I almost forgot—the president will receive diplomatic credentials from the ambassadors designate of Greece and Bolivia. That will be in the Oval Office at 2:00 P.M. No coverage.

Q: There's something new and different.

Q: This just in!

Q: Once again—hold the presses!

Q: The president has said he wants to meet this week on the budget with responsible members of the opposition party. How will he know them?

Q: He'll put an ad in the paper.

Q: Speaking of ads in the paper, what's your reaction to the one in the classifieds today that reads: white house in D.C. for sale, large, well-manicured lawn, tight security, large upstairs bedrooms—

Q: —complete with your own set of round-the-clock demonstrators camped directly across the street.

Q: Can you confirm that the White House has 32 bathrooms?

Q: When you gotta go, you gotta go.

MR. ST. LOUIS: The White House is not for sale. I can confirm that. (Laughter.) (Applause.)

Q: The union is preserved.

Q: Stop the presses!

Q: Again!

Q: This just in!

Q: It's a banner day on the news front.

Q: —all quiet on—

Q: Sox, you'd better have nine lives today.

MR. ST. LOUIS: I was only born once.

Q: Looks like you're about eight short.

Q: Not enough, pal. Not today.

Q: Back to the Russians—are we talking to them about a meeting— Crayon and Navikoff?

MR. ST. LOUIS: Without commenting on the possibility of any specific talks, let me just say that our channels of communication with the Russians are open and meetings at various diplomatic levels occur frequently. This is all part of a process—a general pattern of consultation on issues on the U.S.-Russian agenda across the board.

Q: There's some Sox-speak.

Q: Do you mind if I doze off for a while?

Q: What does "channels of communication" mean?

Q: Selling the president.

Q: I tried to tell everyone in this room that Sox didn't know anything, but no one would listen.

Q: These talks—they're open?

Q: Hate to think they'd be closed.

MR. ST. LOUIS: The president and the secretary of state have indicated frequently our commitment to an open and ongoing dialogue with the Russians—talks in various fora that can serve to eliminate U.S.-Russian differences.

Q: Fora?

Q: Flora?

Q: Fauna?

Q: Has the president signed the proclamation declaring National Poison Prevention Week?

Q: Wait a second!

Q: Do you deny that the leaders are planning a meeting?

Q: Are there any preconditions for such a meeting as to venue or schedule?

MR. ST. LOUIS: Preconditions?

Q: Yeah, is there anything we'd have to promise the Russians to assure their participation in these talks?

Q: The home telephone number of the babe currently sunbathing in Lafayette Park.

Q: What's the president's reaction to suggestions from the congressional leadership that he should meet with Navikoff soon?

MR. ST. LOUIS: The president always welcomes the views of the congressional leadership.

Q: In hearing what views?

MR. ST. LOUIS: —hearing suggestions from leaders on the Hill.

Q: What hill?

Q: Blueberry.

Q: He's interested in hearing suggestions from both sides of the aisle?

MR. ST. LOUIS: Yes.

Q: Since when?

Q: Do the president and speaker speak with one voice?

Q: When they speak low.

Q: When a press spokesman drops his voice low, look out.

Q: When a press spokesman drops his pants low, look out.

MR. ST. LOUIS: The president is keenly aware of the interest in this matter from leaders in both parties and welcomes their input.

Q: Where will Crayon and Navikoff meet and when?

Q: Yeah—

Q: —and what did the president know and when did he know it?

Q: What issues will be on the agenda when they meet?

Q: Financial aid?

Q: Trade?

Q: Terrorism?

Q: The Orioles game?

MR. ST. LOUIS: When we have something to announce—

Q: —we'll announce it.

Q: Jesus Christ.

MR. ST. LOUIS: Look, I've said all I'm going to say on this. I've taken you as far as I can right now. We can stay in this room all day, if you like—

Q: Jeez, we're sorry.

Q: Forgive and forget.

Q: —cease-fire—

Q: —and we'll start all over again.

Q: Are you trying to cut off democracy?

MR. ST. LOUIS: Look, you can bang me all day—

Q: Bang you?

Q: All day?

Q: All night?

Q: Really?

MR. ST. LOUIS: O.K., you can bang on me all day—-

Q: Bang you?

Q: Anyone want to bang Sox?

Q: —not my type—

Q: But does he kiss on the first date?

MR. ST. LOUIS: —banging *on* me, but I'll stand on what I previously said, when we have something to announce—

Q: —we'll announce it.

Q: Yeah, yeah, yeah.

Q: Ab-so-lute-ly unacceptable!

Q: Just out of curiosity, why did the president and Mrs. Crayon keep the motorcade waiting for over thirty minutes before departing for the event at the Kennedy Center last night?

Q: Their tray tables weren't in the upright and locked position.

MR. ST. LOUIS: No particular reason of which I am aware.

Q: —aware of anything?

Q: But you really don't know?

MR. ST. LOUIS: I do know this—and so do you—that delays, unexpected delays, sometimes happen.

Q: Does it bother you that about seventy-five percent of our time on this job is wasted while sitting in motorcades waiting on those two people to depart the residence?

MR. ST. LOUIS: That's life in the presidential travel pool fast lane.

Q: I'll just grab a cab next time.

Q: Did the delay have anything to do with security?

MR. ST. LOUIS: If it did, you know our policy is not to discuss security matters from this podium.

Q: So did it have anything to do with security?

Q: Crayon had to stop to use the indoor plumbing.

MR. ST. LOUIS: No, the delay was not security-related. They were just running late.

Q: Sox, there's a story in the paper today attributed to reliable sources that says the president may be backing off on the idea of proposing new tax cuts. That seems to be a difference in position from what he suggested in his speech to the business leaders earlier this week.

MR. ST. LOUIS: Your comments are noted.

Q: Obviously, someone has gotten to him on this since then.

Q: Who was it?

Q: Late last night?

Q: A phone solicitor trying to sell him steak knives got him to change his mind.

MR. ST. LOUIS: The president has been reviewing a range of options on such proposals with his economic advisors and—

Q: Well, exactly what is his position?

Q: Missionary.

Q: Last night?

MR. ST. LOUIS: Stay tuned. He is continuing to review options and receive the views of White House economic advisors and others in government agencies concerned with domestic and economic policy.

Q: Without confirming whether or not there are plans for Crayon and Navikoff to meet, what would you say is our biggest area of disagreement with the Russians?

Q: That would be the debate over who'll pick up the check for dinner if they do meet.

Q: Sox, a question on—

Q: Sox—

Q: Sox, you said—

Q: But it looks as if the budget process may have stalled—-

Q: And sources indicate that talks may have fallen through on the Hill this week.

Q: And Congress has just overridden his veto of the jobs bill. What's your reaction?

MR. ST. LOUIS: Yes, but we're okay right now in the Middle East. Hey, that's one out of three.

Q: —what—

Q: Did you misspeak on the Navikoff rumor?

Q: No, he screwed up.

Q: Anything else you want to say about that?

MR. ST. LOUIS: Not really, but with regard to the Russians, we always stand ready to promote stable and constructive relations between our two countries—

Q: —*non-answer*—

MR. ST. LOUIS: —and maintaining a continuing dialogue to that end.

Q: *The end.*

Q: *The millennium.*

Q: *Whew.*

Q: *Stop the presses.*

Q: *Stop the bleeding.*

Q: *Are the president and the Treasury secretary speaking with one voice on the tax cut issue?*

MR. ST. LOUIS: Yes, publicly.

Q: *Nice save, Sox.*

Q: *I'm—*

Q: *—confused. Aren't we all?*

Q: *I take it the answer suggests there is some difference of opinion within the administration?*

MR. ST. LOUIS: You can take it any way you want, but—

Q: *The president welcomes—*

MR. ST. LOUIS: —the president welcomes the counsel of all his economic advisory team as we move forward in the appropriations process.

Q: *Yeah, yeah, yeah.*

Q: *Are those the same economic advisors whose idea of kicks is a guided tour of the Federal Reserve Board?*

Q: In God we blind trust.

Q: What about the idea of a prime-time speech on the economy to activate public support and get the leadership off its duff?

MR. ST. LOUIS: What about it?

Q: Well, is it under consideration?

MR. ST. LOUIS: I have nothing for you on that.

Q: That's not a denial.

MR. ST. LOUIS: I have nothing for you on that.

Q: Can you rule out such a possibility?

MR. ST. LOUIS: I don't respond to rule in or rule out questions.

Q: Or to any questions.

Q: No, wait—

Q: Are the wise men around the president, his domestic policy gurus, thinking about such a speech?

MR. ST. LOUIS: Look, I told you, I have nothing for you on that.

Q: What exactly does that mean?

MR. ST. LOUIS: It means exactly that.

Q: What?

MR. ST. LOUIS: I…have…nothing…for…you…on…that.

Q: That's the most meaningless statement I have ever heard.

MR. ST. LOUIS: Hey, you're a quick study. You catch on fast.

Q: Are you embarrassed that the rate of inflation hasn't dropped like the president predicted?

MR. ST. LOUIS: I haven't been embarrassed since I first wet my pants.

Q: In the first grade?

Q: No, in high school.

Q: There's been another baby born into the president of France's family. What do the president and Mrs. Crayon plan to give the baby?

Q: A pair of ballet shoes.

MR. ST. LOUIS: I don't know. Check with the First Lady's press office.

Q: What will it take for the administration to strike a deal with Congress on the Defense budget? What sort of compromise?

MR. ST. LOUIS: Never say. Never say.

Q: Are the current funding levels unacceptable to the administration?

MR. ST. LOUIS: We'll just have to wait and see as deliberations with the Hill continue.

Q: —singing that old tune again.

Q: I've heard it all before.

Q: If budget cuts force us to find new ways for launch and delivery of our missile systems, what will the president propose?

Q: That we call UPS.

Q: Dial 9-1-1.

MR. ST. LOUIS: It would serve no useful purpose to speculate further on this.

Q: What needs to occur for the administration to compromise on this?

MR. ST. LOUIS: I'm not going to analyze the situation from this podium—

Q: —how about from the floor?

MR. ST. LOUIS: —so we will continue to work with the Congress in a bipartisan fashion to try and reach a solution.

Q: Sox, another subject?

MR. ST. LOUIS: Yes.

Q: When does the president plan to have his next physical exam?

MR. ST. LOUIS: I don't know exactly.

Q: You don't know?

MR. ST. LOUIS: As you are well aware, he has a complete medical exam each year, and those results are released to you.

Q: But isn't he due?

Q: Yeah, and he's expecting twins.

MR. ST. LOUIS: I'll have to take your question and check when the next exam is scheduled. I'm almost certain it hasn't been a year since his last one.

Q: Refresh my memory—were there any results from last time that required monitoring in the future?

Q: Yeah, excessive passing of wind.

Q: The old bladder buster.

Q: His gut grumbles.

MR. ST. LOUIS: Nothing that I recall out of the ordinary.

Q: How do you define ordinary?

MR. ST. LOUIS: Look, the president is in excellent health. When it's time for his next physical, we'll let you know.

Q: Is he currently taking any medication?

MR. ST. LOUIS: I don't know.

Q: Shouldn't you know?

MR. ST. LOUIS: Sparta once told me that press spokesmen shouldn't be expected to know everything.

Q: But you will check on that?

MR. ST. LOUIS: Yes.

Q: Poor Sox.

Q: Do you know how many times a day the president goes to the bathroom?

Q: Jesus Christ.

Q: Can you tell us why the vice president was selected to head up a task force to review the tax code?

Q: He flipped a coin with the president and lost.

MR. ST. LOUIS: Because the president felt he was the best person for the job.

Q: I'd hate to hear what was second prize.

Q: Fact-finding in Antarctica.

Q: Does the president plan to meet anytime soon with the bipartisan members of the Social Security Task Force?

MR. ST. LOUIS: He is currently reviewing their report.

Q: As we speak?

MR. ST. LOUIS: It's on his desk.

Q: So is my letter requesting an interview.

MR. ST. LOUIS: He is reviewing their recommendations.

Q: Was the president so bereft of his own ideas on Social Security reform that he needed this commission to come up with theirs?

Q: What does bereft mean?

Q: It means we're closed for business here.

Q: The White House is closed?

MR. ST. LOUIS: The president has his views. He welcomes those of the commission.

Q: Has he spoken to anybody lately on the commission?

Q: Has he spoken to anybody lately?

Q: About anything?

MR. ST. LOUIS: I'm sure the president is maintaining an open line of communication with members of the commission.

Q: You're sure?

MR. ST. LOUIS: Yes.

Q: Is that on the record?

Q: Well, what might they be communicating about?

MR. ST. LOUIS: About Social Security.

Q: That's a pretty broad subject.

Q: Yeah, and broads are a pretty subject.

MR. ST. LOUIS: Look, I've taken you as far as I can on this one.

Q: —not exactly stretching the outer limits of the information envelope.

Q: To go back to this Russian thing—

Q: What—

Q: —Russian's thing?

Q: Where?

Q: Navikoff has already been talking about a meeting on economic meas-ures of mutual interest to the two countries. Will that be their main focus?

MR. ST. LOUIS: I understand he has made such comments. I will let those comments speak for themselves.

Q: Comments can speak?

Q: So you are confirming they are going to meet?

Q: Yeah, and I'd still like an answer to my question about the dinner check.

Q: Let the record show that silence flowed from the podium.

Q: Do you mind if I doze off for a while?

Q: Sox, earlier this week the president played golf.

MR. ST. LOUIS: Correct.

Q: Did his wife approve that?

Q: What was his score?

Q: Less than three numbers?

Q: Less than the federal deficit?

Q: I don't care about his score. I would like to know, however, was he wearing insect repellent as the press pool was advised to do?

MR. ST. LOUIS: I don't know. Out of respect, I don't think the bugs would have chosen to bother him anyway.

Q: Anything new on the immigration reform bill?

MR. ST. LOUIS: The administration believes there is definitely a need for reform in this area. We will actively work toward passage of an immigration reform bill and believe it is an issue worthy of bipartisan effort. There are no easy answers but the president is hopeful the Congress will move forward on this. For more specific comments, I refer you to the Department of Justice which is the lead government agency on this issue.

Q: For more specific comments on anything, I refer you to—

Q: —anybody.

Q: Not here.

MR. ST. LOUIS: Anything else?

Q: Plenty.

Q: —just getting started—

Q: How about some answers to—

Q: What can you tell us about the president's meeting with the Fed chairman?

MR. ST. LOUIS: They had—

Q: —now that unemployment has gone up—

Q: Wait a minute.

MR. ST. LOUIS: —a cordial visit and—

Q: Get serious.

MR. ST. LOUIS: —and that was basically it.

Q: Did they discuss the new unemployment figures?

MR. ST. LOUIS: As you are aware, we make it a practice not to discuss the content of meetings between the president and the chairman.

Q: —make it a policy not to discuss anything.

Q: How about a new policy?

Q: How long did the meeting last?

MR. ST. LOUIS: It was scheduled for thirty minutes.

Q: Hey, gang, this may be as good as we're going to get today.

Q: Did they discuss interest rates?

Q: Did they discuss anything of interest?

Q: Trade dirty jokes?

Q: Was it a courtesy call or a business meeting?

Q: Just the fate of the U.S. economy.

MR. ST. LOUIS: As you know, they periodically meet. That's all I can tell you.

Q: Do you think you'll survive this briefing?

MR. ST. LOUIS: I survived high school math, so I guess—(Laughter.)

Q: Do you have any other pieces of paper up there with guidances on anything we haven't asked you?

Q: Sox, could I ask just one other question—

Q: No, we've all had enough.

Q: What is the deputy press secretary's salary?

Q: It's in three figures.

Q: Sox—

Q: Sox, you have—

Q: Oh, well—

Q: Do you want fries or coleslaw?

Q: Do you have anything else for us that would pass as news?

MR. ST. LOUIS: Not really.

Q: To say that's an understatement would be an overstatement.

Q: Thank you, linesmen. Thank you, ball boys.

THE PRESS: Thank you.

12:58 P.M. EST

END

CHAPTER NINE

REPORTER: What does the president hope to avoid in this campaign?

SPOKESMAN: Random and voluntary testing of the electorate for boredom.

"Crisis! Urgent!"

"Whaaa…?"

Pulling his notes together while still feeling a bit shell-shocked, Sox swallowed hard, lowered his head and began surging past reporters who were now pressing close to the briefing platform, all the while his eyes remaining cocked on the sliding doors and the prospect of escape that lay just beyond.

"Crisis! Urgent!"

Crisis? What crisis? Crisis—a shrill and unnerving word—was an instant antenna-raiser for any press spokesman. He grimaced at the fuss of reporters now causing gridlock. It was the usual tribe of post-briefing hangers-on, pesky diehards waiting to dog his every step back to the upper press office with follow-up questions. To make matters worse, they were being further incited by a rowdy in their ranks popping off about a crisis. But what crisis? At such moments he was reminded of a warning from J.Y.: "The most dangerous time for a spokesman is coming off the podium right after a briefing. You mentally let go. You think it's over. You think you're finished. But you're not. You're never finished. The briefing is mental masturbation. After the briefing is *relaxus interruptus.*

You're tempted to unwind and savor the act just completed. But you can't. They won't let you. The press is still there, clawing. They haven't let up. But they hope you have. They keep badgering, trying to make you bend, finally prying out some news you really didn't want to make. And, in frustration, you say something flip. Next morning, you wake up and read what you wish you hadn't said. You've been jerked around alright— by the press."

He had no intention today of playing the "I gotcha!" game, the verbal sparring that followed every briefing and escorted every briefer out of the room. The "I gotcha!" game went like this: "Wait a minute— you're answering my question differently from the way you did at the podium—I gotcha!" Whatever the game's form, he was determined to make it back to his office without making news. Still there was no escaping the urgent cry that continued to rise from the pack.

"Dammit, crisis! Urgent! Please…please…do something!"

By now the source of the plea had ceased to be a mystery. Soldier Paintbrush was elbowing through the swarm, squarely into Sox's path. A marginal member of the press corps as a radio reporter, Soldier was rumored to have filed news dispatches that seldom went more than ten yards beyond the Potomac River, if that far. One member of the press corps claimed to have once heard one of Soldier's reports on a rural Louisiana radio station, but no further confirmation. Shriveled to pint-size, Soldier was a 70-year-old journalistic nomad given to a daily regimen of idly wandering about the press room before and after the briefing, rummaging in other people's business. In so doing, he remained blissfully absorbed, although no one was ever quite sure with what. His primary business remained feeding the press room rumor mill and, when possible, feeding himself from the unattended lunch sacks of others. Mostly, he just roamed around pretending to be an integral part of the daily scene, but was seen and heard much more on days when news was slow. A court jester, a press room appendage, he was tolerated but not taken seriously.

Now here he was making noise about a crisis and bobbing along in Sox's face, keeping windowpane close and joined by others who were all angling for some tidbit of news the briefing had failed to yield. They knew it was a futile exercise, but having nothing else to do were willing to play the game until Sox bolted free. Which is exactly what he was attempting to do despite Soldier's clinging to him.

"Huh, Sox? Huh? What? What? Tell us what you're going to do about it," Soldier huffed as they moved along.

"About what?"

"This crisis!"

"Dammit, Soldier, what crisis? Where?"

"Right here."

"Right where?"

"In this briefing room."

"So call 9-1-1."

"That's a nonstarter, Sox. What I'm talking about is serious. Mega bad."

"Okay, did I start World War III with something I said in the briefing?"

"Well, actually, no…"

"Gee, I'm off the respirator. Western civilization can breathe easy again."

"Not funny, Sox. We've got a problem here, and you'd better focus on it."

"And…?"

"I'm dead serious."

"So tell me quick," Sox challenged, a note of mild concern edging into his voice.

Soldier fell silent, ruminating on a thought that seemed to have overtaken him. The pause lasted only a couple of blinks before he began rattling on again in fragmented bursts.

"Well…did you know…uh…oh…that is…did you know…that…right now…uh…at this moment…I mean, right now…there are…I mean, there are…count them…there are…one thousand little black ants crawling around the back of this room…and…and…uh…hey, that's not all… no…there is…come see…yeah, come see…confirm it…for yourself…there is also one large brown roach…"

As the little man continued to spew forth, the group, a moving knot of hubbub, passed by the security post where the uniformed guard behind the desk remained stoically nonplussed. And why not? He had seen such mildly chaotic scenes many times following the briefing. In most cases the fits of hysteria that fueled them usually burned out by the time they reached his post. Today was no exception. With a blunt arm-thrusting surge that was equal parts relief and futility, Sox pushed his way around the wide arc of the desk, turned right into the hallway and broke into a slow trot that left those behind mumbling low curses. At last he could quit worrying about anything he had said during the briefing. Then again, why should he be worrying? He had watched two reporters in the third row sleep through the entire exercise. If Soldier was any barometer, the briefing had produced zilch from a news standpoint. No controversy. No sound bites. No alarm bells. Such bland fare that even Soldier's attention remained focused on the White House comings and goings of its ant population.

He slammed his office door. Thank God, it was over. Done. On an Olympic rating scale most of his responses had barely nudged the performance meter—maybe one or two 9.5s, but the rest had been pretty pedestrian stuff. Even though the 40 minutes had seemed to last just short of forever, the good news was he had at least staggered through it without opening mouth and inserting foot. He hadn't said anything erroneous. He hadn't stirred any controversy. He hadn't caused heartburn for anyone on the senior staff. So far, at least. He hadn't wandered into any substantive issue discussions. And he hadn't lied. Basically, he hadn't said anything. A fact which now voided him of any feeling of pride. Indeed, the experience had reduced him to a lump of emptiness, his spirits nagged by taunting thoughts of inadequacy. He was alone in his own briefing backwash where sometimes silence could render a cruel judgment, too. Outside his door it sounded like a library—leaf-falling calm. Not a single reporter parked out there ragging on him. He couldn't blame them. After all, he hadn't given them the slightest whiff of a story anywhere in the claptrap he had just dished out.

The only remaining question was: had he made an utter fool of himself?

The door cracked open and J.Y. slipped in.

"It wasn't pretty, but you did manage to avoid being maimed or killed," the press secretary chuckled.

"Thanks," Sox responded dryly.

"At one point, I thought you got a bit distracted by something. Were you?"

"What made you think that?"

"The blonde fluff on the back row, the one filling out the red sweater. She just signed on as the number three in the booth for one of the networks."

"I noticed the sweater."

"I thought you danced sideways okay on the Navikoff questions."

"It's called tap dancing on eggshells. It's what you do when you don't exactly have a pipeline to a sack full of facts."

J.Y. smiled knowingly and turned to ease back out the door, but stopped.

"Funny thing about the briefing, after you've done it a dozen or so times, you develop a kind of rhythm for the questions. There's nothing you feel you can't answer with some kind of non-answer that sounds like an answer. It's a parlor trick."

"Yeah, sort of like enjoying playing in traffic," Sox said thickly.

"C'mon, you should take the plunge more often. You might actually start liking it."

"That's kind of like wishing for leprosy."

"Hey, you're here because you want to be a press spokesman, right? So quit whining and be a press spokesman," J.Y. scolded, shaking his finger as he departed.

Sox stared listlessly at the door. Inwardly he was tossing with the discontent that comes to those who depart a battlefield uncertain of whether to declare victory or admit defeat.

"Press spokesman, hell, I do this so I can impress chicks," he muttered to himself.

Slowly sinking into depression's arms, he was interrupted by the phone's disruptive ring.

"Hi, Sox. It's Flaxen."

Boom! Back from the dead! Yes! Who says there isn't a God in the White House heaven?

"What timing, what absolute ten-strike, killer timing," he gushed into the receiver.

"You mean it's a bad time?"

"No, I mean I was having this attitude thing, sort of like I was earning frequent flyer miles in hell. The briefing can do that to a person. I just came from there—nearly an hour of wading around in that swampland of press zingers."

"I'm sorry it has you so low. Anything I can do?"

Sure, he thought, how about just panting into the phone for a couple of hours.

"Look," she continued, "maybe I was a little quick on the trigger last week. It's just that, well, you were jerking me around there…and…well…I didn't really appreciate it. Fair enough?"

Fair enough? What isn't fair, he thought, is that a human body of such flawless contour should ever be allowed into any riot-prone country, much less to wiggle up and down the crowded aisles of airliners while dispensing drinks and peanuts. Sheer criminality! Sure, he had tried to con her. Sure, he had jerked her around. But he had gotten caught. He'd paid his penance. He was eager to start anew. In fact, what he really wanted to tell her right now was that she was so damn good-looking that he'd even be willing to go ahead and start the lovemaking without her. She could catch up later.

Instead, he chuckled and said: "As we sometimes say in the briefing room, your point is noted."

"Look," she said, her voice rising with plucky fervor, "I'm thirty years old. I have thirty-one goldfish. I've flown to Europe thirty-two times. I've taken thirty-three hours of cooking lessons. I wore number thirty-four on my high school volleyball team. I have thirty-five-inch hips and a thirty-six-inch bust. Don't you think all that deserves better than some amateur-hour scam at the White House? Enough of the 'I'm a big man with the big man' crap. Okay?"

He paused for a long moment, lending more than just a passing thought to each of the points she had made, particularly focusing on the last number referenced.

"That last thing you mentioned," he finally said, "would that be a C or D cup?"

"That's for me to know and you to try to find out," she said firmly.

He wasn't quite sure how to respond to that challenge, his mind racing, his thoughts a scramble, unfocused, like they were being planned by a committee. Finally, he decided on the direct approach.

"I'm willing."

Evidently, she had made the same choice.

"When?"

While her directness surprised him, he didn't hesitate to seize the advantage. "Today would be nice. Tonight would be even better."

"How about soon?" she countered.

"So where does that leave us?"

"I don't know about you, but I'm in Cleveland," she said simply.

"Beats the hell out of being in this office."

"What's wrong with your office?"

"It's a crawl space for nonstop nagging. It's where I live with reporters for fourteen to sixteen hours a day, sometimes six and seven days a week."

"Hey, quit the mealy-mouthing. You don't have to do that. A lot of people would kill for the chance to be there."

"Yeah, and after they've been here a while, a lot of people might kill for the chance to get out of here, too."

"So why do it?"

"I always had this thing about working in a circus. I finally got my chance."

"I know the feeling. I have that on the plane every day."

"Then that makes us even. And I've got another idea for making the score even. The president has a trip to Houston next week for a major fund-raising speech. How about us meeting there and letting me make it up to you? That event should be over early, and we can make a night of it."

"Make a night of what?" she asked coyly.

"We can put a dent in some of Houston's more dimly lit emporiums of entertainment. We'll have a great time."

"Well, I'll have to do some trip-trading," she said. "I guess I could…"

"C'mon, it'll be a blast," he urged.

"But I've got a promise from you, right? No more 'I'm a big shot' scams?"

"Right. It'll be just you and me. If the president calls, he goes on hold."

"And if there's any more of the phony razzle-dazzle for the flight attendant stuff, then you go on permanent hold," she emphasized.

"It's a deal," he agreed.

"So how will I know where to meet you?"

"I'll check with the Advance Office and find out our hotel there, probably downtown since the event is at the Convention Center. I'll let you know."

"Will that be separate rooms?" she added lightly. The vagueness in her tone perplexed him as to whether or not that was an endorsement or rejection of such a suggestion.

Before he could respond, his attention was diverted to a commotion occurring outside. Swiveling around to the window, he watched as a group of Roman Catholic priests, including a fully robed cardinal, passed by en route to the press stand-up area. They were accompanied by Sparta as their eager escort. He remembered they had been there for a courtesy call on the president, a brief handshake and photo for which no press coverage had been planned or anticipated. Now here they were approaching the cameras and microphones. Ouch!

Obviously, since he had made little or no news at the briefing, the day was looming as a nonstarter on the news front. It was a pretty safe bet that no White House correspondent was going to have any face-time on tonight's newscasts. Thus, any comment today from any visitor, no matter how seemingly mundane, would be worth pursuing on the chance that someone might utter something worthy of a sound bite. And after all, these were priests. How about their thoughts on Crayon's foreign policy? Rumors about meeting with Navikoff? Tax cuts affecting the education budget? And, oh, yes, the president's pro-choice position on abortion?

Christ, Sox thought (in this case invoking the deity's name did not seem inappropriate), the last thing he needed today was Sparta badgering those unsuspecting priests. They shouldn't be out there anyway. He shouldn't have been on this phone. He should have been escorting them out to make sure when departing the West Wing entrance, they turned left instead of right. The turn to the left represented an unwritten rule with the press, signaling that a visitor was off-limits and not interested in talking to the media. Turning right, however, toward the stand-up area, made any visitor, regardless of status, head of state, etc., fair game. Exasperated, he knew he had neglected his duty in favor of this phone tryst with Flaxen. He had let the priests run free, roaming without a chaperone. Now they were about to step in front of cameras and microphones.

"We've got a news break," he gasped into the phone, his voice filling with urgency. "I've got to scramble. We'll talk later."

His abruptness surprised her.

"Well, okay…I was just…bye," she sputtered, her final words being met by his click.

Hurrying out onto the driveway, he peeled his way past the clergymen, reaching the microphone stand and grabbing Sparta who was poised to ask the first question.

"What the shit, Sparta, there was no coverage of this group!"

Her eyes instantly widened as if pleading surprise. "Sox, please watch your language, these are men of the cloth," she mildly scolded, her tongue remaining firmly planted in her cheek.

He glared harshly at her while trying to suppress a smile over his errant obscenity, yet trying to appear annoyed by her rebuke and trying to assure she understood he was royally pissed at her brazenness in dragging the priests out there—lambs to the slaughter.

"Their visit was not on the public schedule. There's no news here. It was only a handshake and a photo op. I'm hauling them outta here."

"Wait," she pleaded. "You're right, but it's so slow today, such a yawner that I asked politely, and they said they'd be willing to answer a few questions. What's the harm?"

"What few questions?" he asked suspiciously. "Give me chapter and verse."

"Strictly slow balls," she insisted. "We've got a story scheduled for tonight about drunk driving. I'll ask them about that. Maybe we can wrap one of their comments into the piece. C'mon, drunk driving—it's a slam dunk for these guys."

Still uneasy, he dawdled between the priests and the microphones, his body serving as a buffer zone. Sparta's eyes continued to plead as she was joined by three other reporters who strolled up and were nodding supportively. One of them was Soldier.

"It's harmless, Sox," Soldier said, a comment which, considering the source, added little to Sparta's case or Sox's peace of mind. With a feint of his head, Sox directed Sparta to walk up the driveway with him to where they would be out of earshot of the priests.

"Give me your word," he said firmly, "that there'll be no bad behavior. These are priests, not politicians. They're not used to this sideshow. Show them respect, particularly in your questions, keep it brief and just on the drunk-driving stuff. I'm giving you a break."

As he spoke, ragged tufts of gray rain clouds rolled by overhead, releasing a slow, filmy drizzle. Sparta didn't wait. She took off immediately back to the stand-up area to gather the priests lest the opportunity be washed out. Hurriedly bunching them together in front of the camera, she gestured upward and implored the heavens: "Can't you say something to stop this rain?"

One of the priests smiled and shrugged. "Sorry, we're in sales, not management."

Pulling his coat over his head, Sox started jogging back to his office, skidding on the slick pavement and then veering to avoid a limousine that had accelerated near the West Wing portico and turned sharply to avoid one of the priests. The car bore diplomatic license plates, a fact that failed to deter Sox from harshly venting his wrath at the driver: "Hey, hot rod, you almost hit a man of God!"

As he stepped to the microphone, the cardinal felt compelled to pause: "They get hit, too!" he shouted toward Sox.

In the West Wing lobby, Sox passed by the Senate majority and minority leaders, both of whom had just come from a brief Oval Office drop-by, an attempt to break the logjam on the budget negotiations between the Hill and the White House. Their visit, too, had not been on the public schedule. And for good reason. Privately the president was backing off his publicly stated position favoring cuts in several departmental budgets. The ugly "C" word was being whispered in the halls: Compromise. If one were going to have to choke it down, as this president was, then no better place to do so than in the privacy of the Oval Office. Just the three of them. No staff. No press. No leaks. Sox had carefully danced around the issue at the briefing. There'd be time later for the president to put the best possible public spin on it.

Exiting the lobby, the senators automatically turned left. Over at the stand-up area, Sparta had begun interviewing the priests but, spotting the departing senators out of the corner of her eye, dropped everything to take off after them, urgently waving her cameraman to follow. With a twenty-yard lead, the senators quickly disappeared down the steps leading to West Executive Avenue and into a waiting chauffeur-driven car.

Sox watched helplessly as the befuddled priests, microphones dangling in the wind, tried to make sense of her sudden dash across the driveway, their faces frozen in a wonderment that said: "What in God's name is going on here?" The cardinal looked even more shocked, like someone had stuck an electric cattle prod under the posterior portions of his ecclesiastical robes.

To hell with it, Sox thought, she broke the deal. Rushing out the door, he caught up to her, jerking her around forcefully so they were face-to-face.

"We had an agreement, remember? Your best behavior, remember?

Look at those priests over there—they think they've stepped into the front pew of hell. I don't blame them. They don't know what's going on, so how about getting your ass back over there and offering a big-time-network-correspondent-type apology? You owe them that. You owe me that."

Still breathing heavily from the run, Sparta studied him for a long moment, glanced over at the waiting priests, then nodded. "You're right. You are absolutely right. I'll take care of it."

"Thank you," he said, watching attentively as she returned to the stand-up area.

She reached the cardinal, braced both her hands against the startled prelate's shoulders and drew him close. She glanced over at Sox to make sure he was watching, then looked squarely into the cardinal's eyes.

"Hey, man, lookit, I'm sorry for having bolted like that. But it's like this—when the big hitters come out, we've gotta go for 'em."

CHAPTER TEN

REPORTER: I've heard the president is ruthless, demanding, and a loner. Is that an accurate description?

SPOKESMAN: No. Absolutely not. I have never heard the president called a loner.

THE WHITE HOUSE
Office of the Press Secretary

FOR YOUR USE AND INFORMATION

TRIP OF THE PRESIDENT
TO HOUSTON, TEXAS

OCTOBER 31–NOVEMBER 1

Weather: Partly cloudy and warm, with temperatures in the low 60s to mid-80s

FRIDAY, OCTOBER 31

12:00 n EST	Press check-in at Andrews AFB
12:45 pm EST	Press charter departs Andrews AFB en route Houston, Texas
	Flying time: 2 hours 50 minutes
	Food service: lunch
	Time change: -1 hour

1:15 pm EST   Press Pool #1 check-in at Andrews AFB

1:30 pm EST   The President departs the White House en route
Andrews AFB, via Marine One
Open Press Coverage

1:45 pm EST   The President arrives Andrews AFB
Open Press Coverage

1:50 pm EST   The President departs Andrews AFB en route
Houston, Texas via Air Force One
Open Press Coverage
Press Pool #1 accompanies
Flying time: 2 hours 50 minutes
Food service: snacks
Time change: -1 hour

2:35 pm CST / 3:35 pm EST
Press Charter arrives Houston Hobby Airport
PRESS NOTE: Members of the press wishing to
proceed directly to the hotel should board buses
1 and 2. Those in PRESS POOL #2 and those
wishing to cover the arrival of The President
should remain at airport. Following the arrival
of The President, press bus 3 will proceed to
the hotel.

2:50 pm CST / 3:50 pm EST
Press buses 1 and 2 depart Houston Hobby Airport en route hotel

3:20 pm CST / 4:20 pm EST
Press buses 1 and 2 arrive hotel
PRESS NOTE: The White House Press Filing
Center is located in the Gulf Coast Room. Room
keys will be available at Filing Center and baggage
will be delivered to sleeping rooms.

3:40 pm CST / 4:40 pm EST

> The President arrives Houston Hobby Airport
> Open Press Coverage
> PRESS NOTE: Facilities include: camera plat-
> form,100' throw, head-on, 6 LDs

3:45 pm CST / 4:45 pm EST

> The President departs Houston Hobby Airport
> en route hotel, via motorcade
> Press Pool #2 accompanies

3:50 pm CST / 4:50 pm EST

> Press bus 3 departs Houston Hobby Airport en
> route hotel

4:15 pm CST / 5:15 pm EST

> The President arrives hotel and proceeds to suite
> for personal/staff time.

4:20 pm CST / 5:20 pm EST

> Press bus 3 arrives hotel

6:30 pm CST. / 7:30 pm EST

> Press Pool #3 assembles in White House Press
> Filing Center and is escorted to motorcade

6:55 pm CST / 7:55 pm EST

> The President departs hotel en route George R.
> Brown Convention Center via motorcade.
> Press Pool #3 accompanies

7:05 pm CST / 8:05 pm EST

> The President arrives George R. Brown Conven-
> tion Center and proceeds to reception
> Closed Press Coverage
> PRESS NOTE: Press Pool #3 will be escorted to
> designated area in the Ballroom where facilities
> include: camera platform, 100' throw, head-on,
> lighted for TV, mult, 6 LDs, remarks piped to
> Hotel Filing Center

7:05 pm CST / 8:05 pm EST
> Press buses depart Hotel en route George R. Brown Convention Center

7:15 pm CST / 8:15 pm EST
> Press buses arrive George R. Brown Convention Center

8:05 pm CST / 9:05 pm EST
> The President enters ballroom for fundraising dinner
> Open Press Coverage

9:45 pm CST / 10:45 pm EST
> Remarks of the President to fundraising dinner
> Open Press Coverage

10:15 pm CST / 11:15 pm EST
> Presidential remarks conclude

10:30 pm CST / 11:30 pm EST
> The President departs George R. Brown Convention Center en route hotel, via motorcade.
> Press Pool #3 accompanies

10:40 pm CST / 11:40 pm EST
> The President arrives hotel and proceeds to suite

10:35 pm CST / 11:35 pm EST
> Press buses depart George R. Brown Convention Center en route hotel

10:45 pm CST / 11:45 pm EST
> Press buses arrive hotel

OVERNIGHT: Houston, Texas

The chartered press plane was a zoo. But that was often the case. Sort of like Halloween. To make matters worse, it *was* Halloween.

Filing on board, reporters were greeted by flight attendants in witch costumes encouraging celebration of the trick-or-treat spirit. One of the flight attendants, whose costume with several moving parts was a work in progress, was attempting to dispense drinks while maneuvering up and down the crowded aisles. As always, the bar was open prior to takeoff. Two rows behind Sox a group of print reporters was gulping straight shots of bourbon. Sox marveled at their stamina. Noontime. Long day ahead. Long night ahead. A speech still to cover. A story to be written. Copy to be filed. Those were hall of fame livers. Had to be. But the bar was always open early and would remain so, or until empty.

Today, takeoff was still ten minutes away and the games had already begun. Bathroom doors were barricaded with occupants inside. Fruit was being tossed around with a particular preference for slightly overripe grapes. A bowling ball had been set free and was rolling in a zigzag pattern, its progress intermittently halted by bumps into seats and contact with the feet and legs of passengers. Everywhere the cabin was festooned in Halloween colors, orange and black crepe paper hanging from the overhead compartments and strewn across aisles, forming a stringy labyrinth. The squawk of noisemakers filled the cabin and randomly tossed confetti hung in the air, drifting so it gradually settled like gentle snow. A Gregorian chant was blasting away at full volume over the intercom system. In the war against chaos on the press plane, chaos was clearly winning.

The press plane operated on a caste system, the larger, more prestigious and financially robust news organizations filling most of the seats in first class and the front areas of the coach section. All seats were assigned, with correspondents at the front and technicians and other support staff in the back. Mixed in were members of the press office staff, stenographers and Secret Service agents not travelling on Air Force One.

One of the few constants aboard was Sox's assigned seat, front row by the window in first class. A lower press office staffer usually sat next to him on the aisle, a strategic ploy which made it logistically harder for reporters to reach and pester him.

"Hey, Sox!"

He heard it, but wished he hadn't. The voice had a tinny, forceful and irritating bite that cut sharply through the noise and chatter, making it sound as if its owner spoke only in capital letters. Pretending he hadn't heard it and hoping it would go away, Sox inched down lower in his seat, the back of his head disappearing from view.

"Hey, Sox!"

He didn't need to look. He knew it was Tommy Tuff, a magazine reporter recently assigned to the beat. Young, brash, eager to impress and certainly self-impressed, Tuff was an irritant to be avoided whenever possible. Sox would rather scratch dandruff on a dragonfly's dick than deal with this prima donna. But here on the plane it was either listen to the guy, or else open the door and step into eternity at 30,000 feet. A couple of non-choices, to be sure. Tommy Tuff. The last name was appropriate, even if it was misspelled. It hadn't taken long for him to adapt to the pell-mell pace of being a White House reporter, or savoring the hijinks on the press plane and in the briefing room.

"Hey, Sox!"

Already Tuff had become a ringleader, this while still going through his rites of passage to earn the welcome of colleagues in the press corps, a coveted badge of acceptance which never came easy for rookies.

"Hey, hey, Sox!" he continued to shout, cupping his hands oval-like around his mouth to simulate a megaphone.

Sox raised up slowly, narrowing his eyes and hesitantly peering over the top of the seat. A ragged conga line was winding serpentine-like through the rows, some of its members having donned Halloween masks as part of the carnival revelry. Those of more serious purpose had taken their seats and were attempting to read or work at laptop computers. Their efforts were futile, such good intentions being rewarded by rock candy tossed their way, also an errant Frisbee and a barf bag filled with water which splattered wildly upon hitting its intended target—a rotund cameraman. Remaining stationary today on the plane was going to be hazardous.

"Hey, St. Louis, I've got a great idea for a free lance article."

"What article, Tuff?" Sox reluctantly answered.

"Just an idea I had." Tuff's palms turned outward in a simple declaration. "A fresh White House angle."

"There are no fresh White House angles."

"Sure there are, but this is a little different. Yeah, it's a lot different. Lots of public clamor for this one. I'll bet it's never been done before."

"Bet me," Sox whispered under his breath.

"Okay, how about this for a title: *The Nation's Poster Boy for Non-Answers—Sox St. Louis. His silence speaks volumes.*"

It wasn't necessary for Sox to respond. He couldn't be heard anyway. Someone had cranked up the volume on the Gregorian chant to such a blaring level that along with shrieks from the conga-line gang, the cabin was a noisy mess.

Two hours later the chaos had calmed. Most of the Halloween celebrants were in their seats, heads tucked down reading the advance text of the president's speech, some pecking away at their laptops, but others preferring to engage in the game of picking the speech apart.

"Say, Soxeroo, how about the second page, third graph? He refers to the importance of modern-day patriots. Who in the hell is he talking about—the New England Patriots?"

Sox didn't immediately recognize the voice which came from the section of reporters seated directly behind him. It was promptly followed by others.

"Yeah, and on the next page he talks about us having pride as a country and holding our skirts up for all the world to see. Isn't that against the indecent exposure laws?"

"This speech is crapola."

"K-rap in saran wrap."

"Carl Crayon e pluribus drivel."

"Nothing in here about meeting with the Russians…"

"Yeah, are they screwing him?"

"I'm not."

"Yeah, but you're not getting any from anybody."

"What about it, Sox, can you confirm the rumors about a terrorism summit?"

Sox couldn't confirm anything. To answer the last question, he fell back on that lamest of dodges: "We don't confirm rumors." Pure dung for an answer, but at least it wasn't "no comment," although everyone recognized it for what it basically was, just another face-saving way of saying "no comment." At least it would tide him over until Houston. He'd check with J.Y. and Quad there to see if there was any new guidance or if he could advance the story "on background." Good ol' "on background." It was one of the four basic ground rules by which business was conducted with the press.

Two of the four, "deep background" and "off the record," were little used. But "on background" was a staple of the daily reporting scene, every bit as much as "on the record." Maybe more. Its use permitted many stories to reach the airwaves or get into print that might not otherwise. It meant being able to feed information to a reporter without having one's name appear in the story. It was instead attributed to "a high government official" or some similar cover. A favorite technique of leakers, it protected the source while boosting one's ego, not to mention one's stock with the fortunate reporter. Its constant use also led to overuse. An oft-used reporter's ploy that never failed to bemuse Sox went thusly: "Okay, you've told me 'no comment' on the record, now tell me the facts on background." With only rare exceptions, his response was always the same: "I've taken you as far as I can using any ground rule. And that's on the record."

"Ach-tung! Ach-tung!" an imposing voice boomed out over the plane's intercom. "Your attention, please, for several vitally important announcements."

Despite the voice's authoritative tone, it was clear that control of the microphone had been wrested from the airline staff and was once again in the hands of rowdies. Realizing the animals were loose again, Sox slumped back down in his seat.

"First," the voice intoned, "would all those wishing free tickets to this Sunday's Redskins game please report to seat 23C."

An instant stampede erupted, heated clawing and thunder among those seeking to be first to reach the indicated seat. Most of those engaged in the hand-to-hand combat were relative newcomers to the White House beat and press plane foolishness. Old hands knew better. 23C was Soldier's seat. One could only hope that by the time the plane was on the ground, order would be restored and Soldier's dwarfish body would still be intact, this despite the grappling rush to his seat in quest of the hoped-for ducats. There were none, of course, and Soldier's angry protestations only served to incite a stream of spiteful taunts from the mob. It was a cruel game, but one the little man had angrily endured in the Crayon administration.

"Secondly," the intercom voice continued, "I would like to thank Sox St. Louis for those confidential notes from yesterday's National Security Council meeting. Don't worry, Sox, I'll get them back to you right after our newscast tonight." This announcement, too, drew only scattered murmurs, the veterans greeting it with yawning indifference. It was an old scam meant to titillate the novices aboard.

Approaching Houston, the plane began slowly knifing downward through great billows of clouds, massive white puffs, one after another, until it seemed they were laced endlessly together throughout the sky. As the plane swayed lightly back and forth in its descent, Sox stood up and stretched, surveying the first class cabin. Patrick Y was asleep. Above his seat, someone had posted a crudely lettered sign. It read: *Got laid last night.*

"Sox, before we land, let me swab you on this rumor thing," Sparta growled from behind, moving up and thrusting herself into the empty seat next to him.

"All crap aside, what can you tell me about this Russian meeting?" As she spoke, she hissed directly in his face, spewing forth a mouthful of stale vapors in bad need of a breath mint. "One of my sources tells me it's a done deal. Any chance Crayon will spring the announcement on this trip?"

Sox turned away without responding, staring vacantly out the window. One reason for turning away was he didn't have an answer.

Flourishes

Another equally important reason was he didn't have a breath mint to offer, and the fumes coming his way were enough to melt the chrome on an armored car.

"Well?" she insisted.

He looked down, up, out—anywhere to avoid eye contact. One good read of his face would confirm he was running on empty. He knew she sensed that. So probably did the newscast producers back at her network, but for lack of any breaking news had no doubt bugged her to seek him out and at least give it a try. Spin the wheel on the chance he might actually have some nugget of news to offer.

What could he say? How to respond to keep her a peg off balance? To keep the game interesting? To at least make her think he might be in the information loop on this one, even if he was only on the edges. Or the edge of the edges. To make her think he did know something about the Russian meeting but just couldn't talk. Perception. It was everything in Washington. But here on the press plane, perception was a tough sell. Here there was no podium. No place behind which to hide notes and scraps of wisdom that could make a spokesman seem spontaneously eloquent. No place behind which to hide prepared guidances for responding to killer questions. Here one had to improvise and play it off the top, the kind of ad-lib verbal dodgeball that had never been one of Sox's strengths.

Peering out the aisle seat's tiny window, his eyes rhythmically followed the weaving of the plane's wing as it gracefully dipped in and out of the clouds. At this point any stall to delay dealing with Sparta was a welcome diversion.

Remaining glued to the window, he coughed and hesitantly cleared his throat. "I'd like to quote an old American proverb which I just made up on the spot," he said.

"Which is?"

Which is, he thought, that a hungry press corps is a pain in the ass. Instead, he answered: "Which is, stay tuned."

"What does that mean?"

"It means stay tuned."

"For what? When?"

His coyness had only encouraged her to keep sniffing. Good God, he wondered, how long does it take a plane on final descent to finally touch down? Now she was dishing out questions which he couldn't possibly answer and making the damn flight seem interminable.

"You'll just have to stay tuned," he said, doing his best to project an air of calmness. What a charade! Calm? His insides were roiling hell. They always were when having to deal with her.

"I still don't know what that means," she grumbled.

"It means I just can't take you any further right now."

"Right now? Does that mean you might have something for me later?"

"No."

"Not even on background?"

He shifted in his seat, glaring forcefully at her, the dark scowl crossing his face providing her answer.

"Okay," she continued, "but just remember that I do have a source who is confirming this…and…well…uh…if I can get another source… well…I can go with it on tonight's newscast."

"Noted," he shrugged.

"What does that mean?"

Goddammit, he thought, it means get this plane down pronto and get this ball-busting bitch off my case. Unfortunately, he had created a situation for which he had only himself to blame. She'd have been back in her seat by now if he hadn't tossed out those noncommittal hints. If he had just refrained from trying to be a big shot. Big man. Big deal. Big-time press spokesman. He knew nothing about the damn terrorism meeting. Well, close to nothing. She thought he knew nothing but wasn't completely sure. So here they were sparring about what he might know. Or, more precisely, sparring to keep her from knowing how little he knew. God bless the government and the press.

The plane continued to surge downward, lower and lower until finally it broke free from the cloud cover and out into an expanse of pure blue sky that stretched endlessly across the horizon.

She clicked her chair into its upright position and leaned over, the stagnancy escaping her mouth forcing him back into the deepest recesses of his seat.

"You know how to stay ahead in this arena, don't you?" she asked.

"Yeah, get a good pair of track shoes," he laughed weakly. "It's always hard to hit a moving target."

"There's also another way."

"Which is?"

"Which is to have information that only a few others have and which—

"—just can't be leaked."

"Even on background?"

"Not even on deep, deep, deep, deep, deep background."

She hesitated for a moment, visually measuring him. "Has Crayon said anything around you about this Russian thing?"

What now? Lie? Sure, they had discussed it, although that was most definitely a generous characterization of what had actually occurred. More accurately, he had gotten his ass chewed out in the Oval Office by the president of the United States. And, oh, yes, the topic was mentioned.

"About what Russian thing?"

"Plans for a terrorism summit."

"We discuss a lot of things."

"Yeah, like what's your name—Bill?" she grunted sarcastically. "I heard about that."

"I think the president's got that one down now," he said, awkwardly clearing his throat.

"And?"

"And what?"

"And how about the Rooskies?"

"And…stay tuned."

She slumped back in her seat, a retreat he hoped would be a realization that this was going to prove a lame exercise, one non-answer after another. Still she made no indication of abandoning the effort.

"I love surprises," she said, winking. "Just so long as I know about them in advance."

He didn't need a United Nations translator to interpret that message:

In other words, just be sure all leaks go to her first.

Once again it was diversion time. "Has it ever occurred to you, Sparta, that maybe only one-tenth of one percent of the people in this country are interested in this?"

"I don't give a farmer's frig if there's just one world-class idiot out there who's interested—just make sure when it's leaked that I'm not off somewhere taking a leak. Okay?"

He had no answer that could possibly satisfy that request. The good news was that his wish for the flight to end was nearing reality, the rumbling of the landing gear being lowered and locked into place providing that reminder. At last, wheels down.

"Well, thanks, young man," she said. "For what, I'm not sure."

He frowned at her. "Young man? Don't you know there are no young men in the White House? Only old young men."

All of a sudden, the plane veered sharply, a jolt in the midst of what had been a smooth descent. The abrupt jerk stirred catcalls from some of the reporters, one of them using the intercom to bellow: "Whoa!"

The sudden lurch recalled for Sox the time when the press plane had gone into a serious nosedive, an abortive maneuver to avoid a small private plane that had blindly cut across their bow. Thanks to instant reaction work by the flight crew, a horrific crash was averted. In the midst of the pilot's heroic handling of the near-crisis, a surly radio reporter, Baytown Baker, had hysterically run down the aisle, banging on the cockpit door and demanding: "Would someone in there get out here and explain what in the hell is going on!" Fortunately the crew, which had been otherwise occupied, had not responded to that press request.

Today, though, things seemed to have finally calmed for the landing. Leaning out over the aisle to survey the rows behind, Sox was amazed to see everyone in their seat. Then it occurred to him that he was experiencing a press plane phenomenon. There was quiet.

CHAPTER ELEVEN

REPORTER: What is the White House policy with regard to staff members and their receipt of gifts?

SPOKESMAN: It is more blessed to give than to receive.

"Signal to all cars and stations, signal depart, depart," crackled the command over radios throughout the motorcade.

It was nearing rush hour in Houston as the long line of cars snaked its way out onto the Gulf Freeway. Rush hour. Another presidential motorcade. Streets sealed off. Intersections blocked. Commuter traffic halted and stacked up for miles. A sure-fire formula for off-pissing thousands of potential voters.

Motorcades. Sox never tired of them. Even though it was a monotonously similar routine in city after city, it was a monotony shadowed by fear of unpredictability.

Then, too, there were always the faces flowing past, a coming-out party for America to see a president…black, white, brown, the awed, the unimpressed, the curious and those just caught in traffic…past construction workers…taverns…children running alongside trying to keep pace, then falling back with shouts of "I just missed seeing him"…past ghettos…signs… flags…crowds…and always in every city, lonely figures in the distance shading their eyes, perplexed by the complexity of it all, yet others looking nonplussed and not seeming to care at all.

Inside the two overly crowded press pool vans, TV reporters were bitching. They were facing evening news deadlines. They didn't give a damn that an advance man was advising them that the Gulf Freeway was not the most scenic route for entering the city. They just wanted to get to the hotel filing center—fast.

Motorcycle policemen sped by, leapfrogging ahead to seal off intersections and provide safe escort. Sox watched impassively as the van in which he was riding passed by a gaudy sign displaying silhouetted figures of two sparsely clad females with epic chest endowments. He wondered if up ahead the president had noticed it. Then again, how could the president or anyone in the motorcade have missed taking a peek at that display of unsheathed flesh? Another garish sign was in close proximity, this one pocked with holes from missing light bulbs but retaining enough firepower to flash its message: *Turn here for the Tastiest Torsos and Bustiest Babes in Texas. Total 100% All Nude Revue. 24 Hours a Day.* Hanging below that sign was a large piece of cardboard, temporarily attached there. Its handwritten scrawl read*: We Welcome You to Houston, President Crayon.* The lead van rocked with appreciative howls, the vehicle's driver responding to requests to slow down for a more comprehensive viewing before resuming speed and closing ranks with the rest of the motorcade.

"Shit, Sox, tell Crayon he needs those babes in D.C. With those figures, they could balance the budget."

"Sox, you think you work hard, how about this place—24 hours a day."

"Kind of makes you proud of the American free-enterprise system, doesn't it?"

"Yeah, you gotta like that can-do Texas spirit."

"Spirit-schmirit. Get me some reaction from Crayon on all this."

"And the phone numbers of the two chesties."

Sox laughed nervously at their jibes, a reaction to cover his more immediate concern for the route they were taking into town. Knowing Houston, he recognized their course as one heading away from downtown and the hotel. They now were going west on the Southwest Freeway, a troubling turn as this represented the most direct route to the city's Medical Center.

Knowing the networks monitored the White House radio frequencies, he was hesitant to query J.Y. up ahead in the motorcade. The word *hospital* uttered over the airwaves would set off a firestorm. But why were they headed this way when the schedule had called for a direct airport-to-hotel arrival scenario?

He stared anxiously out the window as they picked up speed. That, too, was a worrisome omen. Pressing against the glass for a better angle of vision, he could see the lead cars in the distance, including the presidential limousine, an undulant line of vehicles veering right and taking the Greenbriar exit. That could only mean the worst—they were indeed headed for the Medical Center. What had happened? Heart attack? Stroke? Gall bladder? Diarrhea? It had to be serious; otherwise, the president's personal doctor who always traveled with them would have waited and handled it at the hotel.

Sox's mind raged with questions—his own and the barrage the reporters would heap on him the instant they got a whiff as to their new destination. When did it occur? Before the stock market closed? Is it life-threatening? Vital signs? Where is the vice president? He thought of his recent briefing and how they had pressed him about the president's health. Had he lied? The motorcade continued to move faster, swinging wide left onto Greenbriar and heading south, away from downtown and the hotel.

"Sox, how much longer to the hotel?" Patrick Y wondered out loud.

"Yeah, let's get somewhere soon or else—"

"—or else take us to that busty babes place," a network technician added, his suggestion being greeted by lusty cheering.

What was supposed to have been a routine 30-minute ride into town had for Sox become an inwardly jolting experience. Now they were turning onto Holcombe Boulevard, which meant just a few more blocks before hospital row would loom into view. They were only moments away from someone catching on.

As they passed the intersection of Holcombe and Main, Sparta's antenna shot up. "Aren't we in the neighborhood where the Shamrock Hotel used to be?"

"Yeah," another voice followed, "and when did they get these fast-food joints downtown?"

"Damn-a-rama!" Sparta shouted, her mouth dropping open as she caught sight of the imposing facades of hospitals looming ahead. "We're bound for the Medical Center! Crayon's had a heart attack!"

It was that once-in-a-lifetime bell-ringer moment for a reporter on the White House beat. The Russians, terrorism, a summit, news leaks—all were instant ancient history. Now—this moment—was everything, a moment they knew might never come again. Nothing else mattered. Sox knew it, too. But he also knew what he didn't know—whether or not the president had suffered a heart attack.

As the motorcade turned into the complex, the press van in which Sox was riding careened wildly over the curb, nearly spinning out of control, the driver hanging on and managing to steer it back into line. His rescue effort was no small feat, considering the state of panic that had now seized the vehicle's occupants. Cameras were being hastily strapped to shoulders, microphones connected, lights extended, cell phones cradled on shoulders, laptops activated and notepads urgently whipped open.

No one knew exactly where they were except they had turned into the Medical Center. It was uninformed frenzy.

"Sox—quick, what's happened? What can you tell me?" Sparta gushed, grabbing his shoulders from behind.

Sox could only resort to one of the first rules he had learned upon entering the press secretarying business: in times of crisis, stay calm and say nothing, absolutely nothing, until hard facts surface. Above all, don't play the rumor game. It was impossible to respond anyway, for once again he knew nothing. Still, it was not a situation to relish. What in hell's name was happening?

The motorcade began to slow, crawling to a stop in the driveway facing Texas Children's Hospital. There were two entrances with identifying designations over each. One read: *West Tower*. The other read: *Emergency Center*.

"Why a children's hospital?" someone shouted.

"It was the closest—they obviously had to get him somewhere quick!" another voice shouted.

"The president has had a heart attack!" a voice shrieked.

"Sox, can you confirm that?" Sparta urged. "We need an answer now!"

Of course he couldn't confirm that. Instead, he remained mute and allowed himself to be pulled from the van, swept along with the surge of bodies rushing toward the front entrance where the presidential limousine had pulled up. Without delay, the president climbed out and without any noticeable infirmity walked unaided into the West Tower entrance.

Moments before, the area had been a medical village at peace. Now in a blink it had been transformed into a scene of media violence. A cameraman emerging from the first van stumbled and was trampled as reporters and technicians poured out of the second van and pounded over him. A brace of Secret Service agents quickly aligned to create a formidable human wall in front of the West Tower's glass doors, a perimeter beyond which no press access was allowed. Cameras at that spot were thrown onto tripods, small arc lamps popping on and adding artificial luster to the scrambling urgency.

Tommy Tuff elbowed his way to the front and grabbed Sox. "What do you know? What can you tell us? Is it a heart attack or worse?"

"I'm on my way inside," Sox said, kneading his way through the crowd.

"Tell! Tell! Tell!" screamed Baytown Baker. "We're on deadline! Was there an accident? A heart attack? Has the man got major league hemorrhoids? A bad case of the runs? What is it? I've got to put something on the air now!"

"And why a children's hospital?" Patrick Y repeated.

"St. Louis, you'd better get someone out here damn quick with some answers," Tuff insisted.

Sox shoved by two cameramen, brandished his White House pass and trip ID pin for the agents at the entrance, then brushed past into the hospital's lobby.

Compared to the turmoil outside, the lobby was eerily calm. Quad stood off to one side, casually reading a briefing paper held in one hand while nursing a soft drink with the other. He seemed strangely oblivious to the disruption outside.

As Sox approached, he glanced up from his reading. "Hey, hey, it's the

Sox man. Welcome to Houston."

"Is J.Y. with you?" Sox asked, perplexed by the chief of staff's laid-back attitude.

"No, he went upstairs with the old man. He said you could handle the press pool."

Sox hesitated, catching his breath and waiting for further explanation, but none came. From past experience he was familiar with Quad's glibness. It invariably meant further probing was required.

"We've got a press gang out there who've gone ballistic—a prison riot. I need a quick fill on what's going down here."

Quad's eyes wandered back down to the briefing paper in his hand. "So they're in a stew out there, huh?" he asked nonchalantly.

"Yeah, they're setting up for live shots—everything—the full-court press."

Quad drew a leisurely swallow from the soft drink.

"Live shots? Really? Just because of this stop?"

"Crap, Quad, they're a hiccup away from reporting that the president has had a heart attack!"

The chief of staff raised his eyebrows in mock surprise but remained silent.

"So what do I say?" Sox asked, his voice growing weary with exasperation.

Quad turned and tilted his head for a better view of the spectacle outside. "So what's everyone trying to do—write a headline that says 'President Near Death'?"

"I'm not worried so much about what they're trying to do," Sox said, "as I am about what I need to do. In the next minute I've got to come up with an answer to this question: why has the president of the United States unexpectedly gone to a hospital?"

Quad bent down to the briefcase at his side, extracted a letter from a manila folder and handed it to him. "This letter was in the president's weekly reading file. There's a ten-year-old boy here who may not make it to his eleventh birthday. This is from his mother. The president read it on the way here and said why not stop by and say hello."

Sox's eyes raced over the letter, then glanced up to check the press boil outside. It now occurred to him that it would be his unenviable task to tell them they had speculated the president into a heart attack minus any hard facts. But before doing that, his press spokesman's instinct told him he needed to press Quad one more time. He had learned the hard way that extracting information from members of the senior staff often required asking not only the right question, but the right question asked with specificity. It was never just: "How's the economy?" It was: "How's the economy *today*?"

"So it's all about this kid and has absolutely nothing to do with the president's health, right?"

Quad smiled. "Don't worry, Sox, I'm not rolling you. Today the old man just decided to be an impromptu Boy Scout. There is no other story. Go tell the bastards in that shark patrol they can stand down."

On the one hand, Sox was going to savor this moment, the collective sigh of press disappointment, but there would also be a downside—their rage. Massive abuse would be heaped on him from those who felt they had been toyed with to the point of nearly interrupting network programming with news flashes. They'd chew his ass out for having led them to the edge of a near press catastrophe. They hadn't been lied to, but they had been made fools. They would be pissed for having been duped. They wouldn't really be embarrassed; most of them were too hard-nosed to carry such an emotion. There would be, though, that lingering regret over having been deprived of the big story, the supreme career-making moment. But he'd take comfort in knowing that their journalistic "me first" greed was the source of their near undoing, not any White House misinformation.

Leaving Quad and hurrying across the lobby, he reached the glass doors and passed through, stepping out and squinting into the harsh blaze of cameras now haphazardly massed across the driveway so they seemed mangled together almost as a single glob rather than separate units. A torrent of screams flowed from the temporary press pen, anguish pouring from the mouths of the desperate. He stopped when he had come to within arm's length of their frenzy, a hue and cry that had now become a giant verbal spasm on autopilot.

"Did it happen on the flight?"

"Sox, Sox…"

"…how many…"

"…confirm…a heart attack?"

"…doctors are attending him?"

"Has he been sedated?"

"Yeah, for several years."

"…rumor of seizure and…"

"Has Mrs. Crayon been notified?"

"When will the doctor brief us?"

"…an incident during the motorcade…"

"…under anesthetic?"

"… military forces…on alert?"

"Will he temporarily have to transfer power to the vice president?"

"Sox…"

"…sick or just hurt?"

"What…"

"Sox, we need to know if…"

"Should we prepare to go live?"

"Is the president alive?"

Their fury pounded at him, a burst of ceaseless questions until finally he motioned for a halt, raising both arms and extending the palms of his hands. He was surprised by their instant hush, voices falling quiet as faces quivered with expectancy.

"Let me tell you what I know," he said calmly. "The president is inside Texas Children's Hospital."

"Oh, God!" someone screamed.

"Shhh!"

"He has entered the hospital for one reason." As Sox spoke, his eyes settled on their pencils, yellow blurs scratching wildly across notepads. "That one purpose relates to a disease for which the president prays a cure will be found."

"Good God, what does the man have?"

"How long has he had it?"

"Is it curable?"

"When was the diagnosis?"

"Whaa…"

"…heart attack?"

"Stroke?"

"Why weren't we told sooner?"

"Shhh! Let him finish!"

"I can't answer those questions because they do not apply to this situation. What I can tell you, though, is that he is here in response to a letter from a Houston mother whose son is seriously ill and who the president decided to visit while en route to the hotel. I will be glad to give you what details I can about the boy and his family."

His last words were greeted by a collective exhaling, a whoosh of air escaping a deflated balloon. Disappointment had just scored a slam dunk. The press had been had. And they were chapped.

"This is bullshit!" Tuff railed. "You detoured us to this hospital, led us here believing something had happened to the president. Now you're telling us this was all for him to jolly up some kid. Screw this!"

"Wait a minute!" Sox said sharply. "You led each other into thinking that, not Sox St. Louis. The press pack mentality did it, not me. Everyone was so anxious to be first rather than to be sure. That's not my fault."

"So we're here just because of some kid?" Tuff asked mockingly.

"That's right. Not just some kid, either. A very brave kid. Any problem with that?"

Some grumbling erupted from the back of the pen, too garbled for Sox to comprehend before Sparta renewed the attack.

"I'll tell you the problem. We weren't given any warning on why we were stopping, no guidance—zip. Don't you think it's more than a little dangerous, not to mention stupid, to deliver the president of the United States to a hospital without bothering to tell the press why? What the hell were we supposed to think?"

"Yeah, Sox, we came within minutes of messing with network programming to cut in live here," a technician added. "They'd have roasted our ass in New York."

"Well-done or medium?" an anonymous voice shouted.

"All you had to do was tell us the reason, and we wouldn't have had all this rush to judgment," Sparta huffed.

"I hear your pain," Sox said, "but I didn't know the reason myself until we got here. In the meantime, you whipped yourselves into this lather. It was you who decided the president was sick. Your wounds were self-inflicted."

"Yeah, yeah…," Sparta muttered matter-of-factly, reflecting the group's impatience with his explanation.

"I get it," Tuff said sarcastically. "This was just a game, wasn't it? Crayon just wanted to jerk us around, didn't he?"

"…jerk us around damn good…"

"…tool job…"

Sox ignored their grousing. "For those of you that are interested, I'll be glad to provide some background information on the boy and his illness."

There were a few takers on his offer, but most continued to whine about what had occurred. Meanwhile, the cameras and lights were dismantled. Others hung around the front of the motorcade in anticipation of the president's departure, while the rest drifted back to the vans to phone their desks with word that there would be no news, after all, from this stop.

Twenty minutes later the president still remained inside. During the wait, and in the absence of the president having suffered a heart attack, another press interest had developed: food. Someone in one of the press vans had resourcefully found a way to clear access for a pizza parlor bicycle delivery into the motorcade area, with two large boxes being deposited there, one with anchovies, one without.

The aroma wafted seductively over the area in such a pronounced way that congestion engulfed the area around one of the vans, so much so that it briefly aroused suspicion by Secret Service agents who, upon discovering the commotion was pizza-related, relaxed. The area which only moments before had been a storm center of press turmoil had now been transformed into the site of an impromptu junk-food binge.

The deliveryman thanked his patrons, spun his bicycle around and took off, seemingly unimpressed that it was probably the first time in history there had been a pizza delivery to a presidential motorcade.

The devouring of the pizza and the departure of the president coincided. Excellent timing, everyone agreed, an occurrence that lifted spirits even though chatter in both waiting vans consisted mostly of barking about the president's slickness in keeping them in the dark. Sox sat in the front seat of the lead van, munching on pizza crust and dutifully watching as the president emerged and headed directly for his limousine, undeterred by the knot of reporters who lingered near the entrance to shout and taunt him.

"Mr. President, do you think it was smart to stop at a hospital without telling the press in advance?"

"Mr. President, do you enjoy playing let's fool the press?"

"How's the kid you visited?"

"Did you talk to him on the record or on background?"

"Did the kid ask you about your proposed budget cuts?"

"How about telling us the next time you want to make an unscheduled stop?"

"Where else are we going to stop today? How about some bowling?"

The president glowered in the direction of the questioners, hesitating as if to respond, then thought better of it and ducked into the limousine.

As the motorcade got under way, moving away from the hospital and gaining speed, Sox noticed the lead cars turning right onto Holcombe Boulevard, once again an opposite direction from the shortest route to downtown, but at least heading away from the Medical Center and health worries. But why this way? If downtown and the hotel were the next stop, this was a decidedly longer course by which to weave a motorcade through town, especially at the busiest traffic time of the day. Quad hadn't mentioned anything else, but neither had Sox asked the specific question he should have asked: were there going to be any more surprise stops today? Surely they wouldn't do that without telling him. Surely they didn't want him hammered once more today by the press. Enough of the abuse!

They crossed back over Main Street heading west, their police escorts holding back cars for several blocks, an action serving to delay and rile rush-hour commuters. The procession didn't get far before braking and easing to a stop, another unscheduled blip that once again set off a scramble from the press vans, the passengers in each piling into the street and running en masse toward the front of the now nearly stationary motorcade. The presidential limousine had slowed, too, but not completely as it turned right into a driveway fifty yards ahead and gradually disappeared from view. The motorcade cars behind it immediately followed.

"What the hell is this?" Tuff wheezed, breathless and straining to keep up with the pack. "Is he headed back to the hospital?"

Sox sprinted ahead, not looking back or answering, his eyes remaining riveted on the driveway where the president had turned.

"Katy to St. Louis…Katy to St. Louis," crackled J.Y.'s voice over the staff radio channel.

Sox awkwardly pressed his walkie-talkie against his lips as he ran. "Go ahead."

"Tell the pool it's another brief stop, but no need for any alarm bells. The president will not disembark, so hold everyone in the vans."

"Too late, no can do," Sox replied. "The genie's already out of the bottle and coming your way. And what's the purpose of this stop?" He made sure his voice placed emphasis on *this*.

There was a crash of static, then J.Y.'s voice came through loud, clear and calm.

"That would be for a burger, fries and a malt."

"Say again," Sox radioed, confused.

"He's having the Number Two," J.Y. responded simply.

Racing to stay ahead, Sox reached the driveway first. There he could see that it led past the take-out window of a fast-food restaurant where the presidential limousine was currently idling. Another first for a presidential motorcade, he thought. All the other cars immediately behind were patiently waiting for the president to complete his order. Sox watched in wonderment as a hand extended through the opening in the glass window and placed in the president's extended hand a sack containing his order—a Number Two. By now, members of the pool were catching up and witnessing the purpose of the stop. They staggered up to Sox's vantage point where they could see the president of the United States was in a drive-thru lane en route to getting a junk-food fix. Even though many of them were winded from the run, fighting for gulps of air, huffing with hands on their knees, their quest for a fresh news lead had not waned.

"Sox, we need a briefing on this."

"We demand a briefing on this."

"You bet…we need to know—is Crayon anti-pizza?"

"Can you confirm…whether or not that burger had onions?"

"Can we get a readout on his exact meal order?"

"And why he chose to stop here?"

"And why couldn't he wait until he got to the hotel?"

"And doesn't he feel this is risky from a security standpoint?"

"Is the Secret Service going to inspect that burger before he bites into it?"

"What flavor is the drink he ordered?"

"…cost of the meal?"

"Did he pay for it or did one of the agents?"

"Can you give us the exact exchange of dialogue that occurred over the speaker between the president and the order-taker?"

Sox stood there, defenseless, a dartboard. He was tired. He was hungry. He looked at his watch. Quarter after five. With the president's dinner speech still ahead, there would be at least five more hours of this pissy press hand-holding before the traveling Office of the Press Secretary could declare a news lid for the evening and he could concentrate on Flaxen. Ah, Flaxen. Just the thought of her made him feel better, a beguiling image to help tune out this latest rash of unanswerable questions. He looked up at the sky. This was one of those times when he wondered if it all was worth it. Did being a part of history in the making really mean that much? Did it really matter? Who cares about all of this? And who really gives a rat's ass about what kind of hamburger the president ordered? His attitude had gone raw.

Then a soothing thought came over him. He, too, needed a burger.

And some fries. And a malt. And right now he'd even eat the plastic off the little ketchup packets. No doubt about it.

CHAPTER TWELVE

REPORTER: The president's wife takes tennis lessons and his
daughter takes piano lessons. What does he take?

SPOKESMAN: Vitamins.

At 11:15 p.m. Sox walked through the hotel's nearly empty Gulf Coast Room which was serving as an on-the-road press filing center and approached the podium. He stopped there, tore off a strip of Scotch tape and stuck a handwritten note on the front side. It read:

> *As of 11:15 p.m. CST, we have a lid for the day until*
> *9:00 a.m. Saturday, November 1.*

As he walked away, tired cheers drifted across the room, limp utterings from the few reporters still there, workaholics with the wire services plus a scattering of bored network technicians idly milling around. One of those technicians, his feet propped up on a worktable, was lazily turning the pages of a book, *History of the San Antonio Light Company.*

"Viva the lid kid," a voice wearily approved.

"…about time…"

"Lid-a-rooski, gang," somebody yawned.

"We're off the resuscitator…"

"Let the games begin…sort of…"

Many in their ranks had already filed their stories, packed their work gear and headed for bed or the hotel bar. With the lid for the day finally posted, attendance at the latter location would now increase.

Pretty amazing, considering some of them had begun early in the day by downing bourbon shots while airborne and were now concluding the evening on land in a similar fashion with more world-class imbibing.

The fund-raising dinner had unfolded without incident, the motorcade to and from the convention center producing no further surprises from the president. There had been one brief ripple of concern for the staff during the dinner when the president's military aide reported there had been a bomb threat.

"Somebody called here and said a bomb was due to go off at 10:45," the aide said.

"So what's our plan?" Sox asked.

"No sweat," the aide shrugged, "we're due out of here at 10:30."

The appointed time of the threatened explosion came and went, and nothing happened. That was often the case with such scares. But one never knew.

Other than that, the event had been devoid of excitement—press-generated or otherwise. Now with the president safely tucked in for the evening, Sox could devote himself to the pleasures that would be afforded by Flaxen's presence.

Just as promised, she was waiting outside in the hallway. With the filing center now virtually absent human traffic or any other activity, he motioned with his head, inviting her into the room. Simultaneously, he started toward her, meeting her halfway and slipping his arms around her supple figure.

"I'll be finished in just a few minutes," he whispered. "Just a few loose ends to cap off, a couple of major issues we're dealing with." As soon as the words left his mouth, he regretted them. There he went again, playing the big shot instead of just being himself. But with such a luscious package as Flaxen, it was damn hard resisting the urge to close the deal, even if it meant embellishing his role a bit. Besides, what the hell did she know of any issues they might be jacking with at the moment?

Releasing his grip from around her waist, he watched as her eyes filled with amazement at the mass of equipment required to make the traveling press office function. She, too, was an observer to the reality that taking the White House out of town was no simple matter.

They moved into the temporary briefing area comprised of the makeshift rows of tables where the press worked. Then to another corner of the room, the Office of the Press Secretary's cramped working area where flimsy blue hotel curtains partitioned J.Y., Sox and their staff from the reporters. Or tried to. Strewn across their worktables were piles of speech transcripts, press releases, trip schedules, newspapers, White House signal phones, a basketball, some clothes and a serving plate of moldy ham sandwiches. Integrated into this were workstations with computer terminals. Another area with curtains on all sides served as J.Y.'s office, although he had been there only to pass through en route to the dinner and briefly upon return. Most of the staff had drifted off, leaving the scatter of debris that now surrounded Sox and Flaxen. The place was a mess. Like it had been hit by whiplash from the tail of a comet.

"It's like a circus coming to town," Flaxen marveled.

"It *is* a circus," Sox laughed.

She turned slowly in a full circle, surveying the clutter, her eyes settling on a pile of steel trunks stacked over five feet high.

"What's all that?"

"That's how they transport us," he said. "The copying machines—all the heavy equipment."

"But don't you sometimes have to travel to two or three cities in a day?"

"How about countries?" he boasted matter-of-factly. "The travel office guys that move us, they're great. They can move anything, anywhere. We've had offices set up in the middle of cornfields."

"Cornfields?"

"Sure, we've operated from the grounds of the Statue of Liberty, in high school gymnasiums. Once we even set up in a boys' locker room."

"Why not in the girls' locker room?"

"It was a space issue. More room in the boys'—fewer stalls."

"Oh."

"Yeah, who would ever guess that statements by a president of the United States were issued from a locker room?"

"What did the statements smell like?" she asked, lightly rubbing her nose at the thought.

He rolled his eyes, avoiding a response, and instead settled into a visually analytical tour of her figure. He had gotten as far as her hips when unexpectedly Soldier burst into their presence, foraging the area in a late night sweep for edibles or anything else of import that might have been left unattended.

"Say, Sox, some people think the president might have dozed off for a few minutes during the dinner. Can you confirm that?"

"No, I can't," Sox answered abruptly. He looked at Flaxen, his eyes apologizing for the interruption. She in turn formed "Who's this?" on her lips.

"You mean you can't deny that he might have fallen asleep?" Soldier insisted.

"That isn't what I said," Sox answered in a bored monotone.

"Well, what are you saying?"

"I'm saying—are you actually writing this for a story or are you asking just to be asking?"

"Does it make a difference? I mean, in either case, should the president be falling asleep at a dinner in his honor?"

"No one ever said he fell asleep."

"Well, are you denying he didn't?" Soldier asked, offering a pixie-like grin in Flaxen's direction.

"Never mind her, Soldier," Sox snapped, his impatience on the rise. "No, the president did not fall asleep at the dinner. Anything else?"

Soldier continued to leer at Flaxen. "And how do you know that? Were you watching him every minute of the night?"

"No, and neither were you. I'm not playing this game any further with you."

"This isn't a game. This is a serious question."

Flaxen's tongue impishly protruded from her cheek as she leaned close, lightly brushing Sox's ear and whispering: "I guess maybe you are too busy for me. These do seem to be major issues you're dealing with."

He didn't need Soldier's babble. Not now. He needed Flaxen. The warmth of her body. The silkiness in her voice. The whisper. The touch. Her smell. Her her. He eased an arm around Soldier's shoulder and walked him away a few steps.

"Tell you what, if you'll meet me in the bar in fifteen minutes, I'll give you a readout on everything. Okay?"

Soldier measured him cautiously, then glanced back at Flaxen.

"She's an old family friend," Sox said, giving him a reassuring pat on the shoulder.

"Nice friend," Soldier said, his eyes twinkling as they remained fixed on her. "If I meet you in the bar, you'll buy?"

"Done deal," Sox winked.

"And you'll bring her?"

Sox bit into his lip to assure remaining calm. "She doesn't have any guidances on any issues you'd be interested in, so maybe I'll just come by myself. Okay?"

Soldier answered with a frown of disappointment as he started to pad toward the hallway. "One other thing!" he shouted, pausing at the door. "Can you also confirm that after the president arrived back at the hotel tonight, he had a massage?"

Sox's eyes narrowed harshly, their intensity directing Soldier out the door.

That irritant dismissed, he returned to Flaxen, continuing to visually drink her in.

"My anticipation meter has been running on high all day."

"And?"

"And…you wanna go to a party?"

She smiled agreeably. "Well, I didn't come here to spend the night knitting."

He liked the suggestive ring of that phrase—"spend the night." "If you're up for a one-way trip down exhaustion street, then let's rip."

Thirty minutes later they were poolside at a trendy apartment complex, swaying to rhythms bubbling from the center of a frenzied party scene. It had already reached the point where fully clothed bodies were frolicking in the pool—coats, ties, suits, dresses—all soaked and no one seeming to give a damn. Males were immersed in the water, hoisting females on their shoulders for hand-to-hand jousting matches.

"What's the occasion for all this?" Flaxen asked, her voice competing with the clamor.

"J.Y. knows someone who knows someone who's celebrating something."

The dawning apprehension in her face suggested his vagueness would not go unchallenged.

"Is J.Y. here?" she pressed.

Surveying the patio area, his attention ultimately was diverted back to the pool where the ferocity of squeals had increased along with the thrashing of bodies.

"If he's here, he's probably gonna need a new suit," he observed, pulling her back from errant sprays of water.

"Are any of the reporters here?"

He looked around nervously. He couldn't imagine any of them being there, but her question warranted that he'd better make certain. A cursory visual check indicated none were around. Good. No sign of J.Y. either. Bad. Continuing to scan the crowd, he realized that actually he hardly knew anyone there.

"If any members of the press are here, we're all gonna need to find new jobs," he said, watching as one of the more active females in the pool pulled a scarf from her soaked hair, wadded it into a ball and tossed it at his feet.

Blasts of thumping rock music boomed over the area, punctuated by erratic screams from the activity in the pool. Some of the delirium was in response to a new wave of bodies swelling the pool's population. While taking note of that development, the greater part of Sox's attention was now directed to the second floor. Lights had clicked on in all the apartment units above where curious eyes peeked between finger-separated slits in otherwise closed blinds. Other tenants stood on balconies, some in bathrobes and pajamas, watching dispassionately.

"Do you know any of these people?" Flaxen asked insistently.

His eyes searched the balcony level on the chance that J.Y. might have joined the ranks of the non-participating onlookers.

"Doesn't look like this event is peopled by a lot of our gang, does it?" he laughed weakly.

"So do you know any of these people?"

Another female tossed another wet and wadded scarf, this time upward at the unappreciative audience glaring down from above. An eruption of screams arose from another fully clothed couple careening wildly down the slide into the pool. The man bobbed to the surface, spewing water from between his teeth, a human geyser flashing a gap-toothed smile.

Flaxen pawed the ground uneasily.

"Yeah, okay," Sox agreed, "it does look like these folks are shooting to kill, not wound. The children here are really starting to act up, so maybe we should just ease outta here, back to the hotel…and…"

"…and…?"

Out on the diving board two more fully clothed men sprang off, fanning out in opposite directions cannonball-style, their impact sending gushers of pool water to near second-story level. On the far side two women were being swung back and forth by hands and legs, then tossed high so that both smacked the water hard, pancake-style. More bodies continued to recklessly grapple down the slide as dogfights in the pool intensified.

Sox and Flaxen started to leave but were distracted by a muffled female voice crying out for attention. Looking around, they were confronted by a row of clothes dryers. One of the dryers was spinning in slow motion like it was on reduced power. Occupying the entire porthole space of its tiny Plexiglas window was the smiling face of a girl who seemed giddily happy with the confines of her temporarily rotating home. She continued to spin, her eyes dancing merrily as she peered out, her head making a continual 360-degree rotation.

"Heavy on the starch in the eyeballs," said Flaxen dryly.

"Obviously she's feeling no pain. Looks like she might have downed a few pints of lighter fluid."

"Or antifreeze."

They began to laugh, a short-lived moment of craziness interrupted by the hiccuping yodel of a fast-approaching police siren. Sox looked up at the grim-faced tenants on the balcony, none of whom seemed to be sharing in the rampant giddiness below. His gaze shifted back to the girl in the dryer, still spinning. The siren's blare was growing closer.

"I don't think this is our kind of news event," he said nervously. He grabbed Flaxen's hand and led her through a darkened area away from the pool in a direction opposite to the staccato beat of the siren which was now loud enough to signal it had reached the complex. This was further confirmed by the squad car's flashing red light, its rotating beam now methodically splashing across the complex's front wall every few seconds.

Beating it back to the hotel, Sox mentally patted himself on the shoulder for having earned new spurs in spin control artistry—namely, having had the sense to haul their asses out of there.

His new concern was his next move, geographically speaking. The choices were:

a) Invite her to his room

b) Invite himself to her room

c) Suggest they have a nightcap in the dimly lit hotel bar

d) Shake hands and say goodnight in the lobby

e) Grab her

f) None of the above.

Obviously "c" was the safe choice, particularly since his strategy was to avoid the full-court press. Better to ease into it.

An hour later, after drinks laced with vintage product from Scotland, Flaxen had mellowed. Enough so that Sox's suggestion to visit his room had been greeted with a surprisingly acquiescent "Okay."

Once inside, the strategic maneuvering had begun, but in measured steps. There were certain women for whom one was willing to wait. And wait. For Flaxen Day, one was not only willing to wait, but wait longer. And then wait some more.

Battlefield geography in mind, he watched with a sense of silent victory as she dropped onto the king-size bed, sinking herself into its downy pillows.

"You've got two telephones," she noticed, pointing to the nearby table. "Expecting a lot of calls?"

"I hope not. Not at this hour."

"So why two phones?"

"One of them is a White House signal phone, strictly for use by the staff while on trips. It links all the traveling staff together and directly back to the White House. That way, we can still reach each other in case our hotel phone is tied up with calls from reporters or other outsiders."

The words had barely left his mouth when a sharp ring rattled the signal phone.

"Hold on," he nodded, promptly grabbing the receiver. She sat up on the bed, angling herself to hear better.

"Yeah…yeah…no…right, no…not on the record…but just put this response on background…the president wants to review the bill carefully before taking any action…yeah, that's right, attribute that to a White House official…no…no, we won't have any further comment beyond that…and say, just out of curiosity, how did you get this number…the signal line? And also, why is it necessary at this hour to know the president's position on the clean water bill?…uh, huh…yeah, I know you work for a wire service and the news never stops, but how about not calling me anymore tonight unless you hear that American ground forces are attacking at brigade strength…anywhere!" He slammed the phone down.

Flaxen slumped back into the pillows. "Problem?"

"Not anymore. Someone gave one of the wire service reporters the signal phone number. We won't hear that phone ring anymore tonight unless the president calls."

"Will he?" she asked, coyly.

"If he does, I can assure you it won't be about the clean water bill."

"Maybe he'll just be checking up on his press spokesman," she said, uncoiling and languidly stretching her legs.

As he eased close to the bed, she responded with a playful shrug he found difficult to interpret as either a rejection or an invitation. He was poised to slide down next to her when another ring interrupted, this time being the hotel phone which meant it was probably a reporter. Agitated, he yanked up the receiver.

"Yeah?…well, why don't you read your trip schedule? Baggage call is from 8:00 to 9:00 a.m. in the Filing Center. Got it? Adios!"

"Stop the hemorrhaging and give the man a break," Flaxen laughed, shifting slightly on the bed as he sat down next to her.

He shook his head in frustration. He was tired of the calls, the questions interruptus. And he sensed that she was, too. He was ready to enjoy her, to lose himself in her, to put the world of White House reporters on hold for a few hours. Finally, he had gotten her into bed. Never mind that they were both still fully clothed. She laughed again, her soft lips peeling apart with a come-hither allure that had him flushed with an ache to consume her. In a moment their lips would be joined. But not just yet. That moment was again delayed by a telephone, this time the ring of the signal phone again. He slowly turned his head toward the instrument, shaking with exasperation, then settling back on her. The glow of eagerness that had only moments before filled her face had now given way to a blank stare.

"You have to answer that, don't you?"

"Maybe it's the wrong number."

"But it's the White House line."

"Yeah, unfortunately, it is," he shrugged.

As he reached for the signal line, the hotel phone began ringing, too. Flustered, he grabbed both in unison, shouting first into one, then the other: "Hold on!"

He pulled the signal line to his ear first.

"Yes?…okay, I'll hold…"

He dropped the signal line and pulled the hotel phone to his other ear.

"Yeah!…" His face hardened as he listened to the voice on the other end.

"No, dammit, I don't know if pink peonies are the kind of flowers that bloom in the spring on the South Lawn!" Pounding the receiver down, he quickly switched gears, smiling anxiously at Flaxen who was now sitting on the edge of the bed making minor repairs to her slightly rumpled skirt. He continued to hold onto the signal line.

"Yes," he huffed, "I'm still here."

Thirty seconds passed while he remained glued on her as she continued arranging her clothes.

"Yes," he said into the phone, "uh, huh…no, I'm not…well…no, I haven't gotten any calls tonight on that…there was some nosing around earlier on the press plane but nothing tonight…uh, well, the other calls haven't really been too significant…the clean water bill…the travel schedule…and—"

"—the pink peonies," Flaxen curtly injected.

He held a finger to his lips.

"No, no," he repeated into the phone, "it's nobody—just hotel room service."

She glowered at him, signaling a mild contempt for this ruse.

"Yes," he continued, "I'll be up in five minutes. What's your room number?"

He scribbled across a notepad, pausing to listen once more, then said, "Okay" before dropping the signal phone back in its receiver.

"I've got to get up to Quad Sands' room."

What he couldn't explain to her was that Quad had been out having drinks with some reporters who had pressed him about rumors regarding the terrorism summit. Quad wanted to go over the press guidance with J.Y and Sox, just to make sure they would all be responding with the same line. They'd need it tomorrow on the flight back, both for the Air Force One press pool and for reporters on the press charter.

"What's the matter, the pink peonies having trouble blooming?" Flaxen asked sarcastically.

"Look, I'm sorry. This just happens. It's the nature of the work. It's like being a doctor, you're on call 24 hours a day. Just hang loose, and I'll be back shortly—probably less than 30 minutes."

"Probably?"

"As soon as possible."

"That's press secretary babble. Why don't you just say it might be longer."

"Okay, it might be longer, but get comfortable. I'll be back soon."

The signal phone began ringing again. In another instant it was again joined by the hotel phone. It was apparent that the night was going to be one of continuous interruption.

She abruptly stood up and began heading toward the door.

"Where are you going?"

"To escort myself to my room," she said stiffly.

"C'mon, chill out," he implored, a scolded puppy pulling at her sleeve.

"No, it's clear this isn't going to get any better. There won't be any whoopee here tonight. You're already in love—with that." She nodded at the phones. "You whine, but you love it. You love this. You love this—this, this. This nonstop mill drill. Anyone else around is just on deck in case there's a spare minute. That's how it is. There's no denying it. But that's not me. I'm not vying for Miss Instant Availability of the week. I'm checking out of Hotel Hectic. And that, my friend, is on-the-record."

She flung the door open and disappeared into the hallway. He started to chase after her, but held up. It was hopeless and he was helpless. He was too tired to argue. He was just too tired. What could he say? Besides, the sad part of it was, she wasn't all wrong.

CHAPTER THIRTEEN

REPORTER: Are members of this administration deaf when it
comes to questions about the budget?

SPOKESMAN: I'm sorry, I didn't hear the question.

Sox sat at his manual typewriter composing a memorandum. It was
the only manual typewriter to be found in the compound, a companion
to his computer. He had rescued it from a dust-choked room in the
bowels of the Executive Office Building, a machine that had been
consigned to relic status in the wake of the computer blitzkrieg.

"I think better on a typewriter," he once explained to a curious reporter.
"You can think on that?" the reporter had chided him.

As far as he was concerned, computers were not made to be easy.
Typewriters, on the other hand, were pure vanilla. This one was his best
friend. And in this White House any friend—animal, mineral, vegetable
or human—was to be nurtured.

Like most White House memoranda, the one he was typing would
probably wind its way through the system with ultimately little notice
taken. It would dribble off into forgotten history, the place where many
such documents went to die.

As his fingers pecked across the keys, his eyes danced intently over the
pages, taking full measure of their content. It was a memorandum for a
press strategy for launching the terrorism summit. He wasn't trying to
reinvent the wheel, he was just trying to get credit for an idea. More like
retooling the wheel.

When he finished, he pulled the paper from the machine, staring in wonder at the document he had created. At once he was proud, yet somewhat amazed by his authorship. Slowly, he read it over.

THE WHITE HOUSE
WASHINGTON

MEMORANDUM

FOR: J.Y. KATY

FROM: SOX ST. LOUIS

SUBJECT: VICTORY OVER TERRORISM

With what will surely be success for the president in his upcoming meeting on terrorism with President Navikoff, we should move promptly to create an appropriate event following the announcement and preceding their meeting that sets a positive tone and keeps the president's efforts indelible in the minds of the American people and the international community. Thus, this suggestion.

With the president issuing the invitation, why not convene an anti-terrorism, anti-hijack event in the East Room to show support for the president's vision in taking this initiative.

The invitees could include American hostages who have previously been captured and released by terrorists, and members of their families.

In effect, this could provide an opportunity for a united show of support against terrorism, all in a White House setting, by those who know the story best, those who have lived it. Above all, it would provide a visual scene of dramatic impact.

The program could include:

• Some of the attendees telling their dramatic stories
• Remarks by the president
• Prayer
• A reception
• A press availability

If this is to be done, we should move promptly to schedule it following the announcement of the terrorism summit.

An hour later, he was on the second floor of the West Wing, hand-
carrying copies of the memo to other key officials—the White House
counsel, the assistant to the president for political affairs and anyone else
he thought might be willing to buy into his suggestion. It was the school
of overkill. Hand out a lot of paper on the theory that sheer volume was
bound to generate a few takers. He had already covered his bases with J.Y.
as well as the key foreign and domestic policy advisors. Also, in personally
walking it around, he was able to make sure it reached the intended desti-
nations without getting cut off at any earlier points.

He moved past the tiny interior office he had once occupied up there,
dodging a ladder in the hallway placed there by two maintenance workers who were painting, scrubbing and making minor cosmetic repairs. He
couldn't help overhearing their conversation and being troubled by its
dark edge.

"You a German?" one of the workers asked his companion.

"Well," the other retorted gruffly, "my name's Mueller."

"Yeah, you're a kraut."

All of a sudden, Mueller, a massive human brickbat, hulking and
yam-armed, stood up from where they had been painting the baseboards.
He leaned over his accuser, forcibly punching him in the chest with
a forefinger.

"Damn right, asshole, I'm a kraut. So what? I'm damn proud of it. It
took the whole world to lick us twice. Now cork your mouth before I kick
your ass."

Sox moved past them and down the narrow stairway. Returning to
his office, he found that conversation turning over in his mind, worrisome that he should have heard such an exchange in the White House of
all places, a temple dedicated to the pursuit of peace. A workingman's

ethnic hurt, embedded in him by history, had surfaced here in this citadel where blueprints for those two lickings had been drawn up. Sox wondered if Mueller had thought of that bit of irony.

"The old man wants to meet with us right now to strategize about press spin for the Navikoff meeting," J.Y. said, interrupting Sox's thoughts.

Okay, Plan B. If no one else had liked the ideas in his memo, here was a chance to cut out all the small-fry middlemen and bring them up directly with the president. Minutes later, the elevator opened and dispensed them at the living quarters. It was only the second time Sox had been upstairs in the residence area. Once before, he had made it as far as the hallway. That had been in the role of playing kiss-ass to Mrs. Crayon by offering to carry her luggage.

"For some reason, the president wants to meet in the Lincoln Bedroom," J.Y. shrugged.

As they entered the room the president and Quad were talking quietly in front of the fireplace, the president shooting a quick glance at them in the course of finishing his conversation. J.Y. and Sox waited, taking in the historic trappings of the room until the president turned fully in their direction as he began to make his motive clear.

"I thought it might be helpful to have our conversation here, particularly since we're planning an event which will hopefully have an impact on future generations. The fellow who slept in this room would understand that."

As the president continued to speak, Sox visually toured the surroundings. Over near the windows that looked out on the South Lawn was a small desk. He edged a few steps closer to where he could see there were three pages of framed script. It was the Gettysburg Address, signed by Abraham Lincoln and dated November 19, 1863. He read the inscription: *The Gettysburg Address. President Abraham Lincoln delivered this address on November 19, 1863, at the dedication of the Gettysburg National Cemetery. In March, 1864, he prepared this fifth and final copy, the only one to be titled, signed and dated, for reproduction for a war charity.*

Quad's blunt tone snapped his attention back to the business at hand.

"J.Y. and Sox, the president wants your recommendations on how to announce the terrorism summit. We don't want this meeting to be played by the media as just Russian-U.S. busywork. We want to showcase this one— with banner headlines."

"Has to be prime time, East Room news conference—the full package," J.Y. responded without hesitation.

The president remained silent, his blank expression giving no hint of approval or dislike for that suggestion. Except for the pop of sparks from the fireplace, the room was quiet. The president gazed out the windows, seeming to ponder J.Y.'s words. Slowly he turned back toward the fireplace and focused on the plaque there. He leaned closer, his eyes tracing over the lines as his lips moved silently. Then he began to read out loud: "In this room Abraham Lincoln signed the Emancipation Proclamation of January 1, 1863, whereby four million slaves were given their freedom and slavery forever prohibited in these United States."

As the president read, Sox's attention again drifted, this time to a sculpture of Lincoln positioned in front of the fireplace. It depicted him seated with his arms crossed. What would Lincoln have thought of this discussion, Sox wondered.

The urgency in the president's voice suddenly jolted him from his Lincolnesque daydream. "What do you think, Sox? You agree with J.Y.?"

"Uh, yes, sir," he stammered. "I think if you're going for the maximum ride on this one, then prime time in the East Room is the way to knock a home run."

"Rather than just dropping by the briefing room and doing it there?"

"Mr. President, that's sort of like asking would you rather take a step into history or a step into hell?"

"I guess you're right," the president agreed. "More drama to the East Room. Prime time. Big audience. More impact. But, dammit, they'll get off the terrorism summit quick and onto other issues. That's the downside."

"Yes, sir, but watch out coming off the podium after you've finished. Don't relax. They love to swarm around you and ask follow-up questions."

The president nodded, then looked out to the South Lawn and beyond, his face growing pensive in the way of a man who has just become privy to a vision. Once again everyone fell silent, waiting for a cue, some indication that it was okay to speak, to utter a word other than "yes" or, even more boldly, to offer an opinion that might be at odds with the leader of the Free World. It was quiet enough, Sox thought, to hear a pen drop. Or even a pin. The president moved slightly, his eyes shifting to seek out the Washington Monument, its jutting image an eternal and comforting presence on the skyline.

"So, for the news conference, what sort of questions do you think I'll get?" he asked, still looking away.

J.Y. edged slightly forward. "Mr. President, maybe we should consider a prep session in the theatre to review possible questions and answers."

On rare occasions they had conducted press conference practice sessions in the theatre, none of which the president had been enthusiastic about but had agreed to do at the staff's urging. During the last of these sessions, his disdain for such rehearsal had been reflected through a series of sarcasm-drenched answers. One of the exchanges had gone thusly:

"Mr. President, you have indicated an interest in your next Supreme Court nominee being another female. What qualifications are you looking for?"

"A babe who has enough curves under one of those damn robes to stop traffic on Constitution Avenue."

After that session no one had had the guts to suggest they do it again until this moment.

"Quad, do you really think we need that?" the president challenged.

Quad moved next to J.Y. "Well, do you feel completely up to speed on this one, Mr. President?"

"Up the flagpole—the damn meeting is my idea! If I can't defend it without you geniuses trying to help me explain it, then we shouldn't be doing it. If you guys need to sit around and think up answers to feed me, then I'm in the wrong job in the wrong house. Might as well be a damn ventriloquist. I mean, why am I president?"

"Frankly, Mr. President, I'm not worried about your handling the press on this," Quad said. "It's coordinating timing of the announcement with the Russians that's my greater worry."

"And avoiding leaks," Sox added.

"This place sucks when it comes to leaks," the president snapped, eyeing Sox out of the corner of his eye. "This is Niagara Falls."

"Just what we want to avoid in this case," Quad said.

"It rains more indoors in this damn place than anywhere else in America!" the president growled.

As Crayon's rage over leaks continued, Sox's eyes wandered to the bed with its large headboard. On the wall above it was a painting with the inscription: *Mary Todd Lincoln. Wife of President Abraham Lincoln…* As he looked at her he wondered what she might think of how they were going to announce the terrorism summit. Any thoughts, Mary?

"So what kinds of questions will I get?" the president asked, continuing to press.

"I think there will be a great deal of interest in the discussions you and Navikoff have had leading up to this," J.Y. said.

"The who-called-who-first kind of thing," Quad added.

"But the way this press corps would put it," Sox added, "is do the president and Navikoff go both ways?" As soon as the words left his mouth, he knew he had phrased it wrong, a belief affirmed by glares trained on him.

Still, the president had other targets for his wrath. "To hell with the press corps," he snapped.

Everyone pondered that thought, as a low growling began to erupt from the pit of Sox's stomach. He hadn't eaten since last night. Arriving home late, and his stove in need of repair, he had had to resort to using a hair dryer to warm up a two-day-old pizza. The result had been a soggy goo that did little to salve his hunger. Hoping others in the room wouldn't notice his gut's restive gurgling, he half-turned, pointing himself toward another painting in the room. Its inscription read: *President Abraham Lincoln and his Cabinet, Unknown Artist…*

"Mr. President, would you like me to go ahead and begin coordinating this with the Russians—the timing of the announcement?" Quad asked.

"Yes, do it," the president replied. "And be sure to ask them if they're prepared for good news," he added, the corners of his mouth curving slightly upward in a faint smile.

"We'll start work on an opening statement for the news conference," Quad said.

"Tell those speechwriters not to overwrite," the president emphasized. "I'll probably do a good chunk of it myself. I want Carl Crayon's footprints all over this one, not some damn ghostwriter's."

"What dates are we aiming for?" J.Y. asked.

"Let me talk to the Russians," Quad said. "Stroke 'em. It's our show—the president's announcement. I'll get back to you on timing."

"Do you anticipate there will be a communiqué at the end of the meetings?" J.Y. asked, continuing to rattle off questions he knew would be raised later by the press.

"We'll just play that one from the heels," the president said. "What we don't want is this to be just another meeting remembered because at the end we issued another soon-to-be-forgotten 50-page document held together by three big staples."

Everyone nodded compliantly.

"But, hell, who's for terrorism?" the president added. "We can't lose on this one, and neither can they. We're partners in peace."

He paused, seeming to enjoy a moment of self-indulgence over what he had just uttered.

"Partners in peace…that's not a bad theme line. What the hell do I need you press flacks for? Now I'm doing your job."

Great, Sox thought, now we have Carl Crayon, statesman turned pr spinmeister. And still no mention of Sox's memo by anyone. Evidently it was an idea that had died for lack of a second. But what the hell, might as well trot it out here and at least know for sure that it had its moment of consideration with the president.

"Has…uh…any thought been given…uh…to the idea of… maybe…doing an event prior to the summit? Something to kind of tee it up and get good press, too. The mo and mo factor."

"Mo and mo factor?" the president asked, looking confused.

Quad smiled. "Yeah, mo and mo? What do the Three Stooges have to do with this?"

"Uh, I'm talking about momentum and more press coverage," Sox explained.

J.Y. put his hand on Sox's shoulder. "Mr. President, Sox wrote up a memo proposing—-"

"I saw it," Quad interrupted. "It made some interesting points but—"

"Did I see it?" the president asked, mildly intrigued.

"No, sir," Quad said. "It had some ideas for a pre-summit event with released hostages."

The president coughed and cleared his throat. "We don't want to compete with our own event, do we?"

Everyone in the room looked down at their shoes, shuffling back and forth. Sox figured with that kind of gushing indifference he had nothing to lose in pressing forward.

"Mr. President, I was just looking for ways to make sure you were positioned at the front of the war on terrorism."

The president paused, thoughtfully scanning the semicircle of faces.

"I'm going to have Navikoff here in my lap for two days. Maybe we do need to look at creating some ways to keep the news fresh. Pretty soon the fact that we're just meeting, nodding and yessing gets to be refried beans. After the first fifteen minutes when we've agreed we're against terrorists—then what? Start telling lame jokes? Why don't we add a few wrinkles—bring in some of the released hostages, let them tell their stories."

Sox couldn't believe it—-buy-in on his idea. And by the president. His elation, though, was tempered by the reminder that this was the White House—the place where any idea endorsed by the president soon had 100 authors. Sort of like the time Sox received a memo from a senior staff member outlining ideas that sounded more than vaguely familiar. It was plagiarism cum laude. Sox had, in fact, made the very same recommendations in a memo six months earlier. The author of the new memo hadn't even bothered to change most of the language, even the incorrect grammar and misspellings. It began: "The president likes the suggestions I have made in this memo and is anxious for you to implement them." Sox sent it back to the pirate with a copy of his earlier memo, adding this notation: "Your ideas are great. Glad the president likes them. So do I. Wish I had thought of them. In fact, I did."

"We'll work on some ideas for sprucing up the summit, Mr. President," Quad said, trying to steer things to closure. "A prep session in the theatre—yes or no?"

"Do you honestly think there's any question about this that I can't answer, or at least tap-dance on?" The president's eyebrows rose slightly.

"Be careful with any stray subject questions, Mr. President—issues not related to the summit," J.Y. said.

"Like, how's Navikoff gonna get here if the flight attendants fulfill their threat to go on strike?" Sox kidded.

Everyone in the room stared at him for a long moment. It was like they had heard him say it but didn't want to believe he had said it. The president was still shaking his head as he headed for the door, only to pause there and turn back.

"Sox, how do you think Abraham Lincoln might have handled such a situation?"

Sox looked incredulously at the president, then at his colleagues' expectant faces.

Feebly, he repeated the question. "What do I think President Lincoln would have thought about the possibility of flight attendants going on strike?"

"That's right," the president replied, waiting patiently.

Sox shifted uneasily, lowered his head, took a deep breath, then peered out from under wary eyelids.

"Well, I guess he might have told his staff: 'Let's be sure Mr. Navikoff checks the bus schedules out of Moscow. And that he can swim.'"

CHAPTER FOURTEEN

REPORTER: Does the Congress know what you're doing about
               new taxes?

SPOKESMAN: No, because we're not sure what we're going to be
             doing about new taxes.

Sox was happy. Things were going his way. The planning team for the terrorism summit had decided to use some of the ideas he had suggested in his memo. Maybe not in the exact form he had proposed them, but close enough.

Some of the released hostages would be invited to meet with the president and Navikoff, tell their stories and make suggestions for combating future acts of terrorism. There would also be a reception. Most importantly, positive press coverage would surely flow. Who says a memo couldn't snake its way through the layers of White House bureaucracy and survive? Of course, it helped that he had had the opportunity to take his case directly to the president, otherwise that piece of paper and the ideas it proposed would now be ancient history. Fodder for the White House recycling bin.

But life was good. He was on a roll. With the president. With the press. Everybody but Flaxen. Oh, sure, he had called her a couple of times and begged for another chance. A lot of good it had done. She had responded to all of it by cutting him off at the knees.

"Glad you could wedge in a few seconds for me between crisis calls on the signal phone. You'd better hang up before the pope calls." Click!

He'd try and think up some kind of strategic game plan while at Camp David this weekend. Since he had nothing going in town, he had decided to take the weekend duty normally assigned to a member of the lower press office and accompany the Crayons there.

Camp David. That grand retreat in the Catoctin Mountains of Maryland. That pastoral vista once known as "Shangri-La," a mystic appellation given to it by President Franklin D. Roosevelt.

He was headed there with the Crayons to relax for the weekend. To sleep. To play tennis on the precisely brushed court. Perhaps to watch a few movies with the First Couple in their cabin—Aspen. To catch lots of snooze-time in the cottage assigned to the press aide—Sycamore. And to avoid the press, who were rarely permitted inside the grounds. Even solo, it wasn't bad duty. If he had stayed in town, he'd have ended up in the office, hassling with correspondents assigned the weekend duty and then probably hanging out in some bar near Wisconsin and M Streets, loading up on various forms of alcoholic-laden grog and inwardly kicking himself for the screwup with Flaxen. So Camp David was the answer. Better to be miserable in that rustic nirvana than staring at the four walls in his cramped apartment. If misery does indeed love company, then being miserable at Camp David was the best of all deals he could possibly cut for himself this weekend.

Otherwise, he was happy. The president had sailed through the news conference in the East Room, announcing the terrorism summit and inviting released hostages to attend the event. For the most part, the news conference had been a tour de force for the president—tough questions met by hard-edged answers. Slam dunks. Including his responses to the irksome follow-up questions. Those nagging follow-ups, the game of nitpicking which Sparta loved to pursue.

"Mr. President, did the Russians seek any preconditions in agreeing to this meeting?…Oh, and I also have a follow-up on the rise in unemployment."

How Sox disdained those follow-ups. Such crap. So transparent in their attempt to throw the president off a peg. Often there was no attempt to marry two subjects. To the contrary, it was a game of disconnect. The more unrelated the topics, the better. Alpha and omega.

"Hey, Mr. President, are you committed to an increase in the Defense budget?…And by the way, what's your position on tractor pulls in domed stadiums?"

Even without a prep session in the theatre (this time it had been in the Oval Office and much briefer), the president had handled Sparta's questions and follow-ups, and everyone else's, without breaking a sweat, a performance that was both a surprise and disappointment to the press. No drama. No misstatements. No verbal stumbles. No negative head-lines—*President Misspeaks*. Just solid answers.

Sox took pleasure in remembering that it was Sparta who had come to him before the news conference and confidently purred: "That press conference platform better be sturdy. I've got the home-run-ball question that's gonna rock him back on the heels of his feet."

Such bravado hadn't bothered Sox. Such boastful predictions were the norm. Lots of posturing. Lots of pre-game trash talk. The result was always the same. A president sometimes nicked, but relatively unscathed. Sox had yet to see the president go limp on the podium under such fire.

The high point for Sox had come midway in the news conference when the president surveyed the throng of reporters on their feet, shout-ing and jousting for attention (the camera's and the president's). He stood idly calm for ten seconds or so and let the cameras roll as America witnessed the White House press corps bellowing their way into a lath-ered state of prime-time chaos. Figuring that the good citizens of the North American continent might not take kindly to such churlish behav-ior from media stars, the president had let it play out before finally extending his arms to implore restoration of order, then pointing at Tommy Tuff.

"Mr. Tuff, I'll have to take you because your shouting is setting off smoke detectors in the West Wing."

The random snickers from colleagues didn't faze Tuff, who remained standing and intently glared at the president.

"Mr. President," he challenged, "what is the first thing you will tell Mr. Navikoff after the two of you sit down?"

"Why, I'll tell him, 'Sergei, I'm sure pleased I pronounced your entire name correctly. Sergei Navikoff—that's longer than the name of the first automobile I owned.'"

That was a Sox kind of response. Answer 'em, yes, but bust 'em in the chops, too. Put the ball back in their end zone.

Afterward, it had rained hard into the night, a hindrance which had not deterred the network correspondents from their on-air work outside. Preparing to tape a segment, Sparta had glanced back at Sox's office where she could see him with his feet propped on the windowsill, smugly watching her watch him. She was rain-soaked and chilled. He was warm and dry.

Later she had passed by his office, shivering and toweling messily matted hair, her dress tightly drenched against her body.

"This sucks," she snarled. "You come out here and do this. See if you like it."

He felt like saying, "Screw you! How about taking on my job—surrounded waist-deep in whining every day!" But he held his tongue. She, however, wasn't finished.

"Another thing is, there aren't enough damn bathrooms in this building."

That was too much. He jerked his feet down, leaning forcefully across the desk, a slow burn edging across his face.

"This isn't Yankee Stadium!"

It was an answer he felt had earned him a small victory, a badge to be valued in jousting with Sparta.

But that was yesterday. Today he felt good. Even better. The terrorism summit was launched. The news conference had been a banner evening for the president. And now he was off to Camp David with the Crayons. His spirits were in good enough shape that he decided to head for the South Lawn and Marine One via the empty briefing room. Passing by the bulletin board in the room's rear, several announcements posted there caught his eye.

Tommy Tuff, your doctor called and said your test for syphilis was positive.

AND: *Patrick Y, your banker called to say that your humility has been*

placed in a blind trust.
AND: *Q: Which color of crayon is named after the president?*
A: Bland.

Ah, that press corps. He would not miss being away from the pack for the next forty-eight hours.

CHAPTER FIFTEEN

REPORTER: What's the outlook for the trade bill?

SPOKESMAN: Clear and sunny.

The barbs posted on the bulletin board had served to jump-start Sox's spirits to a higher level.

Standing in the ground-floor diplomatic entrance while waiting for the Crayons, it felt good to laugh. Fun—even brief fun—was a diversion he had rarely known in recent days. And in recent nights. At least he could laugh at the press, if not with them. It was only temporary relief from the drearies, a Band-Aid, but a welcome intermission.

The problem was that his life had become Flaxen-impaired. Especially the nights. Maybe he'd call her tonight from Camp David. "Hello, Miss Day, this is the operator at Camp David. Could you please hold for Mr. St. Louis?" No. Better not. That was just the kind of big-shotting that had turned her off before. It would be quiet at Camp David. A good place for thinking. For coming up with a strategic game plan. For creating a way to steer her back into the fold. He'd figure out something while there. Maybe he would call her. Maybe tomorrow night. Maybe. He'd figure out something. A plan. Camp David was the place.

Many times he had stood on the South Lawn watching presidential departures, arrivals of heads of state and other ceremonial events. It was the arrival ceremonies he liked best. The ballyhoo. All the military branches there, starchly pressed in full-dress regalia. Sometimes in the midst of heavy summer heat, sun-baked soldiers in those ranks would wilt while standing riveted at attention, falling face-down, human dominos left on the ground untouched and unaided until the ceremony's end.

He ached for those who went down, but absent those unfortunate blips, he loved watching the ranks of gawking onlookers, many of them government employees brought in to provide instant crowds for these ceremonial displays of White House pomp. He similarly enjoyed watching the press scrambling across the lawn for any tidbit to color a story. Most of all, he savored that moment of grandest Washington fanfare— the playing of *Ruffles and Flourishes,* and its accompanying anthem, *Hail to the Chief.* No matter how many hundreds of times he had heard those pieces played to introduce the president, he still quivered in a red and white and blue sort of way. Corny? Sure. He never admitted it to anyone, but it was so. Today's routine departure would be absent any such ceremony. Still, those tunes played in his head as he waited. He was pumped. Just as he was anytime an event drew him to the South Lawn.

Hearing the approaching roar of Marine One's engines, he peered through the swinging door's glass panes, watching the big chopper ease down, its wheels settling precisely onto pods nestled in the lushly thick grass. The accuracy of the pilots in hitting those marks never ceased to amaze him. It seemed as if each landing was a facsimile of the last: perfection. Even the blades of grass being furiously blown in the propeller's backwash always seemed to bend in the same direction—northeast.

As the helicopter settled onto the ground, the churning whir of its propeller never slowed, its rhythmic grinding continuing unabated in methodical, circular sweeps. The fact that the pilot hadn't shut the engines down signaled that departure was imminent and the Crayons must be on their way.

He stepped outside and crossed over to the press pen where cameras and correspondents were squeezed together, so much that Secret Service agents were admonishing those at the front to step back and not push against the restraining rope. An oft-repeated ritual at such departures, the agents' instructions were greeted with the usual reluctance, particularly since every camera wanted to be positioned in front and no one was about to surrender prized turf.

The reporters yelled at Sox for sympathy, but he ignored the pleas, turning away to watch the Crayons as they emerged from the canopied entrance. Even as the door opened, and before they were visible, a panicked burst of cries from the press pen area greeted them.

"Mr. President, can you confirm…"

"…any reaction to the…"

"…increase in the unemployment rate?"

The Crayons ignored the shouts as they walked across the driveway hand-in-hand, like teenagers. Sox veered across and fell in line behind the phalanx of agents surrounding them. He was pleased by their silent response to the incessant press jabber. And why not? This was a game played at every such departure. The winner, if there was one, was the reporter who screamed loudest, causing the president to pause, take the bait and respond. Bingo—a sound bite! Double bingo—an off-the-cuff quip for which the network evening news shows drooled but drew winces from the White House senior staff. On such occasions the scapegoat was always the accompanying press office staffer. "Why did you let him do that?" Today, Sox was going to make sure he wouldn't have to answer that question after tonight's newscasts.

"Has Navikoff indicated…"

"…a decision yet…new Labor secretary?"

"…budget…"

"…anything…negotiations?"

It was a combination of hysteria and desperation in gridlock. As they droned on, Sox maneuvered into a more strategic position directly behind the First Couple. Now on the far side of the driveway, they were chatting with guests and staff gathered there to wave them off.

Seizing the moment, he leaned into the president's ear.

"Mr. President, there is absolutely no need for you to stop by the press area and respond to any questions or have any exchange with them whatsoever."

The president glanced back over his shoulder, then across to the shouting mob, his eyes merry with bemusement at the torment being experienced across the driveway.

"What the hell could they possibly be screaming about? I took 'em head-on last night at the news conference—every possible question."

"Exactly," Sox agreed. "All the more reason to go directly to the chopper."

The president cut a wary eye at Sox, his antenna up.

"What's the matter, Sox, afraid I might wander over there and make some news?"

Bull's-eye, Mr. President, thought Sox. Just get the man on the damn helicopter and out of here. No questions answered.

"Mr. President, you made plenty of news last night."

"So why are they yelling at me today?"

"Mr. President, they like to yell at you anytime they possibly can and about anything they possibly can—even a hangnail. They're always in agony."

"That's their problem. I'm not a doctor."

"Sir, you cleaned their clock last night. Today they're hurting for a new lead."

"New lead? New lead? How about if I drop my pants and those cameras pan the cheeks of my butt? How's that for a star-spangled sound bite?"

"Mr. President, that would most likely bring an orgasm to Sparta's eyeballs."

The president rolled his eyes in silent horror, his forehead wrinkling into furrows.

They proceeded out onto the lawn toward the shiny green-and-white chopper with the presidential seal emblazoned on its side just beneath the pilot's window. The flapping of its giant propeller and throbbing hum of its motors were smothering all sounds from the press area, save for erratic squeals from the most powerful of lungs.

"…anything…"

"…the meetings…"

"Has Navikoff…"

"…anything…"

The president returned the salute of the Marine who was standing brace-firm at the base of the helicopter's steps, then started up the four stairs to board, pausing to wave to members of the staff and guests who had gathered to watch the departure. It always amazed Sox that presidents stopped to do this. Why? Why wave to one's own staff? Why wave to people one sees every day? Generations of presidents had continued to uphold this tradition, cheerily waving to staff members as if they might never see them again. A strange custom, he thought. One of the very few performances by American presidents where a positive audience response is always guaranteed and never a single protestor in sight.

As they filed on board, fragments of desperate press voices managed to still filter through despite the noisy revving of the engines.

"Do you have any reaction to anything? I'll take anything…"

"See you next crisis…"

The doors slammed shut and the engines screeched into full throttle, thrusting the craft into a gradual liftoff.

The president strapped his seat belt tight. Quad followed and settled into his seat.

"Those damn reporters sure waste a lot of time wasting time," the president sighed.

Having offered that observation, he pressed his face lightly against the window, forcing a smile and half-wave as they continued rising up from the lawn, the south portico slowly passing from view underneath. Continuing to ascend, their flight pattern took them in an arc directly over the tennis court where a doubles match was in progress. Unsmiling, the president glared down at the four unsuspecting players as they volleyed the ball back and forth. Glancing at his watch, he forced his face harder against the glass, trying to penetrate the late afternoon haze for a better view.

"Get those names!" he cried.

Sox wasn't sure if he was serious or not. Quickly they passed over, too high to establish the identities of the players, all of whom fast became tiny blurred dots in the distance.

"Who in the blazes was that out there at four o'clock lollypopping tennis balls?"

"I…uh…didn't recognize them, Mr. President," Sox answered shakily. "Did you?" the president challenged Quad. The chief of staff shook his head.

"Well, whoever it is will never have to worry about winning the U.S. Open," the president groused, continuing to strain for a look back.

Sox felt like he had dodged a bullet. There were lots of afternoons when that could just as easily have been him on that court. In fact, he had been out there yesterday with J.Y. A couple of hackers, they both lacked coordination, ball sense, racquet control, any semblance of basic ground strokes or any ability to lend a sense of grace and effortless ability to the game. But so what? It was, after all, tennis on the White House court.

The chopper continued its slow turn away from the grounds, rolling upward toward a massive expanse of blue sky. Looming directly in their path was the Washington Monument, a lonely spire on an endlessly clear horizon. Looking down on the grandeur of the fast-disappearing South Lawn, Sox's thoughts suddenly turned to the loneliness and isolation felt by presidents.

He had ridden only once in the president's limousine, but had never forgotten what occurred. As they had prepared to arrive back at the White House, he had reached over to open the door, only to be abruptly halted by the president.

"Let me do that," the president insisted. "People are always opening doors for me. It's nice to do something for myself."

It was a fleeting occurrence, but one which had never left Sox's mind. The opening of a door. A car door. So simple. So ordinary. So everyday. So taken for granted. And yet, something so alien to the life of a president. The kind of thing never given a thought. Except by a president.

It also made Sox mindful of when the president had once asked a group of aides gathered in the Oval Office: "You know what I'd like to do right now that I'll never be able to do again the rest of my life?"

Puzzled, they had all shaken their heads with curiosity.

"I'll tell you what," the president said, noting their reluctance to respond. "I wish I could walk right out of this office, down Pennsylvania Avenue to the nearest drugstore, go in and read the magazines on the newsstand, including the tabloids. Can you imagine a president, or a former president, trying to do that? Impossible. It would be an instant war zone. But you guys can do it any day, any time, for the rest of your lives. So you want to be president? Think about what you'll be giving up. It's called freedom."

Watching the avenues and monuments disappear below as they flew into the Maryland countryside, Sox's thoughts dwelled on that moment. The president is a prisoner from the day he is elected to the day he dies. Sox could never be president. He liked reading the magazines on the magazine rack. And the tabloids.

Mostly in his thoughts today, though, was wonderment over his own good fortune. He was flying to Camp David. Sox St. Louis on Marine One! Who could have ever predicted it? Maybe somebody smoking curious-smelling cigarettes. It was one of the greatest long shots in American history. Sox St. Louis? A spokesman for the president of the United States? The same kid who in his youth rode the train to summer camp and managed to hold an entire Pullman car hostage with an arsenal of water pistols, one of which he proudly noted at the time had firepower capable of reaching targets over 25 feet away. The same kid who once tapped into his school's intercom system to announce: "Due to a bookkeeping error, all test scores for this semester have been declared null and void." The same kid who as an 11-year-old saved nickels for six months to respond to an enticing mail order advertisement guaranteed to reveal *The World's Best Falsies*, only to experience the disappointment of discovering he had purchased a set of false teeth.

"The first time I read this, it didn't make any sense," said the president, interrupting Sox's daydream. "The last time I read this, it still didn't make any sense."

Sox eased forward on the couch where he was sitting across the aisle from the Crayons.

"What didn't make sense, sir—both times?"

"This!" the president said, flipping a sheaf of papers his way. As they spilled wildly over the couch and floor, Sox could see *DRAFT* was stamped boldly in red ink on one of the pages. He quickly shuffled the sheets into a pile, placing them neatly back in their blue folder.

"It's the first crack at my remarks for the opening of the terrorism meeting," the president added. "Trouble is, this is just puff stuff—enough purple prose to send everyone in the room to Boredom U. No bite. No bugles. Refried rhetoric from the State Department."

"Well, it's a first draft," Sox said, feeling uneasy in defending a work he hadn't read.

"Yeah, and the next draft will be mine," the president said sharply, swiping the folder back. "It's one more thing I've added to my 'to do' list here for the weekend." He tossed the folder into his briefcase, turning away and abruptly picking up a newspaper, seemingly done with the matter.

Sox's eyes wandered to the window, an escape into the cloudless sky through which the chopper was passing, so smooth it seemed as if they were just idling in space, motionless.

Dr. Yell, the presidential physician, leaned over and whispered in his ear: "Great way to fly, huh?" Dr. Yell. Dub Yell. Dr. Double Yell. Double? How did anyone ever get named Double, he wondered. Double Yell? Why not Triple? Or Home Run?

The one person who had yet to voice an opinion, or for that matter to utter a word, was the president's wife, Copper. Sox watched as she continued to read. In her early forties, she looked to him more like late twenties. He turned slightly to better partake of her curvy figure. Clothes didn't drape on her body, they were incorporated by it. Body by fissure. A gymnasium-toned package with well-defined features, she had always been an enticing image. Today, though, the sparkle that often radiated from her presence seemed missing. Her creamy face, normally rosy with the softness of a baby's behind in bath water, looked tired, like she hadn't bothered to take off yesterday's makeup.

For the rest of the flight he hunkered down and stayed glued to the couch, gazing out on passing scenes of unmarred calm and serenity. Soon they passed over a field where a scramble for a loose football was unfolding, some of its young pursuers pausing to lift their heads upward, the rest of their comrades preoccupied and far more concerned with the glide path of the pigskin than that of the president.

Flying on, they crossed over seamless grasslands, catching up with a lone female horseback rider galloping free and immersed in the pure joy of a romp across the countryside. She offered a cheery wave, then turned away, heading off farther into the heartland.

Soon the broad expanses began to give way to more mountainous terrain, a gradual rise indicating they were approaching the outer range of the Catoctin National Park.

Camp David would not be far now. There they would drop down into a cocoon-like security blanket of splendid isolation, an island on a mountain; a compound of cabins, tennis courts, swimming pool and other amenities of rustic life that only a handful of staffers had experienced during the Crayon presidency.

Before landing he decided he'd better glance over his Camp David Fact Sheet.

THE WHITE HOUSE
Office of the Press Secretary

FACT SHEET

CAMP DAVID

…horseback riding along with the Camp's nature trails, daily walks and swimming have been favorite activities of First Families… Camp David has been the scene of many important presidential meetings with heads of state, Members of Congress, the Cabinet and other Administration officials…the president and Mrs. Crayon enjoy the quiet of Camp David, its beauty and offerings in terms of a place to spend time away from the pressures of the nation's capital.

Camp David is a naval installation staffed by permanently assigned naval personnel, a complement of Marines for security, and a contingent of the White House Communications Agency, which provides communication support.

The natural appearance of Camp David has changed little since the original construction in 1942. The cabins are rustic board and batten construction, stained or painted a moss green hue. The native woods have been maintained wherever possible and every effort is made to maintain the natural beauty of the land and retain the flavor of the outdoors.

Laurel Lodge is Camp David's main conference facility. It contains a presidential office, a conference room and dining facilities. Aspen Lodge, the presidential residence at the Camp, is a two-bedroom ranch-style house.

The choppy whir of the propeller revved slower as the Marine pilot gently set them down at the center of the tarmac. Sure, Sox had seen the world, but he was still awestruck to be here at Camp David, where historic moments were a cottage industry. A mini motorcade was waiting, which after negotiating several meandering curves, delivered the Crayons at Aspen and the rest of the party at Laurel.

"This place is overwhelmed with calm," Quad sighed as they wandered through the lodge.

Sox looked out beyond the windows to the wooded thicket that stretched behind the cabin's rear. "Yeah, but I'll bet there are lots of enlisted men in Greenland who would take a bust in rank to draw this straw."

"Not exactly a hardship post," Quad agreed.

"When the assignments include manning a movie projector and shagging golf balls from the par three hole behind the president's cabin? Sign me up."

"So are you ready for 48 hours of this?" Quad asked, taking a long swallow from the soft drink a steward had delivered.

"In other words, a 48-hour pass from the press room?"

Quad chuckled, nodding in agreement. He took another pull on the bottle, his lips lingering to savor the release of the liquid. "How about some tennis tomorrow?"

"Sure, why not?" Sox nodded. "Tennis and women—that's my program for the weekend."

"Women? In these woods?"

"No, not here. This is a long-distance deal I'm trying to negotiate. I'm using this weekend to develop a strategic plan of action."

"Sounds like you'll be busy."

"That's a distinct possibility because I've also got the press weekend phone duty."

"That's kind of like having bad acne for the weekend."

"Or diarrhea."

"Well, don't let it stop you from being at Aspen at eight tomorrow night."

"Purpose?"

"To watch a movie."

"Title?"

"Don't know. It'll be something current."

Twenty-four hours later, he and Quad were ambling down the road toward Aspen. It had rained earlier, leaving in its wake a misty veil hanging over the thickly shrubbed compound. They moved along the winding, leaf-soddened road past two of the guest cabins, Hickory and Sycamore, each of which bore a nameplate carved in wood on its front.

Sycamore was Sox's cabin. One of the first acts he had committed upon settling in was to gather up and pack away one of the available perks—souvenir matches. He made a mental note to save a few for Flaxen, even though she was obviously on guard against the crass use of White House symbols to curry her favor. His heavy-handed stumbles of the past had cost him. Nonetheless, a Camp David perk was still a Camp David perk, something to be prized. And it's not as if this stuff was available for over-the-counter purchase at one's favorite shopping mall. This was the real deal. No credit card, mail order catalog or shopping network could supply access to these presidential goodies. You had to be there.

There was also the Camp David souvenir store—tie bars, cuff links, golf balls, candy jars, coffee and beer mugs. He particularly liked the price of the latter—$4.65.

The road began to narrow, veering off from other cabins and signs of compound life, save for a clearing with a small playground, apparently put there for use by children of the camp personnel.

"You gotta like this place, huh?" Quad said, deeply inhaling the moist air. "That is, if you're a tranquility freak."

"Yeah, it's great," Sox shrugged. "The trouble is, calm can get on your nerves."

Through the haze they could see looming before them the first dewy outlines of Aspen cottage. With a guardhouse in front, it was a tiny compound within a compound.

"What's our game plan here?" Sox asked as they padded along the last few hundred yards.

"What do you mean?"

"I mean, are we just going to catch a flick or have we been invited here for some other reason?"

"Chill out, press spokesman, you're overanalyzing things. I know it's normal in the press office to be on motive alert all the time, but up here you can back off the throttle. Believe me, it's just a night at the movies with the First Family. No hidden agendas. Just kick back and relax."

They were almost to the cabin. The path that had earlier been narrow and flanked by heavy woods now broadened out into a driveway that circled in front of the one-story cabin. The air was heavy with the smell of rain-soaked fir. Ragged puffs of smoke filtered from the cabin's chimney, ghostly drifts clinging in the trees, serving to blot out lingering flickers of daylight.

Sox's mind continued to race as they covered the final steps. The suspicious, inquiring mind of a presidential spokesman. He couldn't help it. Quad was right, motive-seeking was an essential part of the job. Dig. Dig. Dig. There was always a reason behind the reason. Goodness of heart was for fables, not the Office of the Press Secretary. Why were they here? Was it just to watch a movie? Was it that simple? Had he accompanied the First Family here merely to be part of the audience for a night at the cinema, Camp David style? Apparently so. Oh, well, would necking be allowed? Silly thought.

They passed by the guardhouse, a Secret Service outpost manned by an agent who recognized them and nodded approvingly. In the murky distance beyond the cabin they could see the limp silhouette of the flag-stick marking the practice golf green. Moving on past the small pond at the top of the circular driveway, they arrived at the front door. They were five minutes early.

Quad knocked twice and stepped back. After a moment the door swung open to offer the alluring specter of Copper Crayon as she extended a welcoming handshake.

"You guys are better than being on time—you're early."

"We wanted to be sure we got a good seat," Quad smiled.

"And a chance at the popcorn before it turned stale," Sox added lightly.

"Honey, the A team is here," she cried out, her eyes never leaving them. As they entered the room, the president joined them, nodding "hello." He was dressed casually in a checkered shirt, tan slacks and penny loafers, his relaxed manner suggesting that being at Camp David for 24 hours had already proved a therapeutic balm for his spirits.

A steward appeared and offered soft drinks all around—Quad, Sox and Dr. Yell. Sox noted that the president was delivered a liquid in a high-ball glass that appeared to be less soft. He silently wished for the same, but dutifully selected a cola from the steward's tray.

"You guys up for an evening at the Aspen cinema?" the president asked, moving in front of the fireplace to warm his hands.

Everyone smiled, shuffled, then mumbled "yesses" and "sures" in such meek voices that Sox decided to jump in more assertively.

"Mr. President, I'm grateful for the chance to watch anything other than the press." As he spoke, he realized he was focusing on Copper, a pleasure to be sure, but a slippery slope lest someone notice his leering. Someone like the president. Quickly he turned to the others.

"Then I think you'll like this film," the president responded, oblivious to Sox's brief fixation. "It's one of those spy intrigue numbers where a reporter goes berserk on a plane and causes mayhem."

"I know that scene," Sox laughed. "Sounds just like the press plane. I think I've seen this movie with the original cast."

"And the beauty of watching a movie here is that you don't have to pay," Dr. Yell injected.

Pay? Paying for a movie was the least of Sox's worries. He just hoped he'd be able to pay attention for the next hour and a half.

Over near the couch the steward again appeared and flipped a switch which activated the lowering of a wall-size screen. Everyone stood silently, watching as the gray-glittered screen slowly creaked down until it finally clanked against the floor.

"Well, let's dim the lights," said the president, grabbing Copper's hand and guiding her to the couch, front row center. "Grab a seat, guys," he said, nodding at chairs positioned further back.

The lights slowly dimmed as they eased into their seats. After a brief interlude of darkness, there were abrupt flashes of light across the screen, erratic and blurred images that caused Sox to blink in vain as he tried to bring clarity to the hazy blips. From back in the tiny projection room, muffled cursing drifted out, a desperate response to the scenes of fuzziness to which they were being treated. Impatiently, the president swung around to his aides.

"Anyone know how to run a film projector?"

"Sox, isn't that in your job description?" said Quad, adding a playful slap on the back.

"Mr. President, the fact that there's a manual typewriter in my office says a lot about my knowledge of machinery," Sox joked.

"Frankly, I'm not sure what that says," the president responded, "except maybe the high-tech train is leaving the station without you."

"Time out," uttered a frustrated voice from deep in the bowels of the projection booth as the out-of-sync grinding of the projector sputtered to a halt.

The overhead lights clicked on and Copper sprang from her perch, standing hands-on-hips with her back to the empty screen, eyes narrowing and harshly zeroing in on the projection booth.

"This is Camp David," she snapped. "This is the president of the United States. This isn't film editing 101. Get that projector in gear, get that film in focus and get this show rolling!"

The room remained silent, save for the nearby fireplace where ribbons of flame licked at the logs newly added, some of the live coals spilling out onto the hearth and filling the room with energetic crackling.

One hour later, the movie, its focus restored, was proving underwhelming in its ability to grip its audience. Boredom had been bypassed in favor of direct passage to childlike slumber. The president had been the first to succumb, his head nestled peacefully against Copper's shoulder. Quad, too, was a lost cause. His head wasn't leaning on anyone's shoulder, just bobbing up and down, his eyelids vainly fighting the impulse to droop. Even Dr. Yell was tilted back in his chair, his eyes also heavy with flutter. What action there was on the screen seemed to have been successful only in inducing a universal commune with dreamland. The only source of energy left in the room came from the sparks popping in the fire. The noise level from all the snoring, gagging, wheezing, harrumphing and snorting had now resulted in a volume almost equal to that of the film's soundtrack.

This was just like any other neighborhood theatre, Sox thought, where folks dozed off. He was glad he hadn't succumbed to such a fate, particularly since Copper had taken a head count to determine who was responsible for making all the racket. There was nothing to do now but gut it out, try to hang in there, watch the rest of the miserable flick, and, above all, stay awake.

Thirty minutes later, Quad yawned and uncoiled from his snooze, awakened by a scene featuring the obligatory car chase.

He leaned over and tapped Sox lightly on the back. "Do you think the president will miss me if I slip out before the end of the movie? I'm beat."

Miss him? Fat chance. The only thing the president hadn't missed tonight was sleep.

"No sweat… shouldn't be a problem… I'll cover," Sox whispered back.

"Thanks."

They watched a few more minutes of the picture until Quad again tapped Sox from behind.

"I think I'd better go out the back door. That way, I won't

disturb anyone."

Yeah, and more importantly, you won't be noticed by Copper, Sox thought. He noted, however, that the chief of staff did have a serious logistical problem to overcome. The chairs in which they were sitting were positioned so that anyone departing the movie would have to walk in between the projector and the screen, thereby interrupting the action, an act sure to capture the attention of the First Lady. A successful exit would be no simple matter. Better Quad than him. Timing would be everything. Like waiting until she blinked.

Quad decided to wait a few more minutes. Further study of the terrain was required. What it confirmed was that he would have to get down on his hands and knees and crawl under the projector's light beam.

"Think I can get my rump low enough?" he whispered.

It better be lower than the Catoctin Mountains, Sox thought, then watched as Quad eased from his chair into a prone position on the floor, elbows braced, sort of like a scene from boot camp with recruits crawling under low-strung crisscrosses of rope. Tentatively, he began slithering along the floor on his belly, pausing every few seconds to cock an ear in Copper's direction, then edging up to a spot just under the projector's beam. A trickle of sweat crawled down his forehead, pausing to glisten on his nose. He wiped it away and then hunched his full frame closer to the floor and groped his way under the light until he was safely on the other side. Sox couldn't believe what he was watching—the White House chief of staff crawling out of the president's cabin at Camp David.

Safely there, Quad sat up, his eyes rolling with relief, his lips broadly forming the words "I made it." Cautiously he braced his hands and elbows on a small end table, pushed himself up and began tiptoeing toward the back door. As he disappeared into the room's darkness, one of his hands momentarily reappeared, two of its fingers extended behind in a "V for Victory" salute.

Meanwhile, the movie continued to roll on, Sox noting that the president's head had reemerged into sight, the boss apparently reawakened, fresh and once again engaged by the on-screen action.

"Look, Quad, that actor has a desk like yours," the president said, his head swiveling around to search the near darkness for his chief of staff. Sox's eyes shot back and forth from the screen to the president. The desk in the movie scene they were watching bore a striking resemblance to that in Quad's office. The difference was that Quad's desk was always littered with little pieces of pink paper—phone messages arrayed across it in double layers. The word was out in the press corps—if you wanted a call back from Quad Sands, place the call late in the day when your message would be toward the back of his desk, closest to where he might see it. If you called in the morning, forget it. The desk in the movie was uncluttered, a notable contrast.

"Quad?" the president persisted.

Sox looked anxiously from side to side as if a visual search would miraculously produce the chief of staff.

"Quad?"

"Um…"

"Quad?"

"He… uh…"

"He's missing the best part of the movie," said the president, turning to fully face Sox.

"Yes, sir."

"Well, where is he?"

"He… uh…" Sox stammered, looking at Dr. Yell for assistance but getting only a vacant stare in return.

"Where'd he go—the john?"

"No, sir."

"Well?"

"He…"

"Yes."

"He… uh… that is… Mr. President, he crawled off to bed."

CHAPTER SIXTEEN

REPORTER: The president's last name is Crayon.
              Specifically, what is his favorite color?

SPOKESMAN: Plaid.

An hour later, entering Sycamore, Sox swallowed deep of the cool Maryland air. He hadn't lied to the president. Nor had he trashed Quad by revealing the nature of his escape. Both the Crayons had merely shrugged acceptance on hearing the explanation, albeit both mildly perplexed as to how the White House's highest-ranking staff member could exit their cabin without being noticed.

He decided a call to Dr. Yell was in order. Call it a curiosity check. If there had been any repercussions from Quad's creative exit, the Crayons would have confided their displeasure to Dub Yell.

"Hey, hey, hey, Doc, it's the Sox-man just making a pre-bedtime sweep," he chuckled into the phone, a pretense at sounding casual.

"Purpose?" The doctor's voice was no-nonsense. Shrill. Definitely not that of a physician intent on practicing his bedside manner.

Sox hesitated, puzzled by the iciness of the response but resigned to press on.

"Looks like Quad dodged a bullet, huh?" he continued, forcing another chuckle.

"Yes, but how many people do you know who can claim the honor of having snuck out of a room where they've been the guest of the president of the United States?"

"Well…don't you mean *crawled* out?"

"Okay, crawled. Hunkered. Slinked. Snaked. Wormed. Belly-flopped. Can you get any lower than that?"

"Quad can't, that is unless he drops a few pounds."

Clock-ticking silence resonated from the other end of the line. Four, five, six seconds. Enough for Sox to sense there was no need to try and further engage the doctor on this subject. Better to let this one fade into the Camp David mists.

"So how's the president's health chart?" he asked, an upbeat shift to his tone.

"Everything is ticking like it should tick," the doctor answered mechanically. "Everything is flowing and going."

He made a mental asterisk to file away that phrase for the next time he was conducting the press briefing and being pressed about the president's health. The doctor had unwittingly served up a vintage Sox answer—a response shrouded in specific vagueness.

"Frankly, I'm more worried about you," the doctor said. "Have you quit your occasional smoking?"

"What's the worry? Afraid I'll stunt my growth?"

The conversation was seized by another moment of silence before Sox continued. "Not to worry, doc. My mother once told me that midgets can always get a job."

"Thank you for that employment note," the doctor drolly observed. "But I still thought you looked a little green around the gills tonight. An epidemic case of press office pallor, I'd guess."

"Thanks for the diagnosis. Got a cure?"

"In your case, I think we're dealing with another ailment, too."

"My perk-fetish—is it that obvious?"

Frankly, "I think it's a fever that hits those trying to hit on females."

"Oh, really? How could you just look at me and tell that?"

"Oh, hell, I can diagnose that over the telephone."

Some further small talk ensued before they hung up. Sox was bemused that the doctor had so accurately zeroed in on what was ailing him. If only he could have prescribed a Flaxen-specific antidote. Actually, there was one in his hand. The telephone. Sure. Call her up and crawl. That seemed to be a popular activity around Camp David tonight—crawling. What the hell—he'd do it. Just ring her up and beg her forgiveness. A gargantuan grovel.

Four rings later the receiver clicked on.

"Hello…"

"Hi," he said, swallowing hard.

"…I'm sorry I'm not in right now to take your call," her voice continued, "but at the tone you know what to do."

His body sagged dejectedly, the receiver dangling limply against his ear. It was her answering machine. Hope turning to despair, he felt helpless to answer that which her message had presumed. He didn't know what to do. Or say. He hadn't anticipated her being on tape.

Her recorder's beep rang sharply in his ear. He now was down to two choices: hang up or suck up. In the blink of an instant, he decided to go with the latter.

"Hi…Flaxen…it's one of the president's flaks calling…you remember me, the guy with the two phones implanted in his ear…well, that guy misses you…never mind where I am right now other than to say it's in a pretty damn isolated place…and what I dislike most is being isolated from your life…because…because…I really do care…and besides, you're right, no one is that busy…not even the president…and for damn sure, not one of his spokesmen…so call this a world-class crawl…I'm genuflecting at your feet…" As soon as the words left his mouth, he wondered if she might think "genuflecting" was some weird act of sexual depravity, but too late—the recorder's beeping tone cut him off. Should he have gotten heavier into forgiveness? Perhaps. Still, he had made a good plea. For the moment he was awash in the feel-good spirit of having taken his best shot. He did care. He could only hope now that she might wilt and give him another try.

That thought remained at the forefront of his concerns the next morning, that is, until he checked his recorder at home which offered no evidence of a return call from her. There had been only one message—a call from a Midwest-based print reporter with a slow ball: "What does the president want for Christmas?" And it was still November.

Sox had called him back with a blue-ribbon cliché answer: "Peace."

Later that morning he stood shivering at the rear of Aspen Lodge, dutifully watching as the president hit golf balls in the direction of the practice green. Most of the shots were spraying off into the nearby woods, only a few ending up near the target. The man's golf swing was an adventure in agony, Sox thought, his eyes tracing the flight of one ball after another lofted wildly off course by this free-swinging hacker.

He winced in the direction of Buddy Uncertain, one of the cadre of agents on duty, both grimacing in unison as another ball flew wildly across the sky. But the safety of agents posted at intervals between the president and the green was no joke. It was an assignment worthy of hazardous pay considering that the hard little balls were spewing in all directions. Here, one had to be on guard while being on guard. For his part, the president seemed unfazed by his ineptitude, continuing to wind up and swing with reckless gusto. Mercifully, after ten minutes of fruitless pounding away, he was puffing hard and stepped back, propping a five iron under his hip.

"I think I've lost a few."

"Yes, sir."

"But overall, not too bad."

"Yes, sir."

"We'd better go and try to find some of them."

What Sox really wanted to say was, "Hey, fella—you, Mr. President, sir—you just parked two dozen balls in the deep rough. If that's your definition of 'a few,' then somebody needs to check the presidential contact lenses for mossy overhang."

"Let's make a sweep through the woods, then we're out of here—wheels up for the big white house near the Potomac," the president said, smiling.

They took off across the grounds, tramping into the scrub bushes, the president poking and swatting, trying to unearth the tiny white spheres gone astray. It was all too bizarre as Sox watched the nation's chief executive intensify the search, roaming deeper and deeper into the foliage. Here was the president of the United States thrashing around the Maryland backwoods in search of golf balls. Here was a man with the power to impact millions of dollars in the federal budget, searching to recoup at least one ball lost out of that budget.

Later, aboard Marine One heading back to D.C., Sox wondered about what he had witnessed. What if the press ever heard about this? He could just imagine the barrage of questions.

"How many were lost?"

"What type?"

"What color? Were they all white?"

"What impact will their loss have on the budget deficit?"

"Was anyone hurt?"

"At any point was the president in danger? Or anyone else?"

"If the president is such a lousy golfer, why doesn't he take some lessons?"

"If he does take lessons, who'll foot the bill—the taxpayer?"

Even worse, Sox could imagine his blurting out an ill-conceived response: "Yes, I can confirm the president lost his balls."

He stared out the chopper window as the regal presence of the White House's south portico gradually emerged through creamy rays of the late afternoon sun. The blend of white and green hues from the balconies, columns and canopies was a dazzling sight, one that became more defined and imposing as they angled in over the compound, gradually hovering down to a point several feet off the ground, the pilots holding the craft in suspension while making certain of setting down dead center on the white crosshairs so neatly embedded in the lush spread of lawn, the president's backyard.

"Sox, what'll they be yelling at me from the press pen?" the president asked, unbuckling his seat belt.

The chopper's engines throttled back as its wheels gently embraced the ground, the roar suddenly downshifting to a low, humming gnash, then sputtering silent.

"Pretty much the same bill of fare as your departure Friday. Maybe a few new wrinkles."

"If they've got new wrinkles, tell 'em to see a plastic surgeon," the president smiled.

Sox glanced at Copper. She remained expressionless while stuffing the book she had been reading into a bag, then pressing close to the window to survey the small crowd gathered behind ropes on the driveway, mostly friends of staffers on Sunday afternoon West Wing tours pre-positioned to greet their arrival.

"I don't recognize anyone too friendly or too familiar out there," she noted.

Sox bent down by the rear window to better expand his view. "I see Sparta."

"Like I said, I don't see anyone too friendly out there," she repeated.

"Okay, we know who's out there," the president acknowledged. "Now how about the what? What questions will they be tossing out?"

Sox instantly took mental inventory of the press calls he had fielded over the weekend. Most of them had been fluff, nothing of much substance or unusual, except for one call from a local D.C. television station, a reporter chasing a rumor that the president had suffered a stroke. It was totally out of left field and the only call that had come in on that subject. A cautionary check with Dr. Yell had confirmed that it was garbage, a darter out of the blue with no legs. Following the doctor's guidance, he had gotten back to the reporter with as firm a denial as he could muster: "False, absolutely false. Print it, quote me, and use an exclamation point!"

But his spokesman's instinct for always covering one's butt had left him with a mild case of the worrywarts. Now, in the confines of Marine One, his chance to seek an instant cure had come: he could ask the president. What troubled him, though, was how to phrase such a question: "Mr. President, did you suffer a stroke over the weekend? Dr. Yell says you didn't, and I told the press you didn't, but did you?"

He felt like an idiot just for thinking about asking that. But one thing he had learned from survival deep in the innards of the White House: the only dumb questions were those that went unasked. He knew it seemed a ridiculous thing to ask: the president appeared perfectly fit and normal. But what about a minor stroke? Could it be possible? And even if it had happened, how would a weekend reporter at a local television affiliate have gotten wind of it? It was just a fishing expedition, one of those off-the-wall kind of questions that pop up on a slow news day. The "let's try anything" syndrome.

Still, he wanted to ask the president directly, get it from the major domo himself. He knew it was the only way to cleanly spike that tiny cell of doubt nagging him inside and assure that he hadn't committed the home-run sin for a press spokesman: lying.

He edged forward on the couch, studying the president as he stuffed briefing papers into a leather briefcase. It was speak up now or else accept the fact that the president's deputy press secretary was a candy-ass.

"Mr. President…"

"Yes?" the president answered, finishing with his papers, locking his briefcase and looking up. "You were saying about the questions? What's on their menu?"

"It should pretty much be what you heard on departure Friday—expectations for the terrorism summit, when you'll name a new Labor secretary, the jobs bill…"

"You might get something about the congressional leadership meeting tomorrow," Quad added.

"We'll be talking budget there," the president said. "Anything else?"

An impish grin crossed Sox's face. "Well, Mr. President, I doubt if they'll ask anything about your balls."

Copper glared at Sox. The president reached over and gently squeezed her knee. "Not to worry, honey, he's talking about golf balls."

Copper shrugged, her lips pursing as she laid her hand on top of his, her fingers seeking to interlace with her husband's.

Sox lowered his eyes, trying to avoid visually prying into their moment of intimacy. Still, his need to ask the question that needed asking remained. Now it was a question that would have to wait until the president finished playing handsies with his wife.

He leaned back, turning to get a better view out the back window and pinpoint who else might be camped out in the press pen. Usually for Sunday afternoon Camp David arrivals, those gathered were mostly backups to the regular White House correspondents and other general assignment reporters dispatched by the various news organizations. Many times they only had to be there for short duration, particularly if the president walked past them without responding to any shouted questions. Of course, there was always the possibility he might do otherwise and utter words that would virtually assure those lucky correspondents a spot on the evening's newscast or in the Monday morning newspapers. With such exposure would come enhancement of that reporter's image for having been there on such a newsworthy occasion. It all proved one thing. Despite the hype about all the talent, skill, and drive manifested in the White House press corps, being in the right place at the right time often determined whether one exulted in success or sucked wind. When luck visited the White House, careers often soared.

He could see that most of those in the pen were random D.C. newsies, some backups to regulars on the White House beat and some "standees," those from smaller news organizations who stood in the back of the room during press briefings, absent having one of the prized assigned seats.

This was good. Apart from Sparta, most of the questions would be "lob jobs" the president could easily handle. Answers long on syntax, short on specifics. But answers with just enough pith to make it to the evening news shows and morning papers.

"Besides the press, is there anyone else out there for whom our antenna should be up?" the president asked.

Sox bent down to the window for another look. "Not that I'm aware of, Mr. President. Looks like some staff and friends here for tours." That sounded knowledgeable, but of course he was winging it, just guessing.

Copper cocked her head in Sox's direction, eyebrows raised, her offhand expression suggesting that she knew he was guessing.

"Anyone here to meet you, Sox?"

"Just twenty or so of your favorite reporters."

"That's better than forty or so of your favorite reporters," she observed, her eyes narrowing.

He nodded agreement, but inwardly his concern was building that they were about to step onto the lawn without his having alerted the president to the stroke rumor and, equally important, without having heard the president confirm that it was pure drivel. He stepped into the aisle, positioning himself fourth in line behind Quad, Copper and the president, the latter starting to move toward the exit. The moment had come. There was nothing left to do but go for broke.

"Mr. President, there's just one other thing the press might throw at you," he blurted.

The president stopped abruptly, wheeling around. "There's probably a lot of things they'd like to throw at me, starting with various products from the fruit and vegetable families. In lieu of those, what are you talking about?"

"Well…I had phone duty this weekend…"

"And? C'mon, we've got people waiting," the president goaded, his patience starting to thin.

"And one of the calls was a rumor that—"

"I know. Someone saw me shimmy nude up the Washington Monument?"

"I hope not," Copper said, dryly.

"Okay, the Jefferson Monument," the president said, mockingly.

"Sir, it was about your health," Sox continued. He looked behind him at Dr. Yell, seeking visual support, but the doctor remained rigid, staring blankly ahead as if he wasn't hearing any of this.

"Well?" the president challenged.

"Well, sir, there is apparently a rumor that you had a stroke this weekend."

The president's jaw tightened, his teeth grinding back and forth, a flicker of agitation in his eyes. "A stroke?" he growled. "A press rumor that I've had a stroke?"

"Yes, sir."

The president looked past Sox to Dr. Yell, then back to Sox. "And you want to know if it's true?"

"Well…"

"Well, what the hell does it look like?"

"Sir—"

"Dub, have I had a stroke?" the president asked, again looking past Sox to Dr. Yell.

"If so, you are one of the healthiest specimens standing to ever suffer such an affliction," the doctor replied.

"Sounds like some gobbledygook from one of your answers, Sox," the president said, sharply pointing a finger. "Let me give it to you with the bark off the bark. The answer is no! N.O.! Now stroke that." He turned away to depart, but paused again, smiling mischievously, his mood swiftly changing.

"Okay, if these pit bulls in the press think I've had a stroke, then let's play it out. As I come down the chopper steps, I'll stagger and look disoriented, then walk right past 'em like I'm in a daze. Will that do?"

Sox put his hand to his heart in mock cardiac arrest. "Mr. President, please don't do that. If Sparta sees that, she won't even wait till you're on the driveway, she'll bolt for her booth and phone it in right away. There'll be a news flash on the air by the time you hit the second floor."

The president smiled at Copper. "It would be fun, though, to yank their chain, wouldn't it?"

"Yes, but this time Sox is right," she said. "You'd be playing with fire."

The words "this time" troubled Sox, a suggestion that there had been other occasions when she wasn't in his corner, but his bigger concern right now was the president's next move.

"Yeah," the president said, "but it would cure those overanxious story-chasers from going gaga every time some knee-jerk rumor surfaces. Once again, they're more interested in making news than reporting it."

"Amen," Quad chimed in.

"I agree," Sox said, "but if you stumble off this chopper, they won't wait to see that you're kidding. It'll set off bells in newsrooms immediately."

"Okay, okay, I'll behave," said the president, begrudgingly. "But it would have been fun to watch 'em scatter."

"So we have a deal?" Sox asked.

"Yeah, sure. I won't stage any fake strokes if you'll just promise me one thing."

"Yes, sir."

"That you won't talk about my…"

"Balls…sir?"

"Yes…that is, my golf balls."

"Deal," Sox said, smiling with relief.

CHAPTER SEVENTEEN

REPORTER: What is the reason the president is traveling so much?

SPOKESMAN: He needs the frequent flyer miles.

Forty-five minutes later, Sox was headed for Georgetown. Even though his apartment was there, he found his mood more attuned to stopping along the way at one of his favorite bars, a watering hole known for its intimacy, cozy fireplace, subdued lighting and abundance of females.

But tonight's stop was not for that purpose. That was the old Sox. The pre-Flaxen Sox. The Flaxen he'd been trying to reach all weekend but who must have been on a flight. He'd try her again when he got home. Meantime, he'd just drop by an old haunt where he could relax and reflect on events of the weekend, events which had left him giddy. A 48-hour high, to be sure. Camp David had been a gas.

He slapped impatiently at the steering wheel as he turned off M Street, slowing down and angling his car into a tight curbside parking space. Walking along, he passed deep into the bosom of Georgetown nightlife— thumping music, heaving bodies, gluts of sweat and noise. But he'd had enough high octane for one weekend. What he pined for now was something on the softer side—a piano bar, a killer drink and filmy images of Flaxen to take into the night. If any friendly females happened to drift by, he'd review those options on a case-by-case basis. Case-by-case basis? Review options? Even in social diversions he was thinking like a spokesman. Scary. Very scary. He definitely needed a drink.

Reaching his destination, he was glad to see it was not too crowded and easily made his way to the bar, staking out a spot next to an eye-popping blonde. Her most notable feature was the tightness of her dress which was waging war with the fullness of her figure.

"Hi," she giggled, her tongue moistly licking her rum-red lips.

"Hi," he said, ordering his favorite drink, a seabreeze.

"A seabreeze? What's that?"

"A drink."

"I know, but what is it?"

"An alcoholic beverage."

"Gee, you're about as much fun as measles."

"Okay, it's a drink with vodka and other juices mixed together."

Her eyes were busy on him, their watery twinkle suggesting that she had been parked there for a while.

"You come here often?"

"Some."

"Kind of a short hitter when it comes to words, aren't you?"

"Words are my work."

"Oh, yeah? So what do you do when you're not prowling around Georgetown?"

He decided he'd toyed with her long enough. "I serve the public."

"You're a waiter?"

"No, I'm in the government."

"Which one?"

"Ours."

"Oh, yeah? Where?"

"On Pennsylvania Avenue."

Her face furrowed in contemplation as she stepped back to study him more fully, her eyes narrowing into dim bulbs of recognition. She took another long swallow from her drink.

"Pennsylvania Avenue, huh?"

"Yes."

"Something to do with that new restaurant on Pennsylvania?"

"I don't work in a restaurant," he emphasized.

"So what's it called?"

"What?"

"The place where you work."

"It's called the White House."

"Isn't that what that new restaurant is called?"

Before his brain could determine how to respond, or whether he should, his pager went off. It was a sobering reminder that he still had press phone duty, the weekend not yet being over. It was also a welcome diversion from the mindless drift of their conversation.

"S'cuse me, I've got to take a call."

"You a doctor?"

"Yeah, Dr. N. O. Comment."

"My name's Bitsy."

Bitsy? What a misnomer. Bitsy was anything but bitsy. He grasped the single handshake finger she extended, hurriedly shook it, then having left his cell phone in the car, headed for the pay phone in the nearby hallway.

Dialing the White House, he glanced over his shoulder to see that Bitsy had moved down the bar, trying her luck with two guys in gray suits who had the look of bored lobbyists. Or maybe bored husbands. Or both.

"White House," a female voice crisply intoned.

"Operator, this is Sox St. Louis. You paged me?"

"Yes, you have two press calls. Would you like me to get them?"

Her voice was calm and assured, its efficiency manifest in its directness. Even in times of crisis, with thousands of calls barraging the switchboard, White House operators never lost their cool. Sox loved them. They were his buddies. He marveled at their ability to turn stress aside, their voices unflappable tonic for one's spirits. If they did wear emotions on their sleeves, never did those feelings seep into their voices. From their command post deep in the basement of the Executive Office Building, they were tireless in their ability to track anyone down, anywhere.

"Who called?" he asked loudly, sticking a finger in one ear to mute noise from the bar.

"Soldier Paintbrush called earlier, and there was one other just a few minutes ago—"

"Let me guess—Sparta?"

"Yes, sir," she acknowledged, chuckling lightly.

"Imagine Sparta letting two hours go by without checking in or chasing me down."

"Yes, sir."

"She saw me at the arrival. She didn't have anything to pester me about then. No, she waits until now—now when I'm savoring a few seconds of off-the-record peace away from that pain-in-the-ass press room." As the last words left his mouth, he realized he was ranting at the operator.

"Yes, sir," she repeated patiently.

God bless the White House operators, he thought. They not only had fingers capable of nimbly dancing across that busy switchboard, plugging together presidents, heads of state and global power brokers, but they were also part-time psychiatrists, listening to staffers like him vent puny frustrations. God bless them, indeed. They were saints in headsets.

"Shall I get Mr. Paintbrush?"

"Yeah, sure," he said resignedly. He could never say "no" to a White House operator.

She was off-line for only a moment before clicking back on. "I have Mr. Paintbrush."

It was times like these he wished they weren't so damned efficient.

"Hey, Sox, it's Soldier. Hate to bother you on a Sunday night."

"Okay, so much for the pigeon droppings, what do you want?"

"One of my client papers was wondering…"

One of his client papers? The Paintbrush News Wire has a client? Where? Purgatory?

"Wondering about what?" Sox exhaled.

"One of the bills the president plans to sign next week."

"They were wondering about it on Sunday night, I guess?"

"Yes."

"And what were they wondering about one of those bills on Sunday night?"

"Is one of them the bill declaring National Bowling Week?"

Two girls, freshly perfumed preppy types, jostled against Sox in the crowded hallway, laughing their way to the restroom. He stared after them, his agitation with Soldier giving way to faint stirrings of desire. His patience with Soldier had expired. It was time to get back to the bar.

"You tracked me down just to ask me that?" he asked incredulously.

"Yes, I did," Soldier exclaimed. "So?"

"National Bowling Week? National Bowling Week? What's next? National Bent Fender Week? National Butter Bean Month?"

"Are you trashing the bowlers of America?"

"No," Sox said, quickly regaining his composure. "I've been a bowler myself. In fact, I was captain of my high school bowling team."

"That's great. Can I add that to my story?"

"Sure, why not?" Sox sighed.

"But what about the bill-signing? Will there be a ceremony?"

"I don't know. Stay tuned. Gotta go. Bye." Enough of the Soldier. He clicked the phone's hook to retrieve the operator.

"Yes, sir? Are you ready for the other call?"

"That's like saying am I ready for the plague, but, yes, go ahead."

She again clicked off, and within seconds Sparta's voice had replaced Soldier's.

"What's all that noise in the background? You're not in your office?"

"No, unlike you, I do occasionally wander a few hundred yards from the White House in search of a calm we know doesn't exist at the center of a blast furnace's fury. Tonight I happen to be traveling in a northwesterly direction and am currently visiting a dimly lit tavern where spirits are high, not to mention being served."

Aside from the crackle of static, the line was silent. It was one of the few times he had ever pinned her back without an instant response. He savored the moment, a blush of satisfaction at having lobbed some of her bluster back at her.

"This rumor about a stroke—you're knocking that down hard, right?" she finally said. As always, it hadn't taken her long to rebound and resume the probe.

"Right. Absolutely. False with a capital F!"

He wondered how she had gotten wind of it so quickly but knew better than to ask about her source. There was an unwritten code that White House spokesmen didn't ask reporters about their sources. It was considered amateurish, not to mention futile, since no self-respecting reporter would ever reveal a source anyway. Unnamed sources were the lifeblood of the White House press corps. Name your sources? Might as well ask all of them to strip naked and jog leisurely down Pennsylvania Avenue on Inaugural Day.

"I figured it was science fiction," she said. "He certainly looked all right coming off the chopper. So no problems, huh?"

Good old Sparta. Good old young Sparta. Good old semi-young Sparta. Never say die. Never quit. Always ready to test him one more time on the chance he might slip and tap her into a juicy tidbit. Always ready to ask the same question fifty different ways on the chance one of his answers might lead to a bingo.

"No, absolutely no problems."

"When did you say he had his last physical exam?"

Before he could answer, he was reminded of his surroundings by the two girls returning from their visit to the restroom, a trip that had resulted in their applying fresh lipstick, ample layers of red blush that enhanced the plastered smiles they now offered while giggling their way back to the bar. Their suggestive playfulness further reminded that his priority mission of the moment lay elsewhere, not in sparring with Sparta. He couldn't avoid answering the pagers and calls as part of phone duty, but he could keep them short. He was in a bar, not the briefing room.

"Last physical? Less than a year ago."

"And when is his next one scheduled?"

"I don't know. I'll have to check and let you know," he answered, trying to sound casual, but inwardly impatient.

"Can you get that for me tonight?"

"No, I can't," he said, fast tiring of her fishing expedition.

"How about the new Labor secretary?"

"How about him? Or her?"

"Might it be a woman?" she asked, perking up.

"The president is still considering candidates."

"You didn't answer my question. Could the appointment be a female?"

"Whoever it is, the president feels they will be the best qualified person for the job."

"Can you take me further on background?"

"Can't help you further on that one, including mega deep background or any other way. Anything else?"

"What about the congressional leadership meeting tomorrow?"

"What about it?"

"What's on the agenda?"

"Budget." He relished that answer. What could be more vague, stifling and non-news attractive than a meeting with congressional leaders to review agency budget projections? The budget was a bona fide bore. Definitely not headline-grabbing fare for a Sunday night newscast.

"Look, these are all nonstarters," she grumbled. "A lot of bilge and no bite. I've got to have a story. This is unacceptable."

"Accept it," he said, the bland tone in his voice disguising the glee he felt inside.

He hung up feeling good. He had responded to all the questions on her laundry list, yet hadn't advanced any of the stories an inch.

Upon return to the bar he noted that the tempo of activity in the room had been swelled by an influx of fresh bodies, increasing the noise level to where the piano player's offerings were a faintly heard tinkle buried in the clatter.

A quick survey determined that none of the newly arrived females were his type. There were a few head-turners, but the more he looked, the less he wanted to look. It was time to finish his drink, head for home and plead his case to Flaxen.

Burrowing his way back to the spot he had vacated, he could see Bitsy was busy with the two lobbyists. Better that way. She was already proving too much of an intellectual challenge.

The opposite side of the bar had become a hotbed of group activity, the two preppy girls at its center along with a towering brunette, sunny-faced and fully packaged. Encircled by bar rowdies, she held their attention riveted as she clenched a beer mug in her teeth and, without use of either hand, drained its contents dry to the lusty cheers of mostly male onlookers. It was a hearty feat of massive intake. From any viewing point in the room, it was evident that her lungs were up to the challenge, lots of extra luggage there. It was a décolletage of such impressive proportions as to make even Bitsy look bitsy.

Her admirers lost no time in collectively dousing her with full mugs of beer, an instant suds bath that left her deliriously happy and soaking wet. Many of those males pressed close to embrace and congratulate her, some returning for a second embrace.

Sox had had enough of this relaxation. In times past he would have been at the brunette's elbow or trying to jolly the preppy girls. He would have pursued Bitsy. Now he was infected with indifference to it all. He began weaving his way past bodies toward the door and freedom waiting outside. Once there, he peeled off M Street, taking up a hurried walking pace that soon accelerated into a steady jog, passing by his parked car and then covering four blocks of history-rich houses on Georgetown side streets until he rounded the corner in sight of his apartment, furiously sprinting the last fifty yards.

At the top of the stairwell to his basement apartment, he abruptly halted, searching his pockets for his house key and making a troubling discovery. Other than his wallet, both his pockets were bare. No house key. No car keys. Instantly he knew he was the victim of a bad habit that had nagged him for years—locking those keys in his car. To make sure, he took off, jogging back to where he had parked on the street. Lock-in confirmed. His keys were captive inside. He jogged back to the apartment. Slowly. It had been a long day. It was becoming a long night.

He eyed his front door, strategically pondering his predicament. Its windowpanes were narrow but just wide enough to reach an arm through and make what would be a formidable vertical stretch to unlock it. He'd have to break out one or two of the panes, maybe some of the wood frame, but it would be easier than going back to his car and spending an hour engaged in the coat hanger-through-the-window routine to unlock that door. Besides, the cost to replace the front door's panes would be minimal. And inside was another set of keys. And time was passing. He needed to get inside and call Flaxen.

Sizing up the situation, he decided it was probably best to take off his blazer and wrap a fist in his dress shirt before breaking the window. He hated to trash that shirt. He had bought it last week at one of D.C.'s more pricey men's stores. But advancement of his love life was at issue here, not natty grooming.

With teeth clenched, he seesawed back and forth several times to gain forward thrust, then rammed his fist through one of the small panes, the glass shattering into ragged shards that littered the apartment floor. He carefully wiggled his hand back through the hole, peeling the shirt away and examining to see if any cuts had resulted. The hand had survived unscathed, but the shirt was history—shredded wheat.

He eased his hand and arm back into the hole, extending his limb forward and upward. Groping for the lock, he made the unfortunate discovery that it was still out of reach. He needed to either break out a wooden divider or another pane of glass higher up. He started to withdraw his arm, got halfway, then winced as the flesh of his forearm wedged tightly against both sides of the wood frame, all progress halting. He was stuck. He pulled again, trying to jerk the arm free, but the frame had become vise-like and unyielding. Speckles of glass pricked his arm's flesh, forming tiny dots of blood that oozed down his arm, across his hand and trickled onto his apartment's rug. He had just bought that rug two weeks ago—fluffy and white. He watched helplessly as it began acquiring a new texture—soggy and splotched.

"Son of a bitch!" he screamed in lonely frustration. "This is the piss-ant pits!"

Back and forth, back and forth, gingerly he rotated the arm, trying to create some give that would release it from its bondage. It wouldn't budge. Not a centimeter. Thanks to his body being captive to a fetal and fixed position, cramps of fatigue were also settling in, his anger now joined by physical misery.

He stopped. Okay, time to take stock and invoke the credo he had always followed on crazed days in the briefing room: the more frantic the press is, the calmer the spokesman becomes. Take a deep breath.

Despite the discomfort of his contorted position, the pause helped. He was ready to attack the door again in a more positive frame of mind, an attitude that unfortunately lasted only seconds, for now he was being doused by a spray of mildly warm water, spurts of liquid pelting the back of his neck. Great. On top of everything else, he'd now have to contend with rain. Or would he? Hearing movement near the top of the stairs, he swiveled his neck around as far as possible—a human corkscrew—to discover that the glistening moisture he felt was human-generated, some guy taking a pee from above.

"Hey, bozo in the bushes!" he shouted. "Whoever you are, you're bleeding your lizard on somebody down here!"

"Uh, on who?"

"On me, that's who!"

"Sorry, I was aiming for nowhere," the voice said, apologetically.

"Well, this is somewhere. You're pissing on me, you're a lousy shot, and you're trespassing."

He tilted his head at just enough angle to where he could see the man's silhouette outlined among the bushes, the face remaining hidden in the shadows.

"I'm, uh, sorry," the man said, inching slightly forward.

With his face more illuminated, he revealed himself to be older than Sox had thought, grizzled and unshaven, perhaps a homeless street person trying to ferret out a niche of temporary refuge. Sox inched his neck further around, straining to achieve direct eye contact. The old man finished his business, pulling up pants which were soiled and grimy with street stains.

"I really am sorry," the old man mumbled. "I just didn't know anyone was down there."

"Well, I am. You've been squeezing the dew from your tube all over me."

The man pried the bushes further apart and edged closer, peering down for a better look.

"Say, exactly what are you doing down there?"

"I live here," Sox said. "I'm just doing some work on the place."

"This time of night? What kinda work?"

"Look, fella, you're history here. Okay? You've pissed a bucketful, now push off."

The old man shook his head, his scruffy hand pawing at the craggy contours of his face. Sox turned back to the door, dismissing his visitor. Crouched there, immobile, he was vexed by the thought that the old man, having noted his captive position, might decide to venture down and rob him. The more he analyzed the awkward position in which his body was mired, the more such a heist seemed a most remote possibility, one to be considered by only the most desperate of thieves. Penetrating this human Gordian knot to get to his pockets would be a tough and time-consuming challenge for even the most creative wallet-snatcher. He didn't have to worry long, his concern allayed by the sound of twigs breaking underfoot as the old man burrowed his way back to the sidewalk, the plodding scrape of his worn shoes against the pavement gradually fading into the night.

What next, Sox thought. What else could possibly happen to a guy hunched over in the squat position, his body joined to his front door, one arm wedged through a hole in that door and stuck there? A guy who was also now consumed with the overwhelming urge to take his own leak. Sure. Why not? Wet his pants. Make the night complete.

He gave the arm another try—wiggling, twisting, pushing, forcing and finally resorting to pure brute force, a violent pull jerking it free, the bruised limb emerging pocked with splinters of glass and wood. He fell back exhausted and licking his wounds, literally, running his tongue up and down his bloodied arm, drooling excess saliva on the more chafed spots.

Only a few hours ago he had been euphorically roaming the grounds of Camp David, a chummy day with the president of the United States. Now he was feebly huddled in a stairwell, one laden with the stench of urine, his arm throbbing with hurt from glass-inflicted punctures, his body bone-weary, his front door broken, his stomach gurgling with emptiness, his bladder badly in need of relief, phone duty still hanging over his head, and the call to Flaxen yet unmade.

He leaned back against the wall, taking time to gather himself. But soaked in sweat and droplets from another man's bladder, he wasn't about to opt for a long-term stay in his newly gained position and instead hastened to attack the door again. Might as well bust out another pane of glass and be done with this miserable episode.

Once more he covered his fist, using the remains of his shirt as a tightly wound wrap. Once more he reared back and slammed his hand through the glass. He again stretched his arm through the hole, his fingers groping the air in search of the lock. Once found, he nudged the handle unlatched, freeing the door to swing open, his body helplessly lunging forward in tandem, as his arm remained wedged in the framework.

"Hey, buddy!" a voice shouted from above.

Apparently his victory in opening the door had not been achieved in private. Gently, he slid his arm back out of the hole and swung around. It was the old man again. And a cop. A cop with fingers curled tautly around a sidearm. The cop stood glaring down at him menacingly, the old man cowering behind.

"Hey, buddy!" the cop repeated firmly. "Whaddya think you're doin'?"

"What am I doing?"

"Yeah, right. Whatcha doin'?" said the cop, ducking his head under the stairway's arch, his eyes darting from point to point in a closer survey of the stairwell.

"What does it look like I'm doing?" Sox snapped.

"How 'bout breakin' and enterin'?"

Sox looked up at him, rolling his eyes in disbelief. "Breaking and entering? Breaking and entering?"

"That's what we call it, son," the cop said simply.

"Well, this happens to be my home. Yes, I'm guilty of breaking and entering—breaking into and entering my own home."

"Your home?"

"That's what we call it, officer."

"You live here?"

"Who'd you think lives here—President Crayon?"

The cop's face hardened in confusion. "The old man says he watched you for thirty minutes while you tried to break in here. That's why he called us."

Sox shot a glance at the old man who remained positioned squarely behind the cop's shoulders, his head shifting slightly to return Sox's look, then pulling back to safety.

"He watched me? All he watched was his own piss pouring down on me."

The cop half-turned toward the old man, his eyes never leaving Sox, his right hand still kneading his holster.

"That true, old man?"

"Well…uh, yeah, but that ain't no crime," said the old man, pawing at his crotch. "I stopped a crime."

"Crime!" Sox erupted. "What crime?"

"Now don't get pissed off, fella," the cop admonished.

"Pissed off! I got *pissed on!*"

Thirty minutes later, after much explaining, including walking back to his car, jimmying the window, retrieving his keys, returning to his apartment and demonstrating those were the keys to open and close that door, along with producing various forms of identification, including his White House pass, Sox bid farewell to the cop. There was little sorrow to their parting, the befuddled cop shuffling off mumbling about the evening having been one of the "dingdongest doozies" in his law enforcement career.

Sox started to lock the door but then thought, why? Until the panes of glass were replaced, anyone could just reach inside and help themselves. He'd nail some plywood up as a temporary cover. Ready to collapse, he was momentarily revisited by agitation at remembering he still had phone duty. A quick dial of the White House operator brought relief—no new calls awaited.

Covered with grime from his duel with the door, his next stop was the shower, the rush of warm water helping to soothe the quivers of pain lingering in his arm. Toweling down and fresh, he noted it was 11 p.m., a reminder there was only one act left in bringing this flawed weekend to closure. He punched the phone's buttons corresponding to Flaxen's number, a shiver passing over him.

"Hello," she answered softly.

"Hi, it's me—the guy who's ready to do a mega crawl across the country if it leads to that spot in your heart where sympathy for yours truly has a niche." He knew it was gooey, but dammit, it was the truth. So he added: "That's a lot of syrup, I know, but if a press spokesman is known for his credibility, then you just heard mine to the maximum."

Silence occupied the line. Enough that it seemed to him that a world record for dead air between a man and a woman over a telephonic device had been set before she finally spoke.

"Well…" she hesitated.

"Look," he continued, "the nominations are in for jerk of the year, they opened the envelope, and I won. But how about a second chance? Don't I deserve that?"

"I don't know," she said quietly.

"I know this. I care. And I think you care. I'll take the time to make this work. I'll admit I've been an alcoholic hooked on White House junk food—the kind used to feed press needs. But I'm also hooked on you."

"Well…"

"Why don't we consider what happened between us before as the first inning and move on from there?"

"Well…"

"Well, what?"

"I just wasn't expecting this," she said, taking a deep breath.

"What this?" he persisted.

"This… this…"

The fact that she hadn't promptly become defensive and cut him off at the kneecaps buoyed him with hope. He had been braced for failure. Given everything else that had happened tonight, why not? The noncommittal nature of her response convinced him that he had a chance, even if slim.

"You won't believe what happened to me tonight," he said, deciding to shift gears.

"What?"

"Let's just say for starters that I got rained on."

For the next ten minutes there was hardly an exchange between them not laced with fits of laughter, most of it his, but some of it hers. He was making progress, chipping away, enough so that he figured what the deuce, why not drive a stake in the sand and go for it.

"Look, I know I was wrong before, but maybe it's time for you to let me make it right."

"How do I know it won't be the same all over again?"

"Come visit. Let the jury stay out till then. If you get here and it's the same old Sox, then you're on the next plane out. Sox and Flaxen are instant ancient history. But just come. Just try. See."

She hesitated again. He could hear quick intakes of breath, short rapid spurts, a giddyap in her stress level.

"When, where and what did you have in mind?"

Because he hadn't figured on making such progress, he hadn't taken his strategic thinking that far. But he was a press spokesman. Someone capable of wheeling on a dime. Where? What? When? It sounded like the five "W"s of Journalism 101. Why not have her visit in two weeks, right after the terrorism summit? His plate would be clear, and hopefully the president would be on a roll.

"How about weekend after next?"

"Isn't that when the Russians are there?" He was impressed she'd been doing her current events homework and knew the schedule.

"The last meetings are on Friday. You could come for the weekend. Come watch their joint news conference at the end, if you want."

She remained quiet, leaving him to press the receiver tighter against his ear, straining for any hint of response escaping from her barely audible breathing.

"Well?" he asked anxiously.

"Well…"

"Okay?"

For another ten seconds the line remained void of any utterance. Not a static burst. Nothing.

"Well," she finally sighed. "Okay."

His weekend at last was over.

CHAPTER EIGHTEEN

REPORTER: What abilities is the president looking for in a new
            secretary of the Interior?

SPOKESMAN: Someone with environmental qualifications other
            than being able to mow their front lawn.

It was early on Day One of the Crayon-Navikoff meetings on terrorism when the squawk box in the press room crackled with this announcement:

"A statement from the press secretary is now being placed in the bins."

THE WHITE HOUSE
Office of the Press Secretary

FOR IMMEDIATE RELEASE

STATEMENT BY THE PRESS SECRETARY

By mutual agreement between the parties, no specific details regarding content of the meetings between President Crayon and President Navikoff will be provided at the briefing today or tomorrow. Upon conclusion of the two days of meetings, the two leaders will hold a joint news conference in the East Room to review their discussions. This ground rule also includes agreement that there will be no background briefings by officials of either side during this period.

This notice is being posted in the spirit of assuring fairness for all who are covering these talks and to emphasize that there will be no variance from this policy for either side.

The statement had barely left the hands of the lower press office staffers distributing it when howls rumbled up from deep in the bowels of the press room.

"It's all about leaks, guys—"

"Welcome to drip, drip, drip time in our nation's capital!"

"Hang a grip on reality!"

"Let the leaking games begin!"

"Sieve city!"

"Crayon's trying to—"

"—keep the lid on!"

"—you can't stop the leaks!"

"Mark this policy down under the category of 'nice try'!"

Later in the day, as reports out of the initial meeting had begun to move on the wire services and hit the airwaves, it was obvious not everyone had adhered to the agreement. Even with J.Y.'s statement as an attempt at trying to shape the flow of news, there had already been leaking. And spinning. By someone. Or someones. What the leaks confirmed was that the session had not gone well. Despite the president's efforts to keep the talks focused on sanctions against countries sponsoring terrorism, Navikoff and his delegation had continued to bring up the issue of economic guarantees for Russia. Progress had not been a product of the first day.

The fact was that both sides had agreed not to talk to the press, even on background. The fact was that both sides were talking to the press, on background. The result was news leads headlining the fact that President Crayon's highly touted terrorism summit had thus far been idling in neutral. Even though the two leaders had met before and found areas of agreement to plumb, this time they didn't seem to be bonding.

For Sox's part, his ass was in the wringer again, under fire for having made what he thought was harmless small talk with Navikoff during an Oval Office photo op. It had backfired.

While helping usher six separate waves of media into the Oval Office for individual photo sessions with the leaders, he had positioned himself near the fireplace and behind Navikoff who was seated there with the president, each in one of the room's two wingback chairs.

With both men making idle chitchat while trying to fill the interludes between groups of reporters and cameras coming and going, and each growing impatient with the extended process, Sox had leaned over to the Russian translator and said: "You are our friends in this room, not the press."

Apparently the message's intent got garbled in the translation. The president hadn't smiled when Navikoff whispered in his ear and nodded at Sox.

Now Day Two had arrived, a day in which Sox had hoped to avoid contact with the president, yet here he was with J.Y. being summoned at 8 a.m. to the Oval Office.

"How come he wanted me to come with you?" he asked uneasily as they turned into the reception area outside the Oval Office.

"I think he wants to give us the green light to go ahead and play the background game to the hilt," J.Y. said.

The president's secretary nodded them into the room. Once inside, they joined approximately 20 other bodies fawning around the Oval Office desk, each trying to edge close, but not too close, to a president who sat stiffly braced, glaring at his visitors through eyes swollen with irritation. Gathered around him were the highest rank of administration movers and shakers. And a few lesser lights.

They were:

The secretary of State

The secretary of Defense

The director of the National Security Council

Support staffs of all of the above.

The last group, jittery, paper-ladened aides, hovered near their bosses, faces furrowed in meaningful purpose, those faces pretty much unknown to the public and even the press, some of whom Sox recognized while not knowing their names. Like many people in the White House and EOB, he had nodding acquaintances throughout the complex, those to whom he could attach a place but not a name.

Quad stood to the side, nodding silently as they fanned out around the desk, the key players in front. The president's hands gripped the edge of the desk forcefully as he studied the faces studying him. Visually touring the ranks and reaching Sox, his face hardened. He lingered there a moment, pondering, as if retrieving a mental footnote filed earlier, then moved on.

Survey complete, he stood and turned his back on the group, staring out the window at the light rain now sweeping across the lawn and Secret Service command post that sat at the intersection of the walkway from the Oval Office and the driveway. He remained motionless, appearing lost in his thoughts or perhaps mesmerized by the rain's staccato beat against the window. Sox understood. Looking out through the mist, the command post was enshrouded in a watery shimmer, a ghost-like apparition appearing to rise from the bog. Who wouldn't be intrigued by that scene, especially just outside the Oval Office?

Sometimes on rainy days, with the fireplace alive with fresh-crackling embers, the Oval Office could actually feel warm. Not cozy. But warm. No small feat for a large, round room. As they stood waiting, the coals in the fireplace sagged, several stubbily charred bits rolling out onto the hearth and dying. It was an ill omen, Sox thought, the room growing more chill.

The president wheeled around, eyes crisscrossing the group as he leaned forward, palms down on the desk.

"Washington, we've got a problem," he said firmly. "This Russian-U.S. hen party is offtrack. We've got to stop the bleeding, get the meeting up to tempo and back in gear."

All around the room, heads nodded in uniform agreement.

"We've got leaks out the wazoo," the president continued, his tone growing sharper. "War on terrorism? Hell, what we need is a war on leaks. This is the only house in town where it's wetter inside than out."

Again heads nodded, some feet shifting, eyes roaming and shoulders shrugging in "who me?" innocence.

"Look at the damn leads in the papers!" the president exclaimed, grabbing one of the newspapers neatly arrayed on one side of the desk. "'It's slow-going thus far in the initial talks on terrorism, sources said… a case of two leaders groping to find common ground on the issue, those same sources indicated…'"

He tossed the paper aside.

"Sources say, sources say. I say we've worked too hard to have this meeting sabotaged by spinmeisters playing the leak game with the pressies. We cut the meat out of the press briefing for two days in order to keep the lid on this thing. I can damn sure keep my mouth zipped for two days. Anybody here who can't, if I catch you, I'll use the splintered end of a baseball bat to run your butt out of this White House and far from life in this administration."

Quad edged forward into the president's line of sight.

"Mr. President, I think if anyone in this room were doing the leaking, there'd obviously be a more positive slant to the stories."

"I agree!" the president retorted. "But I've also been around this town long enough to know that along the Potomac River reside some people who suffer from ego-driven diarrhea of the mouth. They love for the press to know they have access. They love for the press to think they're a big deal. I'm just not so sure that all this source stuff is dribbling out of the mouths of the fellas from Moscow."

"Mr. President," Quad said, "I think what we need to do is—"

"—make sure everyone here is singing from the same hymnbook," the president interjected. "As far as I'm concerned, we're all humming without lyrics until after Navikoff and I hold our joint press conference tomorrow. Got it?"

Heads all around again uniformly nodded "yes." Other than the president, Sox had yet to encounter a bona fide "no man" in the White House.

"Now that we've all agreed to stick a cork in our mouths, does anyone have any other suggestions?" asked the president.

J.Y. looked left and right in the ranks, then cleared his throat. "Mr. President, in all fairness, just because we agree not to background the press, that won't keep the Russians from cozying up to key reporters. They've learned from us how to play that game. What you're suggesting is that we surrender the opinion-molding turf for two days. I don't think we should do that."

The president scanned the room to see if anyone might be inclined to second that view. None did. Sox wasn't surprised. There were no life rafts for the brave in the Oval Office. Open your mouth in opposition here and be as welcome as a headwind of halitosis.

"J.Y., I appreciate that. Sure, they may well be spinning the press, but I'd like to see if we can pull this thing off on the merits of the message. And what is that message? It's simple. Who is for terrorism? Who is against it? We've got to keep them focused on that and get off the side issues."

The room again fell quiet, the president using the pause to move around from behind his desk, stepping into their midst, like a coach rallying his team with last-minute rah-rah for the ensuing fray.

"Any other ideas?" he asked, his manner becoming more relaxed, an invitation rather than a challenge.

One of the State Department aides spoke up, followed by a National Security Council staffer, offering minor refinements to the talking points the president had used in the first day's meetings, subtle tweaks aimed at keeping the dialogue narrowed to the single issue.

"I know how to follow the script," the president said. "I also know how to ad-lib. Anything else?"

Sox glanced around and saw only reticence. These suggestions were only fancy ribbons and bows tied on words and phrases to use in trying to charm Navikoff. Now it occurred to him that maybe a spontaneous action of some sort might be the twist that the talks needed. Maybe that was the problem—too much talk. Maybe they needed to take this show on the road. Take it to America. Door-to-door. But not too far. The suburbs would be far enough.

"Anyone else?" the president repeated.

Why not give it a shot, Sox thought. Nothing to lose. Go for it. No use in hiding the idea in cold storage in the back of his brain.

"Uh, Mr. President..."

The president peered through the bodies, focusing intently on Sox, headlights fully engaged.

"Another idea, Sox?"

"Well—"

"Before you launch it, let me say that the visit with the former hostages and the reception were probably the high points of yesterday. Great ideas. Good marks."

"Thank you, sir."

"That's the good news. The flip side was yesterday's photo op. I'm sitting there making with the plastic smile, talking the talk, when Navikoff leans over and purrs in my ear that his translator has just told him something about being compared to our press corps. He wasn't exactly belly-laughing when he said it. I'm sitting there trying to figure out where in the hell that came from, and then he points at you."

Sox shifted uneasily. "Mr. President, he misunderstood. I was just making small talk to fill in time between waves of the photo ops."

"Waves! That's exactly what you almost made!"

"I'm sorry, sir."

"So am I," the president said through tightly pursed lips.

As if on cue, there was an accusatory nodding of heads in Sox's direction. Despite an inclination toward disgust and self-pity, his feelings were instead tempered by the thought of having witnessed J.Y.'s unflinching attempt to change the president's mind, a noble, if unsuccessful, try.

What was equally significant to Sox was that despite J.Y. having opposed the president, the course of human events in the Western Hemisphere had amazingly not screeched to a halt just because an aide had had the gall to lob a contrary suggestion right at the man. A rattling discovery, to be sure, the eyes of some of the lower-level hirelings in the room having widened in disbelief as J.Y. made his case. But wonder of wonders, J.Y. had spoken his piece and was still here, still breathing, still standing. Life flight and paramedics had not been rushed to the scene.

Better to be a quasi "no man" than no man at all, Sox thought. If J.Y. had survived, so would he, despite his current residency on the president's probation list. Might as well thrust the shoulders back and give it a go.

"Mr. President, maybe there's another way to get you and Navikoff in better sync—to get him tuned in to your message on terrorism."

The president cocked his head apprehensively.

"Yes?"

"Maybe the two of you need to take a break—something completely away from the to-and-fro of the talks—something that'll have both of you making with pats on the back, slapping palms, and exchanging high fives."

"That should be interesting. And what do you think will make that happen—an alcoholic-induced binge?"

"No, sir. Something spontaneous. An action so spontaneous that no one will have time to leak it to the press."

The president chortled lightly under his breath.

"Imagine that, an action taken by yours truly before it can be leaked, before any source has had time to phone it in. Imagine me being the actual source of news rather than the sources. There's a showstopping twist. Government by action, not by leak. What will people think?"

"You're right, sir. That'll be our result. But there'll be more. What I'm suggesting is a people thing, something that will show Navikoff how you care for people everywhere, the same people who could be victimized by terrorism anywhere."

The president nodded, intrigued. "Go on."

Sox paused, taking stock of faces other than the president's that were sullenly leering at him, including those who before had stood close but now had moved several steps away, their aloofness and raised eyebrows confirming that he was a solo act on this one.

"Sir, there may come a point in the talks today when you can suggest that maybe the two of you need to bail out of here and go take a walk. Better still, a ride and a walk. Just get up and go take him for a ride. In a car, I mean. As you're riding along, just pick a house at random, not some place swarmed on and scouted by the Advance Office, but a totally impromptu stop so Navikoff will see it's not some precooked, staged event. The two of you can go up and knock on the door and see what happens. At the very least, you can point out that these are folks who can be impacted by terrorism at any time, just like regular folks in the suburbs of Moscow. Terrorism doesn't abide city limits. It would get the two of you out of the White House, away from artificiality, talking about people and to people, just regular Joe Six-Packs. It would inject the human element into the talks for both of you."

As he finished, it became completely still in the room, save for jaws dropping in awe. Freeze-frame still. Sticker-shock silence. No one seeming to breathe. Sox shifted uneasily. He wished he had a knife to cut the tension. The president rocked back firmly on his heels, squarely facing him.

"Door-to-door diplomacy, huh?"

"Yes, sir. But just one door."

"Like I'm selling something?"

"Yes, sir. That's exactly what you'd be doing—selling a way of life that's essential to be protected from terrorism."

The president stiffened and turned to the others.

"Comments?"

"Mr. President, we've blocked out today's schedule in terms of the content and participants," the secretary of state interjected. "It's going to be a full day. It would be very tough to shoehorn any other events onto the agenda."

"What about the press?" challenged a National Security Council staffer.

"What about them?" Sox countered.

"The president can't go anywhere off the grounds without the press."

"Hey, you're telling Noah about the flood," Sox said. "No sweat. We'll take them along, a travel pool. We'll give them five minutes notice, a scramble. With such a short fuse, it'll be hard to leak in advance, and it'll be hard to leak specifics that are so nonspecific."

"Anything that's hard to leak, I like," the president declared. "As to whether or not we should consider such a thing, let me point out that I've heard more absurd ideas floated in this room. Thanks, Sox. We'll table it for now."

"Yes, sir."

"Once more it looks like you've managed to work your way off the resuscitator with me," the president grinned. He moved closer and patted Sox lightly on the shoulder, an act of guarded appreciation. Sox relished the moment of recognition, noting envy in some eyes. He also noticed that some had moved closer to him after hearing the president's response, their loyalty seemingly measured in shifting centimeters.

A brief discussion followed regarding the day's meeting schedule, and then all were dismissed except for the inner circle of foreign policy advisors.

"You love to stir-fry the old man's juices with your schemes, don't you?" J.Y. whispered as they exited and made a right turn into the hallway past the Cabinet Room, then to the left for the few remaining steps to the upper press office. Sometimes when leaving the Oval Office, they would cut through the Roosevelt Room, but a meeting in progress this morning precluded using that path.

"Schemes? I prefer to use the proper White House vernacular—short-range scheduling initiatives."

"Fancy rhetoric for a funny idea."

They swung open the door to be greeted by a crowd of reporters blocking the way to their respective offices.

"Nothing for you until the briefing!" J.Y. shouted above the noise, pushing his way past and slamming his door.

"And there'll be nothing then!" Sparta shouted angrily.

The mob swung around and surrounded Sox, who began elbowing bodies in a thrust toward his cubicle.

The level of babble oscillated throughout the room like a radio being tuned between stations.

"Sox, can you confirm the rumor that the talks have bogged down and may be shortened today?"

"What I can confirm is what J.Y. just told you," he said, earnestly pushing free into his office, a collective groan rising up in his wake and settling over his pursuers.

"This place sucks!" screamed a voice in the pack.

"So does my golf game!" added another voice.

"Screw your golf game!"

"Screw you!"

Sox wondered what Abraham Lincoln would have thought about such verbal squalor in the White House.

Three hours later, Sparta's prediction about the briefing proved right. Despite an hour-and-a-half of rumor-inspired questions, J.Y. held the line. Other than basic answers as to the length of the meetings, names of the support-staff participants from each side and what the two leaders would have for lunch, he provided very little substance to advance the story. In fact, none. It hadn't been easy, but he had adhered to the game plan and left it to the president and Navikoff to fill in the blanks tomorrow at their joint news conference.

Shortly after 2 p.m., with the press on hold, Sox felt confident enough to drift downstairs for a late lunch in the White House Mess. Usually he and J.Y. went together, but the latter was occupied with two television reporters intently (albeit unsuccessfully) trying to wheedle leaks from the press secretary.

Entering the intimacy of the Mess, he sat down at the circular staff table. Except for two staffers from the congressional relations office, the room was empty. He always got a buzz from eating in the Mess. A real power trip. Just to have the privilege of dining in that small room was a perk of stature, one pickily bestowed upon those with the rank of special assistant to the president and above. Such status provided access to this room, a club within a house within a compound. An inner sanctum within an inner sanctum. For those who didn't make the cut—that being the larger part of the staff—they were relegated to "carry out"—a tray carried to one's desk. Some of those in the West Wing without Mess privileges walked over to the EOB and used its cafeteria. Although never openly confessing to visiting there, Sox occasionally and quietly sought this latter site as a lunchtime refuge.

Sometimes the strategy backfired, particularly when minions based in the EOB would spot him: "Gee, Mr. St. Louis, why are you having lunch here when you could be in the Mess?" Trying to make some gung-ho junior aide understand the lure of that location's escapism was time-consuming, so usually he just shrugged and replied with tongue planted firmly in cheek: "The food in the Mess is too good. I prefer something more bland."

The Mess steward handed him the four-page menu, its cover adorned in bold blue letters that read: *Welcome to the White House Staff Mess*, above which was a presidential seal. The pages were loosely bound by a twisted blue cord, resembling a mortar board tassel. A sketch of the West Wing façade adorned the back page, one which offered this insight: *The White House Staff Mess, located on the ground floor of the West Wing, was established by President Truman in June, 1951. Today, following years of tradition, the Mess functions much in the same way that it did in its early days.*

Opening it, his eyes scanned the list of items he knew so well, one of the day's specials, however, catching his eye: "Roast capon with seasoned cornbread stuffing, cranberry relish and sautéed zucchini." Somehow it just didn't seem like a sautéed zucchini kind of a day.

But no matter what the food offerings were, the Mess was always a soothing place, quiet, with low conversations, and in addition to the staff table, there were separate dining tables, paneled walls and thick carpet. A safe haven for those seeking hyper-calm.

It was also easy to eavesdrop at the staff table. Its circular pattern, placing diners in close proximity to one another, virtually assured a lack of privacy and a paradise for leakers grubbing around the underbelly of the White House for news. If one was alone, taking a seat at the staff table usually assured not eating alone. This was the White House version of the Algonquin Round Table, sans the flow of quick witticisms. At times, this round table could be pretty square. Talking budget numbers over split pea soup was not spellbinding fare.

As he continued to study the menu, he was interrupted by a steward placing a phone in front of him, its attached cord instantly being plugged into a tableside socket. The efficiency of the act suggested it was an oft-repeated exercise.

Taking a phone call in the Mess was yet another form of White House power trip. It was also an occasional ploy used by staffers to impress other diners. The scam was simple. A friend would call there and the recipient be brought the phone, then answering in a voice loud enough to carry across the room: "Hello…yes, Mr. President…" Games. The Mess was not absent its own forms of self-serving showmanship.

"Hello."

"I called the press office, and they tracked you down," Flaxen's breathy voice intoned.

"Yeah, the White House operators are pretty amazing. They can find spit in the ocean," he answered, fighting to resist a meltdown under her feathery coo.

"That's a nice comparison," she said sarcastically. "That glad to hear from me, huh?"

He swallowed hard, chewing inwardly on himself for the flippancy of his comment.

"Hey, this call is at the top of today's happiness highlight reel. What I meant was, bless those White House operators for being so efficient."

"Speaking of White House *operators*…" her voice trailed off.

He decided to let that dig pass. No need to joust with her. Just get her airborne to D.C.

"Okay, this is on the record—when are you getting here?"

"How about tonight?" she answered bluntly.

He liked that a lot. At least a busy day could now possibly be followed by a busy night. A good kind of busy. "Sure," he enthused. "When?"

"I'm on the Atlanta leg now of a trip that ends later in Baltimore."

"Speaking of legs…" his voice trailed off.

"Down, Rover," she chided. "If I get in a little late, I'll still see you tonight, right?"

"The only way it won't happen is if I step off the edge of the earth."

"There's always that possibility in your job, isn't there?" she laughed.

"Only in the briefing room."

The congressional relations office aides across from him abruptly broke into snorting hoots over a joke one had told.

"Are you in someone else's office?" she asked.

"Mess."

"You're in a mess?"

"Yes, sometimes, but I mean the Mess—the place where we chow down."

"Oh."

"Yeah, it's great. We don't have to lower a tray table to get a meal."

"But I'll bet you don't have that heavyweight champion of hunger-killers sought by parched and weary travelers around the globe."

"That would be the contents of the liquor cart?"

"No, that would be our savory peanuts."

"Right. But when's the last time you served sautéed zucchini on a flight?"

"Is that a meal or a punishment?"

He glanced at his tablemates. They had stopped snickering and were now intently studying him as they followed his side of the conversation.

"Look, I'd better ring off," he said, his voice dropping low. "So what time?"

"Around dusk. Will you still be there?"

"Sure, I'm always here. Besides, we've got the Russians in town. Just check in at the northwest gate when you get here. I'll meet you there."

"Okay."

He wondered why she hadn't asked him where she would stay, a puzzlement that lasted only an instant.

"Where will I stay?"

He, of course, wanted to matter-of-factly say, "At my place." Instead, he opted for a press secretary-ish response.

"Why don't we go by my place first, you can freshen up there, and then we'll see about getting you checked in somewhere before we head off into the night."

He knew it sounded fishy. He knew she knew it sounded fishy. Still, there was little hesitancy in her voice.

"Your place, then someplace, right?"

"Right."

"Northwest gate entrance?"

"Right."

"And then, what was it you said—off into the night?"

"Right. You and me spinning off into the nighttime of our nation's capital."

"In which direction?"

"One guaranteed not to take us in opposite directions."

"I thought press spokesmen never made guarantees."

"At least not on the record."

"And this is…?" she said, her voice again drifting off.

"On the record."

"What about other diversions this time?"

"That's another guarantee. There'll be none."

"What about the Russians?"

"They can go to the singles bars."

"Then I guess I'll see you later."

"I didn't think you made guarantees, either."

"You just heard one, pal. Bye."

Hanging up and giddily emboldened, he decided to order the zucchini. One of the aides at his table winced: "You're a brave man, Sox."

"Hey, St. Louis, was that phone call about making news or just about making somebody?" the other one asked smugly.

He was used to letting such flak slide by. These were BB shots compared to the press blasts endured in his office and the briefing room. He began to attack the newly arrived zucchini, shoveling it down with a dispatch that had the green stuff rapidly disappearing, leaving his table-mates to watch in bemused wonder.

"Maybe with the Russians here we should have had borscht today," one of them quipped.

"Yeah," added the other, "or at least shots of vodka to kill off the zucchini."

He continued to ignore them, preferring to use these free moments to gorge himself. He was hungry and happy. Today's meal could be microwaved manure for all he cared. Tuning out lunchtime jabber by other staffers was a well-nurtured skill, particularly if it meant dismissing their oftentimes preoccupation with "The Hill." Their talk of Congress always seemed to be wrapped in holy-like references to "The Hill." "What's the word from The Hill?" "How will The Hill go on this vote?" "What did The Hill do on the appropriations bill?" The Hill. The Hill.

The Hill.

He had once tried to turn such reverence to his advantage. It was at a party in Georgetown, the target being a buxom lass whose starry-eyed intoxication with political Washington suggested that exalted Hill status might result in a direct route to her heart and elsewhere.

After approaching her and making some perfunctory small talk, the subject of respective work locations had surfaced.

"Where do you work?" she asked.

"On The Hill," he boasted.

She paused, wrinkling her nose in labored confusion.

"Really? What hill?" she giggled.

That cured him. Never again.

All the food on his plate had nearly disappeared by the time the steward again delivered the phone to his seat. Unfortunately, there was no one left to be impressed. The room was now empty, save for him.

"Hello," he said, forking down the last mouthful.

"Get your butt up to the motorcade fast!" J.Y. ordered.

"Whaa?"

"Damned if the president hasn't bought into that dopey drivel of yours about taking Navikoff for a ride. Right in the middle of this afternoon's session, they decided to do it. The motorcade's ready to roll."

"What about the press pool?" Sox asked anxiously.

"Done. They're on the way out. You'd better haul ass. See you there."

Choking on the last gooey remnants of the zucchini, he bolted for the South Lawn driveway, breaking into a full sprint as he reached the colonnade. Along the way he reasoned that if his suggestion was being implemented, then surely the president had decided that the Crayon-Navikoff chemistry needed work. Maybe there wasn't any chemistry at all. Why else would the president resort to this Sox-inspired mobile photo op? And what if it backfired? What if being in the limousine together only made things worse? What if one of them had bad breath? Such worries tormented him as he raced through the ground floor of the residence toward the diplomatic entrance.

Out on the driveway the motorcade was assembled, engines revving and ready to roll. He scrambled for the rear of the line and the two press vans. The first was crammed to capacity with camera equipment and an excess of bodies rubbing grittily against one another, a heaving spasm of flesh.

The second van had an empty seat on its back row. As he wedged into its innards, an authoritative voice boomed out over his staff radio: "To all cars and stations, signal depart, depart."

They were moving, but toward what and where? Only the president could answer that. Sox's suggestion had been that the two leaders just get in a car and take off for nowhere in particular, just drive, chitchat, crack jokes, air things out and then maybe stop somewhere unannounced. Now it was happening, a presidential motorcade passing through the streets of Washington en route to a non-destination destination. Presidential motorcades usually left the grounds knowing their ultimate destination. This might be a first. It could also be a last. He knew if this proved a bust, he had probably earned himself another turn at the podium in the briefing room. Or maybe even being fired. He'd prefer to be fired.

As they gradually picked up speed down the circular driveway, he found himself being whipsawed by reporters who had turned the van into a seething hotbox of rumors.

"Where to, Sox? The boys out for a little fast food—burgers and fries?"

"Or did they get bored and decide to go play miniature golf?"

"I say they're gonna cruise the avenue."

"Whadda ya say, Sox? Where are they headed? Where are we headed?"

"And why?"

"Yeah, what's the guidance?"

"Hey, my coat has lint all over it."

"So what? You don't know the difference between lint and Lent."

"C'mon, Sox, give. What are these guys up to? Where are we going?"

"It's not an emergency, is it?"

That question froze everyone. They were all aware that sometimes in situations like these, such questions were not answered by words tumbling from one's mouth, but more by a look in the eye, a nod, a wink, a feint of the head, a dropping of the eyes. All eyes were now riveted on Sox. Without the benefit of leaks to guide their way, the playing field on this one was level. He was all they had.

Tommy Tuff leaned close, nose-to-nose. "What's the story behind the story? The talks broken down? Why did these fellas just suddenly up and pop for a ride?"

Sox ducked down in his seat, stealing a glance between the bodies to where he could see they had turned left onto Pennsylvania Avenue. Aware that there were hospitals on the route ahead, he needed to respond immediately and with calm.

"There is absolutely no emergency of any kind," he assured. It was a nice try, his subdued manner doing nothing to quell the firestorm that erupted in his face.

"How do you know?"

"How do we know that you know?"

"If it isn't an emergency, then why else would they interrupt the talks?"

"Is it a heart attack?"

"Which one of them is sick?"

"Shh…let him answer."

He turned his palms upward in the cramped space, signaling for calm amidst the clamor.

"Everybody take a chill pill. Let me repeat—there is absolutely no emergency. Nobody's sick. No problem. Nobody's had a heart attack unless it's somebody from bouncing off the walls of this van while going ballistic."

"Cut the snow job, Sox," Tuff snapped. "Is something wrong? We need to know. The American people have a right to know."

"The only thing wrong is that there's a bad case of the berserks running loose in this van," Sox lightly scolded.

"So what's going on?" Tuff insisted.

Sox swallowed and inhaled a deep breath. He needed to buy a little time to keep his cool and make sure their rapid-fire popping off, the intensity of which had now forced him down between sweaty bodies in the back row, wouldn't cause him to lash out and return fire with some in-your-face verbal venom. The thought was extremely tempting. Instead, he shrugged, chewing thoughtfully on his lower lip to assure a measured response that would appear routinely casual.

"The president wanted to take a break and show Navikoff some of the city. That's all."

Having so stated, he could only pray that was still the case. After all, he hadn't even had a chance to ask J.Y. where they were headed. In the meantime he knew this mini press riot needed tamping down instantly or else the rumor mill, fast approaching full throttle, would be a runaway train. Yet there was nothing else he could say. He was caught in guidance limbo, a prisoner in press spokesman's hell.

"Okay, so they're out joyriding," Tuff persisted. "Where do we think they might be going? A tour of the monuments?"

"Would you believe me if I told you I don't know?" Sox said, the hint of futility in his voice unleashing a storm of protest that so fiercely buffeted the vehicle's insides, the van veered out of the motorcade's path for an instant before the driver regained control and wheeled back in line.

"He calls himself a press spokesman for the leader of the Free World, and he's completely tapped out on information. What a joke!"

"Incredible!"

"Implausible."

"Stupid!"

They were right. But he'd have to live with it, make with the press secretaryish-type answers and do the double-talk two-step until they got somewhere. As always, a press spokesman trying to pursue his job without the benefit of information was an empty windsock.

He turned away, trying to escape their ranting for a few seconds and gather his wits. Pressing his face hard against the window, his eyes settled on a solitary figure on the sidewalk, an old man teetering in the wind, hunched and unsteady. After a moment's study, Sox recognized him, a former senator and one-time presidential candidate from three decades past. In his prime he had been a media darling, lionized during his brief stay at the forefront of the national political arena. The citizens of the early primary states had been less enamored, dismissing him in back-to-back losses that hastened his entry into the club reserved for political castoffs, relics of yesterday's news. Now he was a has-been, poking along and so enfeebled that the presence of a nearby presidential motorcade failed to arouse even the cock of his head. Passing by this fallen idol, Sox suddenly felt paralyzed by sadness, a condition he was sure would not be understood by those in the van should he point the man out. He decided to say nothing, leaving the man alone with thoughts that occupy those to whom the political gods have once offered hope, then denied glory. The motorcade continued past, picking up speed as it crossed over the bridge leading onto M Street and into downtown Georgetown. He continued to look back until the man had disappeared, his silhouette swallowed up in the coldness of concrete corridors.

"Oh, I get it," Tuff sneered. "We're going to Georgetown on a shopping junket. Navikoff wants to pick up some curios while he's in town—you know, one of those little glass things that you turn upside down and it's snowing on the Capitol."

Sox shrunk further down in his seat, letting their chatter pass without offering any response. His mind had still not let go of the specter of the old man.

"So where are we going, Sox?"

"And wherever it is, did the president discuss this movement with anyone before deciding to take off?"

"Sure, he discussed it," Tuff injected. "With himself."

"Sox, on the jobs bill—"

"Screw the jobs bill! We've got something much bigger here!"

"Screw the jobs bill? That'll be tough—it's just a piece of paper."

"Yeah, and foreplay with paper is such a messy thing."

"Unless it's toilet paper. Right, Sox?"

As long as they fussed with one another, he didn't need to respond. Not that he could. He had already maxed out on answers. Even though he was the one who had suggested that the president take this impromptu trip, he was just another passenger along for the ride. But to where? And how much further?

"Sox, do you have anything on the mudslide in California—will the president declare it a disaster area?"

Tommy Tuff glared at the reporter who had just asked that question.

"No, he's going to declare your brain a disaster area. Stick to what's happening right now."

"Hey, Tuff, cram a corncob up your ass."

"With a rusty crowbar."

Suddenly Tuff lunged forward across bodies, swinging wildly at the reporter who had offered the last comment, the attempted blow glancing off the right side of his target's face. The reporter, a radio network correspondent, swung around and attempted as best he could in the cramped quarters to strike back, his arms flailing in Tuff's direction, a lot of windmill action but little contact. Still, he didn't let up, continuing to throw left and right combinations, leaning over the seat and pounding against Tuff's forearms which the latter was using shield-like, bending over and protecting his head.

What next? Sox thought. A fistfight in the press van in the midst of a presidential motorcade. Bizarre. Of course there were days in this White House when bizarre was a work in progress. Silently he was rooting for the radio reporter who continued to swing away, albeit with little luck, Tuff having now curled himself into an even tighter and more secure position. Adding a sidebar of color to the fisticuffs was a betting pool that had immediately sprung up in the van's front row, the oddsmakers favoring Tuff's opponent. The enthusiasm for this wagering action and the fact that no other reporter had made the slightest move to break up the fight convinced Sox that maybe he wasn't alone in his preferred choice of combatants. Nor was the audience faint in its thirst for action.

"Beat his butt!"

"Ditto that!"

"Dial that son-of-a-bitch out!"

"Swing now—you've got the wind behind you!"

"Stop the motorcade!"

"Stop the bleeding!"

"The gore, the violence, the daring, the boredom!"

"Let 'em fight. It beats driving to nowhere!"

"Fight? What fight? I've seen better brawls in the boys' bathroom at the junior prom!"

A beefy member of the television pool crew leaned forward and pushed the radio reporter backwards, holding his arms pinned, then turned to Sox. "So much for the dueling peewees. We're ten minutes out of the grounds and still no fix on where we're gonna end up. What's the read, Sox?"

"Yeah!" hissed another reporter. "Damn straight!"

The fight had done nothing to diminish the bottled anger continuing to be vented at Sox.

"If I were a press spokesman for the president of the United States and couldn't answer where in the hell the man was going, I'd have a drooling case of diarrhea of the worry glands."

"Ditto that!"

"Are we just driving around?"

"Or are we lost?"

"Whatever's happening, this sucks, Sox."

Once again, they were right, but what could he do? The fact that his staff radio had been numbly silent since departure told him that perhaps no one, save for the president, knew where they might be headed.

They passed by Key Bridge, moving in tandem with the Potomac River far below as the street's grade rose steadily until it leveled off and the motorcade turned onto MacArthur Boulevard. At least he was familiar with the surroundings, his apartment being nearby. Too, they were only a few blocks from another apartment with which he was familiar, that of a senator's daughter he had once chased, that effort having resulted in a spectacular lack of success. She had denied him early on, the rebuff having added bite in that he discovered that he had been trumped by a White House colleague. That smarted, particularly since his competitor was a minor functionary in the First Lady's office. It was one thing to be beaten out by a big hitter, but to have one's nose rubbed in it by an East Wing flyweight was a jackboot planted firmly in the pit of his overinflated West Wing ego.

On and on the motorcade wound its way deeper into the suburbs, past blurs of houses and apartment units, until there was a gradual slowing down, sending every face in the van hard and alert against the windows, straining to maintain eye contact with the president's limousine ahead.

"Something's happening, gang!" someone yelled.

The television pool crew hurriedly thrust equipment to their shoulders, yanking straps in place.

"We're slowing down."

"Or...turning around."

"What is this?"

"Sox, get on that damn radio and get the word."

He was hesitant to transmit. Virtually nothing had passed over the radio since departure. Unusual, to be sure, but maybe there was a good reason. Maybe the president had wanted it that way. His face pressed firmly against the window, he could see the lead car turning left around the esplanade and slowly crawling back up MacArthur Boulevard the other way. He groped behind him on the seat, reaching for his radio only to have it come alive in his hand with the commanding voice of the base station operator.

"Base to all cars and stations, signal arrive, arrive."

Arrive? Where? In the middle of the street? There was no time to ponder that question as the reporters and camera crew were already grabbing for the doors, scrambling over each other out into the street, across the esplanade and toward the president's limousine which, along with the rest of the motorcade, had eased to a stop.

He peeled through the disembarking bodies and raced ahead, utilizing foot speed that had served him as a high school track standout. Being fast on one's feet as a presidential spokesman sometimes had no relationship to being nimble in answering tough questions. Sometimes it meant just being able to haul ass faster than anyone else.

Reaching the other side of the esplanade, he found J.Y. standing on the curb surveying the one-story house in front of which the lead cars of the motorcade had parked. Paint-chipped and weather-scarred, its weedy front yard was crawling with agents. Normally, they would be combing the grounds. Here there was little ground to comb, save for scraggly patches of crabgrass.

"What's the drill?" Sox panted as he caught up.

J.Y. cocked his head, glaring at him out of the corner of an eye.

"This one's on you, pal. The boss decided to take Navikoff for a spin—your grand idea for showing him a bit of America beyond Pennsylvania Avenue. What we have to do now is figure out what spin to put on this lark."

"Whose house is this?"

"How in the jake would I know? This is your scheme. The president's doing just what you suggested—stopping at some random house so Navikoff won't think it's a precooked deal—the house, the family, nothing rehearsed. No advance person's footprints anywhere."

"But I wonder who does live here?"

"Whoever it is, let's hope they have indoor plumbing."

"And cable TV."

"Yeah, maybe Navikoff and the president can watch some 1960s reruns."

"What about the press pool?"

"Hold 'em out front in the street so they'll have a clean photo of the front-door scene, but far enough away that they can't pick up any audio."

Press pool positioning—an essential in achieving good spin. In making photos that were a slam dunk for the administration. Always make pictures that make the man look presidential. That was the standing order.

Suddenly there was action thirty yards behind them on the esplanade. They turned and watched as two agents maneuvered into place, rigidly bracing themselves in front of the angry press pool and inviting their abuse.

"Hell's bells, would somebody please get these anal Adonises out of the way so we can get to the story!" Sparta screamed.

"Yeah, we need to be across the street!"

"Closer, closer, closer!"

"Crayon supports censorship!"

"Break the blockade!"

"Feed these animals so they'll go back to their cages!"

"Ramming speed!"

"Hey, J.Y., can you confirm the rumor that Crayon has a tattoo of a snake on the right cheek of his butt?"

"Or that Navikoff has a tattoo of Crayon on the left cheek of his butt?"

J.Y. and Sox watched the writhing for a few more seconds, then began walking across the street toward the house.

"Have the agents let them move across the esplanade and out into the street," J.Y. said. "They can establish a temporary pen there."

Sox glanced down the street to the nearby intersection where motorcycle police were holding the traffic in place, securing the several hundred yards of street they were now occupying. The people in those waiting cars would be steamed pissed, but such was the price for presidential spontaneity.

"Once the pool is in place, get back over here," J.Y. ordered. "I want you with us when the two leaders go up to the front door. If this turns out to make headlines for all the wrong reasons, a fiasco in somebody's front yard, I think I'll let you have the privilege of figuring out how to brief the pool."

That was a suggestion with which Sox couldn't argue. After all, here was a presidential movement that had come about through the force of his own creative impulse. J.Y. was right. It was his show to defend. The issue was, would he be explaining a success or a screwup?

Once the pool had moved forward, the television crew having set up its equipment in the middle of the street, Sox gave the "all ready" signal via a wave of his hand. J.Y., in turn, gave a "thumbs up" to the presidential limousine. A door swung open and Quad eased out, nodding for Sox to join them. While watching them intently, Sox let his attention momentarily veer to the house. What amazed him was that with all the commotion outside, there had been no sign of life from inside. Not a peek through the blinds. Nothing. The president had done his part to assure the element of surprise by ordering that no one, not even the agents, was to knock on the door in advance.

His eyes shifted back to Quad and J.Y., who were waving for him to join them. Leaving the pool to supervision by the agents, he headed across the street, picking up the pace by shifting into a trot as Quad started waving his arms in a circular "hurry up" pattern.

"C'mon, sultan of spin," Quad exclaimed. "These world leaders are ready to make a house call."

"The pool's in place," Sox said, shooting a glance back over his shoulder just to make certain.

"It's always reassuring to know that the living rooms of America won't miss out on the sight of the president visiting a living room somewhere in America," Quad observed, his voice thick with sarcasm. "I'm still not sure why we're here, but I'm just a government underling, an order-taker doing what he's been told to do."

J.Y. recoiled with an exaggerated grimace, his hands seizing his throat, as if gagging.

"Some order-taker! This coming from a man who has people whispering in his ear all day in the hope that he'll then whisper the same thing in the president's ear."

Quad half-smiled. It was a short-lived response, his manner abruptly turning serious as he grabbed J.Y. and Sox by their arms, pulling them close.

"Listen, guys, for your guidance only, things have gone good in the car. They needed this blow—away from the bargaining table. It's helped. Amazing how people sometimes change when they get ten yards west of the White House. It happens. It's happening. I think they're getting in lockstep on terrorism with some of the economic sticking points less sticky. We'll see. But that's still close hold – for your ears only."

J.Y. and Sox nodded.

"Oh, and just to give this moment a note of complete credibility, the president tossed it to Navikoff on when and where to stop. This house was his call."

"Why here?" J.Y. asked.

"Who knows, maybe it reminds him of someplace in Russia."

The three of them pondered that thought, their eyes drifting toward the house. Quad took several steps to the side as if to analyze the place from a better angle.

"Two baths, two bedrooms and no flamingos in the front yard,"

J.Y. quipped.

Quad again half-smiled, then turned and walked back over to the president's limousine. A rear window lowered, and the chief of staff eased his head inside for a few seconds before backing away, leaving two rigidly attentive agents poised by the car's door. After a moment the president and Navikoff emerged, both of them pausing tentatively, both seeming uncertain of exactly what to do next. If they were a bit disoriented, it was understandable, Sox thought. Here were two guys used to crowds, cheering, tumult and applause when exiting from cars. Today, the only sound greeting them was howling from back in the street where those in the temporary press pen were jostling for position in the tightly defined area. Such physical exertion had done nothing, however, to lessen their ability to screech uncontrollably at world leaders in hopes of gaining their attention.

"Mr. President, what's the purpose of this visit?"

"Will the terrorism talks continue here?"

"…in the kitchen?"

"Are the talks in a meltdown?"

"What's on the menu for dinner here?"

"Who in the Sam Hill lives here?"

"Who in the Sam Hill is Sam Hill?"

"Are they gonna play on that swing set in the back yard?"

"…tell 'em they need to mow the grass!"

"And fix the roof!"

"And get that dog dung out of the front yard!"

Both leaders kept moving, turning toward the press pool as they walked and holding up the palms of their hands in a sign of futility at trying to answer the spray of questions. Sox found it amusing that Navikoff even bothered to join in the gesture. He didn't understand English and didn't know what he was responding to anyway, just following Crayon's lead.

As they reached the front walk, the commingling of shouts dissolved into a garbled yapping from which no single reporter's voice was definable. Surrounding the two men was a flying wedge of Secret Service agents and Russian security personnel, all their faces taut and expressionless, their heads swiveling left and right, their eyes busily darting everywhere.

Trooping along behind, Sox looked down at the ground they were tramping over, brown and barren, little of it green or growing except for countless ants marching into the knobs of several hills. He marveled at the ants' busyness, then his eyes shifted to the sky and the shadow play of clouds overhead. As he looked upward, his lips moved silently with the murmurings of a prayer. He had good reason to be reaching out at that moment to the Almighty. Seldom was there a presidential movement, other than visits to the presidential commode, when every step wasn't choreographed in advance. Clockwork was the dictum in moving the man around. But right now it was all happening on the fly.

It was also troubling that there still had been no sign of activity from within the house. Maybe they weren't home. But if they were—good God, the presidents of the United States and Russia were about to knock on somebody's front door! It was scary. No one could be sure of anything. No one, except Sox. If this backfired, he could be certain that his White House career was once again on a fast track toward oblivion.

He wouldn't have to wait long to find out—they had reached the base of the house's crumbly front porch. Three steps up, and they would be there. He dropped back into the yard and scrambled around to the side, moving up even with the porch but only a few feet from the two leaders. From there he could better hear the conversation and watch their facial expressions, unimpeded by the layers of U.S. and Russian agents, plus Quad and J.Y., all of whom were bunched up around and behind. If he was going to have to brief the press pool on what was about to happen, it was essential he be strategically positioned where he could see and hear everything. Then he'd at least know what to tell the pool. Or, more importantly, what not to tell them.

When they reached the porch, an agent pulled the screen door open and attempted to peer into one of the wooden front door's two small panes. Standing on tiptoe, his nose rubbed against the decay-pocked surface, a chipped and peeling mural of warped neglect. The president tugged on his arm, nodding him to stop. The agent reluctantly stepped back and watched as the president circled a guiding arm around

Navikoff's shoulder, easing him forward so that they stood side-by-side facing the front door. He then indicated for their fingers to join in pressing the doorbell, a mini symbolic gesture of global unity. As they did so, the president whispered something in one of Navikoff's ears while simultaneous translation was being whispered in the other ear. The comment united them in a short-lived laugh.

Sox tried to move closer, pressing against the edge of the porch's wooden floor slats, its splintered ends gouging into his pants at thigh level. But he had found the perfect niche. From there, if he crouched down slightly, he had a clean, agent-free view of the leaders and whomever might answer the door, albeit from slightly below belt level.

Ten seconds passed. Nothing. Zilch. Not even a muffled voice from inside saying, "I'm coming." Maybe they weren't home. Maybe this could all be chalked up to just a "nice try." These two pit bulls in the battle against terrorism—Carl and Sergei—could slap each other on the back and go back to work. And Sox could swallow deep with relief.

Their forefingers again mashed down on the doorbell, the hum of its erratic buzz suggestive of a bee with bowel discomfort. Another ten seconds. The president's eyes wandered down to the left side of the porch, his raised eyebrows settling on Sox who returned his questioning glare with a "thumbs up" gesture.

Suddenly the door creaked open, diverting the president's attention. At first only a narrow slit was offered, a slice of darkness out of which leered a goggle-eyed face. Slowly the door opened wider until it was imposingly filled with the jiggling girth of a middle-aged man, unshaven, wearing a rumpled T-shirt and cradling a can of beer in one hand.

The president cleared his throat, looking around anxiously, his face stricken with the panic of a hopelessly trapped animal. He pulled Navikoff closer, using the Russian shield-like to better block the view of the press pool, then leaned in closely so that his nose was pressed lightly against the screen door's wire mesh.

"Uh, hello, I am…President Crayon and this is President Navikoff of Russia."

"Yeah, man, I recognize you," the man blustered. "Damn straight.

Right here. My place. The president. And the Russian dude."

"Yes, he's the president of Russia."

The man wearily shook his head, then patted it several times, combing his hair with his hand.

"Man, you guys caught me at a lousy time."

"Lousy?"

"Well, napping," the man said.

"Napping?" the president repeated, waiting for Navikoff's translator, then continuing. "I'm sorry if we interrupted you, but President Navikoff and I have been meeting on the subject of terrorism. In the course of those meetings, we decided it might be interesting to get out of the White House, go for a ride and stop at a random American's house to get their opinion on the subject."

"Random American?" the man challenged. "What kind is that?"

The man's bluntness shifted the president's tone to instant damage control.

"What I meant was that we thought it might help just to stop at a home where no one knew we were coming and get the opinions of the owner, a sort of spontaneous survey. A chance for President Navikoff and myself to visit firsthand with citizens outside the White House and get their take on terrorism and how it endangers us all."

"Terrorism?" the man repeated. He raised his hand to his mouth, wiping it assertively. "I'll tell you about terrorism," he continued, thrusting the beer can enthusiastically at the leaders, an innocent but overt act that stirred the agents. "Hell, guys, I've got a 16-year-old daughter who lives in a pair of tight-fitting shorts. That's terrorism."

The president nodded for the agents to relax, looking on helplessly as the translator whispered the man's response into Navikoff's ear. Navikoff shrugged, mumbling a terse reply back to the translator.

"Mr. President, President Navikoff is not clear how clothes that don't fit an American girl relate to global terrorism," the translator said dutifully.

The president winced, looking over at Sox, then turning back to the screen.

"I'm sorry, sir, I haven't gotten your name."

"No problem. You betcha. The handle is Yikes. Buster Yikes."

What an appropriate name for the moment, Sox thought. Yikes. Exactly what he wanted to scream.

"Mr. Yikes, it's a pleasure to know you," the president said. "Please meet President Navikoff."

Yikes set the beer aside and stepped out onto the front porch, the addition of another body to that space-short area forcing two members of the security detail to step back down into the yard. Yikes proceeded to pump each leader's hand with good-ole-boy gusto.

"You mentioned you were busy…I'm sorry we interrupted you," the president said, struggling to make conversation.

"Naw, never too busy for you guys. It's just me and my wife here right now—daughter's at school. We're gettin' ready to have a late lunch—sardines and crackers. Got plenty for you two guys, but I'm not sure there's enough in the feedbag for all these other folks," he nodded at the agents.

The president grimaced as the translator babbled Russian into Navikoff's ear.

"That's a very thoughtful offer," the president said. "Unfortunately, our schedule is such that we really need to get going."

For the first time since stepping out on the porch, Yikes took notice of the waiting motorcade and, beyond, the press pool.

"Damn, this is some traveling squad. Wish everybody could come in for a visit—"

"That's perfectly understandable," the president interrupted, his hand reaching for Navikoff's shoulder and a move toward departure.

"Hey, Mr. President, on this terrorism thing," Yikes said, his hand lightly grasping the president's arm, an innocent but again overt act that once more seized the rapt attention of the agents, those nearest the president closing ranks around him to block any further physical transgressions.

"Yes, Mr. Yikes."

"Look, I don't watch the TV news much, mostly wrestling, but I know that when it comes to terrorism – well, we've got to do something about it. I'm a butcher by trade, but it could happen to me. To my wife and family. To my kid. To a lot of us ordinary Joes in America and Russia and everywhere. So if you guys can get together and figure out how to stop this, then I'm all for you. Let's kick ass."

He once more extended his bearish hand to the president, forcing a vigorous handshake. Turning to Navikoff, he started to duplicate the gesture but instead raised his hand palm-forward in front of the Russian's face, inviting an exchange of high fives. After explanation by the translator, Navikoff cautiously held up the palm of his left hand which Yikes swatted firmly with his right palm, leaving the Russian to stare in wonderment at the reddened palm, trying to decipher some meaning from the ritual which had just occurred.

"Thank you, Mr. Yikes," the president said. "It has been a pleasure visiting with you. Please forgive us for the interruption. And please give our regards to the rest of your family."

Yikes saluted, then raised both hands in a thumbs-up gesture.

As the entourage descended from the porch, Sox peeled back around to the front yard to advance the pack as it headed toward the line of waiting motorcade vehicles.

"Whoa, Sox!" J.Y. yelled.

Sox didn't want to hear that voice nor any other right now. He just wanted out of there. The sooner this scene was history, the quicker the president's memory might dim that this detour in the talks bore his handprint of responsibility.

J.Y. wasn't about to let it happen. "That was certainly an interesting little episode. Not quite what we had hoped for, I'd say."

"I thought it went okay," Sox said, gamely defensive.

"Yeah, for about five seconds. Most importantly, though, is how are you gonna play this with the pool?"

"Brief the pool? Why me?"

"Your idea, Einstein—remember?"

He frowned at the reminder. Now he wished he'd never sucked up to the president with the damn idea. He wished…it was yesterday. He wished…he was with Flaxen. Tonight seemed a gazillion years away. Only a hundred yards away, the press pool was waiting, their heated cries erupting from across the esplanade.

"Mr. President, what did you discuss on that front porch?"

"…Navikoff almost step in the dog poop?"

"…front door diplomacy?"

"What's the man of the house's name?"

"What was he holding in his hand?"

"Did you guys talk some budget numbers?"

"Human rights?"

"Civil rights?"

"Wrongs and rights?"

"Do's and don'ts?"

"Racetrack results?"

"What was the purpose of all this?"

As the president and Navikoff reached their limousine, the pool broke ranks and started scrambling for the two vans at the rear of the motorcade.

J.Y. shoved Sox. "Get over there quick and tell 'em we're gonna hold the motorcade in place while you give 'em a readout."

Sox's face flushed with exasperation. "But what's the guidance? The line? How am I supposed to play this? How am I supposed to hedge those questions? How am I supposed to dance through this minefield?"

"It's simple—serve up your best purple prose. You know, some rhetorical razzle-dazzle. Just be sure you turn this escapade into a win-win for the president and Navikoff. That's all. Nothing to it. Hey, spinmeister, it was your road show. You spin it."

Sox's eyelids drooped, begging sympathy, but it was too late. The pool had begun to disassemble, its members fanning out across the esplanade, a scrambled mess of bodies. Normally he took delight in watching such scenes of press chaos, especially when the participants were facing deadlines—crunch time. But now he felt anything but glee, watching vacantly as the laggards in the ranks huffed to catch up with their speedier colleagues. In a minute, all of them would be his nemesis, gathered together as one, barking at him with questions whose answers were neither on the tip of his tongue nor part of a growth industry in his brain. This readout would be by the seat of his pants. Sort of like always. Nothing much different from the norm except at this briefing, albeit a mini briefing, there would be no assigned seats. Just standing-room-only in the middle of MacArthur Boulevard.

"Hurry!" J.Y. commanded.

Reluctantly, he began jogging toward the motorcade, angling over to cut off the front-runners in the press pack before they reached the vans. Even with halfhearted exertion, he got there first, stopping ten yards in front of the lead van, bracing his legs wide and throwing up his arms to signal a halt.

His waving attracted instant attention, and the masses surged his way, the stragglers picking up steam as cameras were slung into position, hand recorders clicked on, and notepads flipped to fresh pages. He waited silently as they gathered, paying little heed to their bunching up and milling around him impatiently in an undulant semicircle. He was preoccupied, mentally groping for a sentence or two of salvation—anything to paint a positive spin on what they had just witnessed.

Even under such duress he couldn't help musing about their temporary occupancy of one of the capital's busier streets. In his years of White House travel, he had seen temporary press filing centers set up and briefings conducted on the decks of battleships, in bingo parlors, casinos, bars and manure-laden livestock arenas. Why should conducting a briefing in the middle of a major Washington traffic artery seem weird?

Still, in looking out over the press orgy now engulfing him and beyond to the intersection and the stream of vehicles jammed for blocks waiting on them, he couldn't help but wonder if they weren't prime candidates for admission to the advanced school for the cockeyed. Here he was about to offer words to a waiting world on the latest chapter in U.S.-Russia relations, and he was camped in the middle of MacArthur Boulevard surrounded by a crush of screaming reporters. Lunacy? Perhaps. But damned if it didn't always work. Today was proving it once again. As always, despite rampant disorder, the process of making and gathering the news, the courtship between the White House and the press, was functioning even when taken on the road. Or, in this case, *in* the road.

The last bodies chugged over from the esplanade, joining the grappling and pushing to be up close and in his face. Watching their stress, he couldn't help musing—so much sweat and wrestling—all to hear so little. Quickly, though, they readied for business, expectant hands poised on notepads, eager to record his every utterance. Now if he could just think of some words.

"Let's get going so we can get going," Tommy Tuff ranted.

No matter what the situation, Sox thought, Tuff was always a sure finalist nominee for press corps prick of the moment.

"Lighten the attitude, Tommy. As soon as everyone is ready, we'll start the readout," Sox said, buying a few seconds. "The motorcade is going to hold until we're finished."

"What about filing?" asked a voice from the pack.

"We're going directly back to the White House so you can file there."

"So dish the dirt."

"We're ready."

"Spill."

"Yeah, let's have this nothing statement so we can get back. We're starting to butt up against deadlines."

Sox glanced down at the piece of paper crumpled in his right fist. It contained his hasty scribblings from back at the porch, most of it illegible. He nervously turned it over in his hand. It really didn't matter that he couldn't read most of it. He knew at that moment that any positive news coverage to result from this excursion would have to come from seat-of-the-pants guidance drawn from his own gut, not from any other source.

Even with all the reporters crowded around him and ready, he waited as the stenographer trotted over with her machine. She reached the edge of the crowd, the bodies begrudgingly parting as she burrowed through to the front. Once there, she plopped the machine down, bending over it in a tentative crouch, her reddened face reflecting the discomfort of her constricted position, but nonetheless ready to type. He knew the reporters would be clamoring for the transcript as soon as they were back at the

White House. That wouldn't be a problem. How long could it possibly take to type one page? Maybe two? His problem was thinking of anything in the next few seconds to fill those one or two pages.

Still not certain of what to say, he decided to begin at the beginning.

"It was President Crayon's suggestion that he and President Navikoff take today's totally unplanned trip to the suburbs."

"Why?"

"He felt it might be a productive way for the two leaders to…uh…get the views…unrehearsed…unstaged…unvarnished…the views of average citizens on the subject of terrorism…President Navikoff agreed, and it is my understanding that it was left to him to randomly pick the home where they stopped."

"And who picked the guy with the beer gut—central casting?"

Sox frowned in the direction of the voice. "The more popping off like that, the longer it's going to take to get back and file."

Tommy Tuff half-turned toward the rear. "Yeah, and whoever said that, shut up and ram a Fig Newton up your left nostril."

"Tuff, you fartface—"

From the vicinity of that voice two arms emerged, yanking and pulling bodies in an attempt to get to Tuff. The source of the commotion was the radio reporter seeking a reenactment of his earlier scuffle with Tuff.

"Amateur night!"

"Somebody get these runts out of the way!"

"And change their diapers!"

Two technicians from the network pool television crew forced their way between them, holding each combatant's arms, leaving legs to kick freely, but each only kicking air.

"Knock it off—both of you!" scolded an authoritative voice in the pack. "We're trying to get a handle on some news here!"

"Why not let them fight—it's more interesting than this crock of goo Sox is trying to peddle."

"If Tuff gets his ass kicked, I'm buying the brews," an anonymous voice shouted.

"Shut up! I'm on deadline."

Sox sucked in a deep breath, waiting. The extra thirty seconds was a welcome breather. Still, he'd just have to press on while trying to steer clear of any specifics. Then again, that was nothing new in this job.

"We'll get back shortly to round two of prizefight on the Potomac…an event full of drama, heartache, pathos and body odor…in the meantime, as I was saying…uh…the two leaders felt this was a unique way of…uh…hearing firsthand from citizens in a completely spontaneous way."

"So tell us about the guy at the door!"

"Just wait," Sox said firmly. "I'm getting to that."

"Well, how about trimming the rhetoric and cutting to the chase?"

He ignored the voice as he glanced again at his notes, desperate for any phrase to offer as a "bite." The paper on which the notes were scrawled had become wrinkled and hard to read. It didn't matter—none of it was usable. The president wouldn't want any of that dialogue beamed to evening news audiences or splashed across the front pages of the morning papers. There was nothing else to do but fall back on a phrase he had often heard used by State Department types, a gem of diplomatic vagueness.

"The two presidents had a frank and friendly exchange of views with the homeowner."

"What's his name?"

"Yikes. Mr. Buster Yikes."

"Spell it!"

"Y-I-K-E-S"

"Yikes?"

"Yes. Yikes."

"Can you confirm that that's what Navikoff yelled when he planted his brown brogans flush in that pile of doggie doo—yikes?"

"No, that's—"

"But you are confirming that he got the stinky stuff on his shoes?"

"No, I am not confirming that. I don't have any information on that."

"Well, can you look into it and find out?"

"Sure, I'll rush back pell-mell and ask him. Do you honestly think anyone in Des Moines gives a diddly-squat?"

"Listen, Sox, I do think the diddly-squats in Des Moines care and the American people have a right to know."

"And the folks in Russia, too."

"Yeah, Sox, I'll bet they wake up every day in Moscow worrying whether or not their leader has bowwow barf on his shoes."

"We need to get to the bottom of this."

"Absolutely! Investigate! Investigate!"

"Special prosecutor!"

"Did he get it on his shoelaces, too?"

"Or were they slip-ons?"

"Finish the statement," a voice demanded. "We need to get this show back to Pennsylvania Avenue."

Sox looked over at the presidential limousine, motor idling, agents rigidly standing at the ready. He could imagine the president's mood inside.

"What else, Sox? What did they talk about?"

"Before the president departed, Mr. Yikes spoke warmly about his own family and expressed his support for what the two leaders are doing in seeking ways to combat terrorism…and, uh…pointed out…uh, that his family…and the families in Russia could be impacted by it."

"Give us a quote."

He scanned the messy shorthand of his notes, looking for anything he could Band-Aid together. "His words were…uh…basically these: 'I know that when it comes to terrorism…we've got to do something about it…it could happen to me…my wife and family…my kid. To a lot of us ordinary Joes in America and Russia and everywhere. So if you two guys can get together…and…figure…how to stop this…then I'm all for you.' I think it's fair to say that the two leaders listened attentively to Mr. Yikes' views."

He paused, neglecting to mention that Yikes had concluded with "Let's kick ass." Even though having withheld that morsel, he was relieved to see pencils grinding away against notepads. He waited until everyone had finished.

"That's it," he concluded, turning wistfully toward the vans.

"Wait, wait, wait—a couple of questions," a voice insisted. He cringed on the inside, forcing a frown he hoped would be misinterpreted as self-confidence. The last thing he wanted to do was take any questions. Unfortunately, his anticipative look in the direction of the vans had not energized anyone to bolt that way. He would just have to stand there and endure the agony, abetted by the discomforting thought that the delay was sure to irritate the president.

"Sox, what was the family doing when the presidents knocked on their door?"

"I believe they were napping," he responded quietly, his eyes darting around and noting that virtually everyone was writing down his answers verbatim.

"So they were asleep at this time of day?"

"Napping, yes. That's what Mr. Yikes indicated."

"So everyone in the house was asleep?"

"I didn't go inside…I don't know…what I do know is…uh, there was a time delay…it took several rings of the bell before Mr. Yikes answered the door…so, uh…I assume that he had been sleeping…as he indicated."

"What is Mr. Yikes' profession?"

"He's a butcher."

"Of what—the English language?"

"What was he doing home this time of day?"

"I don't know why he was home. Maybe it was his day off. Maybe he sliced everything thin today and got home early."

"Sort of like these answers—sliced a little thin."

"Did Yikes ask them inside?"

"Actually, he indicated that he would like to do that…the two presidents were welcome to join him in a late lunch, but they respectfully declined."

"What was on the menu—bad breath?"

"That guy looked like he had enough halitosis to make wind shear wilt."

"Is that why the president appeared to be leaning to the north throughout the entire conversation?"

He ignored the comments, continuing to anxiously eye the vans.

"Sox, was that a beer Yikes had in his hand?"

"It was a beverage can."

"What kind?"

"Cold."

"Thank you!" hollered a merciful voice from somewhere deep in the ranks, signaling a mass merge of bodies scrambling for the vans.

Sox stood in place as they pushed by, his shoulders sagging with relief. They had probed, and he had responded. Barely. He had not strayed from the truth in his portrayal of what had occurred on the front porch. He had held back some, yes, but hadn't lied. He hadn't told the entire story, but maybe he had parceled out just enough fragments to satisfy the broadcast producers and print editors to whom this information would now flow. He had delivered the goods—sort of. The key question now was—how would it play? Would the press have enough time to follow up with Yikes? Hopefully not. They'd be on a tight deadline. Or would the president be made to look like a fool for having interrupted the talks to take a frivolous ride into the rudimentary world of Buster Yikes? A distinct possibility.

All he could do now was drag himself onto one of the overcrowded vans, go back to the White House—and pray.

CHAPTER NINETEEN

REPORTER: Will the president talk about hope in his State of the
              Union speech?

SPOKESMAN: Yes, and glory, too.

Perched at his office window, Sox was once again enjoying the temporary relief of pursuing his favorite pastime, observing the late-afternoon
stream of humanity passing along Pennsylvania Avenue, all the while
experiencing a condition heretofore unknown and unheard-of in the
upper press office—solitude. It had been like that since their return from
Yikes' house. Ominously quiet. Quarantine quiet. A creepy stillness that
had rarely, if ever, visited that office.

Listlessly transfixed on the street, he wondered if indeed his White
House career was over. No one had said anything to him since their
return. No expressions of anger. Certainly no praise. No word from the
Oval Office. Nothing from J.Y. No reporters coming to call. Zip. Nothing
for a guy whose idea, endorsed only a few hours ago by presidential
enthusiasm, was now considered a stink bomb. That idea's author, who
had been the early afternoon's hero, was now about to conclude the day
as twilight's leper.

His attention shifted to the lawn where technicians were hustling to
pull rain covers off camera equipment and adjust knobs, a painful
reminder that correspondents would soon be standing in front of those
cameras, reporting to the nation on the net effect of the unexpected ride

taken by the two presidents. Print reporters now busy in their work carrels at the back of the press room would be hammering out similar leads for tomorrow's editions.

Hunkered down in his chair, Sox dourly contemplated what, if any, future remained for him there. He really didn't want to think about it. Then again, thinking about anything right now was a burden. The day's events had left him thought-dead, save for wallowing in regret at having been passed over when God doled out today's rations of good luck.

All he could do now was wait for the other shoe to drop. It would probably happen via a drop-by from J.Y. Or if the president's ire was at rage level, maybe even a call from the Oval Office. How bad would it be? A verbal spanking? Termination? Or the worst—transfer to the public affairs department of a faceless government agency, to be drowned forever in the bowels of a bureaucracy infested with professional paper-shufflers. He'd quit first.

He swung his chair around, leaning across the desk to see who might be in the outer office. "Anyone out there?"

"Just me," Missy answered eagerly.

He was in no mood for her cheeky enthusiasm.

"How about the wire leads?"

"I was just going to pull them," she replied, inching warily into the doorway.

"Why don't you go do that?" he asked tonelessly.

"Were you looking for anything in particular?"

"The wire copy on this afternoon's movement. What else did you think I'd want?"

She blinked nervously, surprised by his brusqueness. "Okay, okay."

"If I'm not here when you come back, just leave them on my desk."

"Sure." She paused, waiting to see if there might be any other requests, but he only continued to stare silently at her.

"Some story, huh?" she said, awkwardly trying to make conversation.

"What does that mean?"

"I heard some of the reporters laughing when they got back. One of them said the president didn't need to leave the White House to meet a fat guy drinking beer—that we had plenty of those right here on the staff."

He fell back in his chair, deflated. "Just go get the wire copy," he repeated. She turned and disappeared around the corner.

He needed to be alone right now. Why not get the deuce out of here and go hide in Lafayette Park? He always felt better over there. It was a view of the White House that was much easier on the nerves than that from the inner recesses of the press office. He eased over to the door, glancing cautiously to assure the room was vacant. Fortunately, Missy had been its only occupant. The others were probably off somewhere helping plan his execution. He slipped out into the West Wing hallway, through the lobby door and out onto the driveway.

Moving past the network camera stands, he ducked his head down, hoping none of the crew members would engage him. None did. They were busy with their setups, hands intently pressed against the headsets covering their ears, receiving instructions for production of the evening's newscasts.

He could just imagine how their reports would open: "Today, the president took a break in his talks with President Navikoff to show his Russian counterpart a typical day in the life of average Americans…typical if your workday has you home in the middle of the afternoon sloshing down suds…the kind of suds that fatten your frame, not clean your clothes…"

He kept moving past them, walking faster.

Once past the gate, across the street and into the park, he slowed up, passing by the statue of Rochambeau nobly pointing his finger at the White House. At least the Frenchman wasn't giving the White House the finger, he thought. Reaching an empty bench, he plopped down, dispirited. From this distance, the house across the street looked peaceful. Just another house across the street from another park. Other than the few technicians moving about on the lawn, it was a still life of serenity. All that majesty on the exterior and all those reporters inside about to dump his career in the toilet, not that he hadn't shown them the way.

Pondering that thought, he was interrupted by an intruder settling in at the opposite end of the bench, a vagrant covered in street dust looking him over with suspicious contemplation. Considering Sox was distinguishable from everyone else in the park for obvious reasons—a coat and tie and a cleanly shaven face—such wariness was understandable. He returned the man's inspection with an uneasy smile, simultaneously dropping his right hand down to pocket level and tapping lightly against his pants leg to reassure the presence of his wallet.

As the man stared, his swollen hand scratched thoughtfully at the gray stubble enveloping his lower face. While harboring compassion for a benchmate who had clearly seen the shorter side of life, Sox also reasoned that it was probably best to avoid further eye contact. Better to move on and surrender the turf, one more defeat in a long day.

There were other good reasons, too, for abandoning his current company. It occurred to him that anyone else watching them might think that a) this was a drug deal going down; b) this was a drug deal gone bad; or c) this was a White House aide who had just been responsible for mucking up the president's day and was now being administered the last rites by a homeless person.

"Hey…"

The gravel-thick utterance from the other end of the bench short-circuited his thought of departure.

"Hey…" Sox answered weakly.

"You from around here?"

"Well, I work around here."

"Work?"

"Yeah, that's what some people call it."

"I'm a college graduate myself," the man blurted.

Must have been the University of Grime, Sox thought. The man looked like he'd just recently been for a swim in a sewer.

"Where's your work at?" the man wheezed, spittle erupting onto his lower lip and dribbling down into his beard.

His mangled grammar usage was a momentary stymie. The ending of a sentence with a preposition had been an irritant for Sox since youth when his mother, a schoolteacher, had rid him of the habit through energetic use of a broom to his butt. Considering the academic neglect that had seemingly befallen his companion, he figured any attempt at corrective instruction would be an exercise in exasperation. He'd already had enough of that today.

"Actually, I work across the street," he finally answered.

The man's head swiveled around toward Jackson Place, its block of row buildings bordering one side of the park.

"No, you're looking in the wrong direction, I work over there," Sox said, nodding toward the White House.

The man's eyes narrowed dubiously.

"Oh, yeah? What are ya doing here? They closed for business over there?"

No such luck, Sox thought. "Let's just say I'm between innings."

The man edged closer. "Do you know that I've been an advisor to three presidents?"

Sox shifted uneasily, moving to the bench's edge, his eyes unblinking and fixed on the man. Absurd as it seemed, could this possibly be some personage he should know? Someone he had failed to recognize under all that muck? Was he indeed in the presence of some down-on-his-luck Washington power player he had failed to recognize under this tattered scruffiness? If so, what should he do? Apologize? Be deferential? Reverential? Or just walk away from the ramblings of a nut? A brief quiz was in order.

"You were an advisor to three presidents?"

"Yeah."

"Really? On what subjects did you advise them?"

"Usual stuff."

"Usual stuff?"

"Yeah, you know…budget deficits…"

"That all?"

"War."

"War?"

"Uh, huh. And peace."

"Peace?"

"Uh, huh. And bobsledding."

Any doubts Sox previously had were now removed. He was conversing with a bona fide Lafayette Park loony. But so what? It had been that kind of day.

"How did you advise them on peace?"

"Well…there was that peace rally…"

"Yeah…"

"It turned into a riot."

"A riot at a peace rally?"

"Uh, huh."

"What did you do?"

"Told the president how to break it up."

"And how was that?"

"Rushed a brass band to the scene."

Sox abruptly stood up. Bad as his options were, life in the White House, even the White House of the last few hours, was still a better deal than this delirium trip. It did occur to him that with limited prospects for his future, possibly not extending beyond today, he might be out here soon, joining this fellow on a permanent basis. He began walking away, but an instinct told him to stop and look back at the man whose head had now sagged down, a late-afternoon snooze taking hold.

"By the way, what did you do after you left the White House?"

The man's head jerked up, his face wrinkling in a toothless smile. "I became a concert violinist," he grinned.

A half-hour later, Sox was back at his desk, still anxious to see the wire service stories. He had taken the long way back, walking up to 17th Street, then cutting over to the Ellipse where its baseball fields had been swarming with activity. Like most days, those fields were a venue for post-work play by government worker-bees, all of whom today had seemed oblivious to their temporary spectator's presence as he paused to follow their anemic attempts at hitting and throwing. As he had watched, it seemed that his world was unraveling.

He had had a definite purpose in delaying his return. The extra time assured that all the network television reporters would have by now completed their "stand-ups" on the lawn. Their day's work would be done. Having returned and now looking out his window, he watched the technicians who remained outside dismantling the high-intensity lights used to enhance the White House backdrop. It was a "put 'em up, then tear 'em down" routine they mechanically carried out day after day.

He dropped into his chair, kicking absentmindedly at the leg of his desk as if such an act would free him from the burden of inevitability. Where were the wire service stories? He'd been gone more than long enough for Missy to produce them. He grabbed the phone and dialed her extension.

"Hello." The squeaky bounce in her voice exuded verbal sunshine.

"I asked you thirty minutes ago to bring me the wire leads. What happened in the meantime—did you fall off the edge of the earth?"

His harshness didn't deter her. "No, but you weren't the only person asking for them."

"J.Y.?"

"Him, too."

"And?"

"And the president."

"The president—what did he say?"

"He said that somebody in the press office better get over there with the wires and break the sound barrier doing it."

"And what happened?"

"And…I didn't break the sound barrier, but I am now the world record holder in the press office to the Oval Office dash on thick carpet while negotiating a curve."

"Congratulations," he said flatly, his annoyance growing. "But what about the wires?"

"What about them?"

"What about the leads—what did they say?"

"I don't know."

"You don't know?"

"Look," she said defensively, "after the president called, there wasn't time to do anything but rip and run. So I did."

He fell back in his chair, frustrated. "Okay," he muttered, dropping the receiver in its cradle.

Thanks to Missy's efficiency, his communion with slow death might now be mercifully brief. The president had the wires. J.Y. was nowhere around. No reporters were hanging around. Just as he had learned from the cruelty of politics, that no one knows instant loneliness better than an election loser, such was also true of any White House aide upon acquiring tarnish to his star. No one wanted to be near quicksand. He was now experiencing on-the-job training for has-beens.

For the first time since his return from the MacArthur Boulevard excursion, his phone rang. Obviously some laggard who hadn't gotten the word of his imminent fall from grace.

"Hello."

"Are you watching the networks?" asked the president sharply.

Though his reaction should have been rooted in terror, Sox felt strangely seized with calm, even as the president snapped at him. At that moment he could only attribute it to the past hour's adventure across the street, a sobering balm for his spirits in helping prepare for this confrontation. If that old man could survive, so would he, even if it meant his next career move was to join him on a more permanent basis on that bench in Lafayette Park. And besides, how many people could travel through life and along the way earn the distinction of being fired personally by the president of the United States?

"The networks…uh, no, sir, I haven't been watching…"

"Not watching the networks?" the president asked, awestruck. "What are you watching?"

My career as it becomes an instant mudslide, he thought.

"Uh, actually a blank screen, Mr. President."

"Oh, really? How are we doing on that one?"

"Uh, you're winning, Mr. President," he said, weakly grasping for humor.

"Have you seen the wires?"

"Actually, no, Mr. President. I believe you are the first."

"What kind of press aide lets the boss see the press coverage first?" The logical answer to that question was: one who's fast sliding into the bog of presidential doghouse doo-doo and about to take his last gasp of White House air.

"Mr. President, we knew you'd be anxious to see the coverage, so—"

"—and I'm also looking at a one-pager just sent over from the News Summary Office. It already has all of tonight's network leads."

"I haven't seen that one either, Mr. President," he sighed mechanically, as if these acknowledgements of his shortcomings were now a routine thing.

"Well, you'd better look at it," the president said forcefully.

"Yes, sir."

"And then let me know how you did it."

"Yes, sir," he sighed again.

"Pretty matter-of-fact about all this, aren't you?"

"Not much else to say, Mr. President."

Please, please, please, just drop the other shoe now, he thought. Plant the boot to the butt. Get it over.

"I guess you're right," the president said, his voice softening.

Sox swallowed hard. He thought it was about to happen. The president was going to fire him. He looked at his watch to record the time. Someday he might be a footnote in somebody's White House book and at least could help them accurately document one of President Crayon's lesser-known ass-kicking actions. Not really a defining moment in his presidency, but certainly a deflating moment for Sox.

"I guess there's nothing else to do but end this by offering congratulations and thanks for all you did today."

"Thanks?…for all…I did today…Mr. President?" Sox mumbled in bewilderment.

"Yes. Absolutely. What I want to know is, what did you tell the press pool out there?"

"Well…uh…frankly, the close-shave truth, sir."

"Well, it damn sure saved the day."

Sox was stunned. Saved the day? Impossible. He hadn't saved anything, including his own ass. He knew he must sound like a lip-drooling fool to the president.

"Mr. President, I—"

"Listen to these leads from the networks… 'Terrorism takes a holiday while world leaders go door-to-door…Today President Crayon wanted to talk terrorism, and President Navikoff wanted to talk economic aid. At President Crayon's suggestion, they compromised and took a ride into Washington's suburbs, eventually stopping to visit the home of a local butcher. The leaders used their change of venue for a chat with the butcher that was characterized by a White House spokesman as frank and friendly. It must have worked, because terrorism talks that were rumored to have been stalled over a Russian push for economic aid have now picked up steam again and, according to administration sources, cooperation in the battle against terrorism, as well as progress in other areas of U.S.-Russia relations, appears to be the result.'"

Sox tossed his head back against his chair, closed his eyes, hung his mouth open and gulped deeply as he listened.

"There's more…'Crayon creates front-door diplomacy…Anyone home? President Crayon today took his anti-terrorism campaign down the road a few minutes from the White House. He had Sergei Navikoff in tow, trying to get their talks back on track. Somewhere along the way, they decided to stop. Next thing, they were on the front porch of a local butcher, Buster Yikes, talking terrorism. According to a White House spokesman, Mr. Yikes engaged them in a way that encouraged the two leaders to listen attentively. It must have worked because administration sources now say that instead of ending tomorrow, the talks have apparently been jump-started again and may even be extended for an additional day…'"

"Mr. President—"

"—and here's the wire stuff…'Butcher tells leaders to get tough on terrorism…The spin on today's White House story is that President Crayon took his Russian counterpart for a spin…'"

Sox sat listening, stupefied.

"Well?" the president asked after he had finally finished.

"Sir, I'd say—"

"—that we knocked a home run in the ninth with the sacks filled."

"Frankly, I'd have settled for a bunt, Mr. President."

"Color it any way you want, we have cleared the track of the high hurdles, at least for today."

"Yes, sir, it sounds like we have," Sox said, taking pleasure in raising his voice to emphasize the *we.*

"The American people know that their president took his case today to grassroots U.S.A. in the person of a salt-of-the-earth meat-cutter."

"Salty, yes, sir."

"And it showed Navikoff something about the belly of America and what's in it."

Sox paused, pursing his lips before responding.

"The heart, you mean, sir?"

"Yeah, the heart, the belly, the solar plexus, the gut—the spirit. Navikoff saw and heard what we're all about. He saw it in that guy's eyes. I think it helped."

"Sergei Navikoff, meet Buster Yikes."

"Sergei Navikoff met America today when he had the grip and grin of Buster Yikes laid on him."

"Maybe you should invite Mr. Yikes over for lunch sometime."

"That's a damn good idea, too. Make sure we have a meat dish. Thanks, Sox."

"Thank you, Mr. President."

As they hung up, Sox extended both arms fully in a victory thrust and whooped, "Yes!" His exertion nearly sent his chair tilting over against his window again, a near repeat of the president of Egypt incident. A desperate grab for the edge of the desk saved him, the latest escape in a day of saves.

He sat limply for a minute, breathing freely while quietly celebrating the removal of the anvil from his shoulders. He had poured virtually every press secretarying skill he had ever learned into today and was drained—emotionally, mentally, physically. But he was comforted in knowing he had danced on the edge of the cliff and survived. The old man in the park would still have to be a solo act. Sox's self-proclaimed White House obituary had been premature. Nor would he have to worry for the time being about being introduced as "the former White House aide." It was tough enough just being a White House aide, much less bearing the stigma of "former." Five minutes as a former White House employee, and one was yesterday's news, especially to the press who craved access to current information, not barroom tales of "how things used to be when I was there…"

Two points were of utmost significance. One, he had kept his job; and two, his life would not be perk-less. He still had Mess privileges. He still had an assigned parking space. And he still had access to the tennis court. Such bits of recognition were to be prized in clubby, power-crazed Washington.

As with much news relevant to the Oval Office, word had already leaked into the West Wing corridors and beyond about the president's "saved the day" phone call. Sox had press corps friends again, those who only an hour ago had been invisible. They drifted by to offer congratulations and pats on the back. Thanks to the events on MacArthur Boulevard and the subsequent positive news coverage, he was here to stay for at least another twelve hours. Then it would start all over again in the morning, a fresh page.

J.Y. ducked his head in the doorway. "Bravo, buddy!"

"Yeah, back from the dead."

"You and your squirrelly ideas. I have to admit, I didn't think this dog would hunt."

"Yeah, about an hour ago the fat lady had sung and they were sweeping the aisles."

"Okay, spin guru, that was an hour ago. Now, how about working up some guidance on the budget negotiations that I can look at first thing in the morning? I'll need it for the briefing tomorrow."

Sure, Sox thought, so much for his eye-blink of glory. Back to business. He felt like the PR man whose client challenged: "So you made me the lead story on the network news tonight, whadda ya got for me tomorrow?"

But J.Y.'s request had served to remind that the reality of the work was that savoring any victory here was a hiccup. If that long.

Now his phone was ringing again, reporters interested in tomorrow's schedule and nibbling for any other bits of color to flesh out their MacArthur Boulevard stories. It was mostly the wires calling and the West Coast papers whose deadlines hadn't yet passed.

Wading through these and filling in what blanks he could, which were basically none, he felt the wise choice was to leave the story free of any more of his fingerprints. It wasn't his story anyway. It was the president's. But at least the phone was ringing again.

"Mr. St. Louis, this is the guard at the northwest gate. You have a visitor here."

Flaxen. Yes! It wasn't that he had forgotten, it was simply that he had been transfixed on the events of the day, her visit being relegated to the rear in his thought process.

"Yes, clear her in," he blurted. "Please tell her I'll meet her in the West Wing lobby."

"Yes, sir."

He darted from his office, veering left across the hall to the bathroom—right in the shadow of the Oval Office. Someday he'd be able to tell his kids about the tiny bathroom right across the hall from the oval-shaped room. Or at least some version of that story. Maybe they'd be Flaxen's kids, too. He fumbled with his pants' zipper, nearly snagging his most vital area in the iron mesh. Another incredible save, he thought. What a near-tragic occurrence at such a crucial time. A splash of cologne, gargle of mouthwash and it was a high-speed dash back to his office.

A glimpse out his window confirmed she was already halfway up the driveway. Unlike her previous visit there, the lawn was nearly deserted, most of the crews having drifted back inside after the evening's newscasts. One crew remained at work, fully staffed, apparently completing a piece for syndication. This time, her walk up the driveway was free from the hoots, whistles and burden of an escort convoy.

He stood savoring the shimmer of her slinky figure, a blurry silhouette floating toward him in the haze of dusk. He couldn't wait any longer, the itch of eagerness driving him into the hallway, through the lobby and out onto the portico, trotting past the microphone stand and reaching her at a point within shadow's length of his office window. Without hesitating, he embraced her fully.

"Well, hello, Mr. Hungry," she smiled, tossing her head back while leaving her arms laced in his.

"Hi," he whispered.

"Busy day?"

"Hey, it's the White House press office."

"I know, I know," she said mockingly. "I've heard this one before—every day here is like stepping into a flying airplane."

"Or some other fun kind of hell."

"So what's next?"

He gently steered her around, clasping her right hand in his left as they walked back toward the West Wing entrance, pausing at the portico's step.

"So where would you like to go tonight?" he asked.

"You choose. Actually, I thought you had chosen."

"How about nowhere?"

"How can you go nowhere in Washington?"

"How about we just stay in?"

She broke into a cautious smile that beamed slowly across her face in a way that stirred his encouragement glands.

"Hey, Sox!" It was Sparta's voice interrupting as it spiked the air from behind. "I've been looking for you all over this yard! We've got a problem! Or should I say, you've got a problem!"

From over Flaxen's shoulder he saw her rounding the corner, urgently panting toward them. Why? Why now? Why her? A confrontation with Sparta was the last thing he needed to end this day. He already had the last thing he needed to end the day standing next to him. He guided Flaxen to join him up on the portico's step. Whatever Sparta wanted, he would at least have the leverage of looking down on her. A false sense of advantage, perhaps, since in any such negotiations the playing field usually seemed tilted her way.

"We've put the MacArthur Boulevard and terrorism talks stories to bed!" he shouted, curving his hands around his mouth. "Besides, your newscast is over."

She trotted up, bending over to catch her breath, then looking up at him harshly.

"No joke, junior. I'm already on to tomorrow's news and beyond—

including that super screwup on the president's schedule for next week."

"What are you talking about?"

"Read my lips. I'm talking about the president's schedule for next week."

He frowned nervously. "That's pretty visionary on your part since we haven't announced it yet. You know we don't release the week-ahead until the Friday briefing."

"Cut the cotton candy! I've got sources."

"So?" He and Flaxen exchanged desirous looks, their mutual eagerness noted by Sparta who nonetheless pressed on.

"So this White House has committed major muck in terms of the president's schedule for next week."

"In what way?"

"Do you know that he's receiving courtesy calls next week from several heads of state, including a king and queen?"

"I'm not confirming that, but even if you are correct, so what? What's the big deal? Those would be protocol-heavy visits—photo ops, tea with the First Lady—you know the drill. What's the problem?"

"There's a big problem."

"You want to be more specific?"

"Sure. Does the president realize that this particular queen on his schedule has been dead for twenty-five years?"

"Dead?"

"Yeah, that's what we call it. Dead. She's been roosting in a pine box for quite a few semesters."

He looked at Flaxen and swallowed heavily, then turned back to Sparta.

"Dead?"

"Yeah," she said forcefully, "explain this one, pal. I want an answer right now. No excuses. No *no comment.* I want you to tell me how the president of the United States can possibly have tea with this queen if the dame's been dead for twenty-five years."

He paused for a long moment, pensive and thoughtful, then cleared his throat.

"Well, I guess it's like this—-maybe there's been a ringer living with the king all these years."

Abruptly swinging around, he gathered in Flaxen under one arm as he rejoiced inwardly that he wouldn't have to conduct tomorrow's briefing. J.Y. would be back in the pit.

Strangely, it was that thought, not the evening's pleasures that lay ahead, that filled him with a soaring elation as they disappeared from sight into the house that was still his home away from home.